D1479136

Desert
DEADLINE

A DANTE & JAZZ MYSTERY

MICHAEL
CRAFT

QUEST
·OVER·
PRESS

Design and typography: M.C. Johnson
Cover art: modified from an image via Shutterstock
Author's photo: Aaron Jay Young

Library of Congress Cataloging-in-Publication Data

Craft, Michael, 1950–
Desert Deadline : a Dante & Jazz mystery / Michael Craft
    ISBN: 979-8-218-13795-3 (hardcover)
    ISBN: 979-8-218-13881-3 (paperback)
    BISAC: FIC011000 Fiction / LGBTQ / Gay
            FIC022100 Fiction / Mystery & Detective / Amateur Sleuth

First hardcover and paperback editions: July 2023

Questover Press
California • Since 2011

DESERT DEADLINE

Dante O'Donnell and Jazz Friendly make an unlikely pair of crime solvers, thrust together by iffy circumstances in the so-called paradise of sunny Palm Springs. He's white and gay, a concierge at a vacation-rental outfit; she's Black and straight, a private eye on the rebound from a failed marriage.

Maude Movay, a reclusive author of romance novels, is facing a tight deadline for a multimillion-dollar deal. So she checks in at one of Dante's rentals intending to write a blockbuster, then checks out on a gurney, feet first.

It was murder, all right, and Jazz steps in to help prove who's guilty. Soon, though, a second tragedy strikes, this one much too close to home.

For both Dante and Jazz, the race is on to name a killer, save a fortune—and rescue an innocent child.

DESERT DEADLINE
Dante & Jazz Mystery #2

"A delicious whodunit. This Palm Springs mystery is as funny as it is thrilling." — *BookLife Reviews* (EDITOR'S PICK)
from the indie review service of *Publishers Weekly*

"It's fun to see Craft, the author of 19 novels, plot the demise of [an] author, which he does with typical ingenuity and precision."
— *Kirkus Reviews*

"Michael Craft is a writer of great charm, and *Desert Deadline* shows him at his most charming. The mystery is cunningly plotted, but it's the characters and their relationships that make for such a memorable read." — *Michael Nava, Lambda Literary Award-winning author of the Henry Rios mysteries*

"On the stiletto heels of the inaugural Dante and Jazz mystery, *Desert Deadline* does not disappoint. Michael Craft imbues his tale with just the right amount of atmospheric magic, both brilliantly sunny and deliciously shady at the same time."
— *Anthony Bidulka, Lambda Literary Award-winning author*

"No one delivers a sharp, stylish whodunit like Michael Craft. Romance on the page turns deadly in the desert when Dante and Jazz return in this delightful—and sexy—sequel."
— *Rob Osler, MWA award-winning author*

"*Desert Deadline* is as much about preserving the magic in relationships as it is about preserving life when a murderer resides too close to home." — *Midwest Book Review, Diane Donovan*

DESERT GETAWAY
Dante & Jazz Mystery #1

• 2023 MWA Edgar nominee: Lilian Jackson Braun Award •

"A wild romp through Palm Springs' glittery underbelly. Fast, funny, and thoroughly enjoyable. An instant classic."
— *Tod Goldberg, New York Times bestselling author*

"In this enjoyable series launch from Craft ... an intriguing puzzle keeps the pages turning."
— *Publishers Weekly*

"Distinctively colorful storytelling ... an immersive first outing for a crime-solving odd couple."
— *Kirkus Reviews*

"Michael Craft delivers an irresistible high-camp twist to the classic detective mystery. A fast-paced and captivating new series."
— *J.D. Horn, Wall Street Journal bestselling author*

"*Desert Getaway* glows with humor, moves at an energetic pace, and is wholly entertaining."
— *John Copenhaver, Macavity and Lambda award-winning author*

"Smart, sophisticated, and ingeniously plotted. I loved it."
— *Ellen Byron, USA Today bestselling author*

"Dante and Jazz show great chemistry in what I hope is the first of many adventures."
— *Michael Nava, Lambda Literary Award-winning author*

"A compelling romp through fiascos, fairy-tale lives, and organized crime."
— *Midwest Book Review, Diane Donovan*

CONTENTS

PART ONE

ROMANCE QUEEN

CHAPTER
ONE

Ever heard of Swedish death cleaning?

It's the practice of decluttering your surroundings, your possessions—your life—so others won't have to pick up the pieces and throw out your stuff when you're gone. It's a serenity thing. It's nice. It's polite.

Agnetha Berg wasn't Swedish, but Norwegian (close enough). She wasn't dying, either. And I couldn't describe her as nice, let alone polite. But she could clean like a dervish, with an obsessive attitude to match.

Earlier that week, I was prepping a newly listed vacation rental in Indian Wells, an enclave of gated country clubs in the California desert, about fifteen miles from Palm Springs. Agnetha, employed by the property owner, was told to be helpful, but to my way of thinking, she was just a pain in the ass.

Maybe she didn't like gay men. Maybe she didn't like men, period. Whatever her hang-up, she didn't like *me*, and I had an inkling she would be the source of future annoyances.

But she was no longer on my mind by Saturday. On that bright, busy morning at the tail end of February, I pulled into the parking lot of a strip mall—a mishmash of shops, galleries, and artists' lofts—on the outskirts of Palm Springs, a short drive from my office at Sunny Junket Vacation Rentals.

The resort town was in high gear, with tourists milling into and out of the storefronts, searching for something small to take home as a remembrance of their visit—or something big to help decorate a bare wall in that new condo that would serve as a winter getaway from Canada or Portland or Detroit.

As I walked across the parking lot, a middle-aged couple was moving in my direction, lugging opposite ends of a five-foot painting. Its palette of sherbet pastels coordinated with their Brooks Brothers shorts and polos. She gushed to her hubby, "It's *perfect* for the guest room."

While passing me, he told her, "I hope it'll fit."

"Of course it will. It's perfect."

"I mean: fit in the *car*."

When I glanced back, they were standing, flummoxed, behind the trunk of a white Lincoln sedan. Nope, I thought, not even close.

I wasn't shopping that morning. Moving through the crowd, then past several storefronts, I made my way to a door of darkly tinted glass, identified only by its address letter, H. Inside, a tiny hot vestibule led to a second door. I buzzed the intercom, and moments later, a man's husky voice asked, "Yeah?"

"It's Dante."

"C'mon up." He buzzed the lock.

I opened the door to a rush of chilled air, walked down a winding hallway, then climbed a long flight of stairs, where the subtle but distinctive smells of linseed oil and turpentine drifted from above. Nearing the top, I heard lighthearted conversation accompanied by a soundtrack of laid-back rock, played low.

The husky voice belonged to Blade Wade, an artist of some renown whose paintings were catching the eye of influential collectors across the country and beyond.

The woman's voice belonged to Jazz Friendly, an ex-cop who had quit the force in Palm Springs and was struggling to establish her own private-eye biz. Both Jazz and Blade were Black, and each was recently, unexpectedly single. Their lives had intersected several months earlier during a murder investigation. Unless I was mistaken, they might now be described as an item.

There was also a third voice that morning, a younger guy's voice I didn't recognize—but I knew a gay lilt when I heard it.

Reaching the top of the stairs, I emerged into the huge space that served as Blade's home and studio. This was no starving artist's garret. It was stunning, the sort of place that ends up in magazines—a melding of industrial chic with designer furnishings, significant art, and a sleek, drop-dead kitchen. Blade's work area contained easels displaying several paintings in progress—dynamic abstractions, most at least eight feet tall, predominantly red. The studio opened into the living room, where a high ribbon of windows framed the interplay of light and shadows on a ruddy expanse of nearby mountainside. A spiral metal staircase at the far end of the room led up to a loft bedroom, where more windows looked out toward the snowy peak of Mount San Jacinto and, hidden in the piney crags beyond, the alpine village of Idyllwild.

Jazz was telling Blade, "So he asked if I could look after Emma today."

"No problem. That little darlin's always—"

"Dante!" said Jazz as I approached. "Thanks for coming over so quick."

"I was running errands, happened to be nearby." Though speaking to Jazz, I was looking at the gay guy, who broke into a smile. I now recognized him as Liam Heimlich, who worked at a gallery that represented Blade. A year out of college, Liam was the nephew of the gallery owner.

"Mr. O'Donnell," he said, stepping over to shake my hand, "it's been *way* too long."

I gave him a wink. At fifty-two, I was probably older than his father, but Liam had never been shy about flirting with me. "You're right," I said. "Last summer—way too long." And our handshake morphed into a quick hug.

Jazz cleared her throat. "The *reason* I called you: my ex needs a rental for someone, but it's a last-minute sorta deal."

I grinned. "Well, this is a switch—you bringing *me* business."

A year ago, when Jazz was getting started as a private investigator, she offered to pay me for tipping her off to potential clients who might have use for her services. My job at Sunny Junket as a field inspector also included duties as a concierge to our VIP guests, and some of them did indeed have "baggage"— of the messed-up sort. This arrangement proved profitable for both Jazz and me, and before long, I took on a more active role in her cases, assisting with occasional side work.

She explained, "Christopher has a new partner in his law firm, a gal who moved from LA, and she's got an old client there who needs to come out here for a while—to hunker down and get some work done."

"What kind of work?"

"It's an author with a big book deal and a tight deadline— wants some fuckin' peace and quiet, I guess."

Jazz had a way with words.

Laughing merrily, she continued, "Incognito, too. Cloak-and-dagger shit."

I noted, "We're smack in the middle of high season. When do they want to book this?"

"Yesterday."

"Impossible."

Jazz planted a hand on a hip. "I know that. *They* know that. That's why I called *you*."

Blade stepped into the conversation, telling Jazz, "You could rent them *your* apartment—and stay here for a while." With a little growl, he added, "Might be fun."

Blade was about my age, fifty or so, but unlike me, he had a massive, solid body—a football build—and spoke in a creamy baritone that sounded seductive even when he wasn't trying.

Jazz, in her mid-thirties, hesitated just long enough to signal that she was tempted. But she tossed her arms, blurting, "It wouldn't work."

"Why not?"

"For starters: I'm sure this snooty author—whoever he is— would find my place a total dump. Second: they need the place for a full month. And third: now that I've got joint custody of Emma, what about *her*?"

Blade made a sweeping gesture that encompassed the tasteful surroundings of the loft, reminding Jazz with a soft laugh, "Emma's been here *lots* of times. She loves it."

"She does," Jazz agreed, "but she's never *slept* here, and as far as she knows, I haven't either. She's four—and I'm not ready for *that* conversation."

Liam Heimlich, standing a few yards away from us, near the entry stairs, must have felt that the discussion had veered to topics not meant for his ears. "Sorry," he said, "I guess this isn't the best time. I could come back later, Mr. Wade, to talk about picking up the new paintings. I can send our truck over whenever you'd—"

"Nah," said Blade, stepping to the young man and clapping

an arm over his shoulders. "Don't rush off. You're not intruding."

With a shrug, Liam shot Blade a smile. Then his eyes slid in my direction. And lingered.

Jazz caught this interplay, gave me a finger-wag, and strolled me toward the kitchen. Clicking her tongue, she said, "He's a little young, Dante."

"A little young for what?"

She stifled a hoot of a laugh. "Don't bullshit *me*, Mr. Innocent. You're thinking with your dick again."

"And how—*exactly*—is that any concern of yours?"

We'd had this conversation before, a righteous tit-for-tat that involved advising each other on perceived mortal flaws. She had been struggling to overcome some self-destructive anger and booze issues, and I wanted to think I'd helped her. In turn, she felt I was wasting my life on misguided dreams and the wrong men, and I wanted to think she was clueless. But she wasn't.

"It concerns me," she said, "because you're attached now."

I said nothing.

She reminded me, "The Brazilian?"

"Isandro and I are not 'attached.' We're ... seeing each other."

This conversation was nipped, thank God, by the sound of the door buzzer. Blade moved to the intercom and spoke into it: "Yeah?"

A child's voice said, "We're here, Mr. Wade."

Blade winked at us. He said to the caller, "Who's 'we'?"

"It's *Emma*. I brought my dad and a lady."

"Okay, darlin', any friend of yours is a friend of mine. C'mon up." And he buzzed the lock.

Wryly, I asked Jazz, "What's this, an ambush?"

"I need to look after Emma while Christopher helps scout for rentals with the new law partner." Jazz leaned close, confiding, "And I wanted to get a look at this gal, so I asked them over."

I heard voices rising from the deep stairwell, dominated by Emma's excited chatter. I'd often spent time with the youngster, finding her delightful, since the early days of my association with her mother. But I'd never met Emma's father, Christopher Friendly, who was white. Jazz had once asked me if I thought Christopher might be gay (because she recalled him describing something as "simply *fab*-ulous"), and I assured her that it was unlikely (although it remained a point of curiosity). When he reached the top of the stairs—holy Christ—I turned to Jazz agog, as if to ask, How the hell did you manage to lose *that* one?

But Jazz didn't see me. She was focused squarely on the new partner in her ex's firm, a good-looking woman, smartly dressed, appearing a few years older than Christopher, who I'd heard was forty. While the woman had abundant style—spike heels, nubby silk suit, and oversize eyeglasses with heavy frames of Porsche red—I was also struck by her manner, which seemed oddly withdrawn and earnest. Almost prim.

Jazz must have noticed this, too. Her tepid smile could not disguise an underlying smirk of satisfaction, which I decoded with ease: Christopher would be steering clear of the company inkwell.

Liam Heimlich—still standing near the stairs as the others arrived—pounced to shake hands with Christopher, passing him a card. "We *do* hope to see you at the gallery sometime."

Introductions were being made as Jazz and I stepped over from the kitchen. Emma already knew everyone, so she scampered off to the studio area, eager to resume working on her latest painting; Blade had been tutoring her, finding uncommon promise in the child's early grasp of composition and abstraction.

Liam quickly confirmed some trucking arrangements with Blade, then gave me a hug, offered a wave of farewell to the others, and headed downstairs.

Jazz made short work of introducing Christopher and me. She paused, swiveling her head toward the other woman. "And this is...?"

"Allison Harper," said the woman, stepping to Jazz, offering her hand for a shake. She smiled. "I've heard so much about you, Jazz. Emma *couldn't* be more adorable. You must be *very* proud of her."

I'd never seen Jazz tongue-tied before, but she was clearly unprepared for the flattery. Finding her voice, she thanked Allison, adding, "Christopher has said many lovely things about you, too."

I doubted if that was true, since Christopher looked a tad surprised—and flustered—by Jazz's words.

"Hey," said Blade, breaking an awkward lull, "why not get comfortable, and I'll open a good bottle of chenin blanc."

It was eleven in the morning, but no one objected, so Blade retreated to the kitchen, and Jazz assumed the role of hostess in his home, leading us to the seating area of the main room. We arranged ourselves on big square leather ottomans around a hefty stone cocktail table.

Jazz said to the others, "I asked Dante to come over because I thought he might be able to help with a rental for Allison's client, but he tells me the town is booked solid."

I raised a finger. "But then you mentioned that the rental would be needed for a full month, and that's a different matter. Some of the resort cities—and some of the property owners—

don't allow short-term rentals for weekend visits, requiring a four-week minimum. There's not as much demand for those, except in high season."

Jazz rolled her eyes. "So we're back to square one. No vacancy."

"Not so fast. Just this week, we've been preparing a property to add to our Luxury Retreats portfolio. We'll post the listing this afternoon, available tomorrow, March first." I took out my phone and handed it to Allison Harper so she could scroll through some photos while Christopher and Jazz got up to peer over her shoulders.

While they shared nods of approval, I explained that the rental property was actually a large guesthouse at an estate in Indian Wells that had been built by a former United States ambassador. Recently, his widow decided to offer the guest quarters for rent to help with the estate's upkeep. Wishing, however, to "preserve appearances," she insisted that the rentals be arranged with discretion and that the renters themselves be screened for propriety.

Jazz looked up from the pictures. "Wow. That's quite a spread."

"It is," I agreed, "and it doesn't come cheap."

"I'm sure," said Christopher.

"How much?" asked Allison.

I told her.

"Not a problem," she said. "Not for *this* client."

Glasses clanged in the kitchen. Blade said, "Hey, Jazz—can you give me a hand?"

While stepping away to help him, Jazz asked Allison, "Your client—the author—who *is* it? Sounds like he's loaded."

"Uh," said Christopher, "Allison's client wants to maintain anonymity. This will be a 'working vacation'—with the emphasis on *working*."

"Keep your secrets," Jazz said with a laugh. "Or *try* to—I'm a private eye, remember?" She returned with two large wineglasses, accompanied by Blade, who carried three.

Blade gave the three glasses of pale yellow wine to Allison, Christopher, and me. Then he sat next to Jazz on one of the ottomans. She handed him his glass of wine; her own glass contained water. I noted there had been no discussion of this—Jazz had sworn off booze, and Blade was totally on board, which implied that their relationship had progressed to an easy, homey stage.

After we skoaled and drank, I set my glass on the table and said to Allison, "If you want the place in Indian Wells, I'll need a decision soon. Once the listing is posted, it'll get snapped up."

She nodded. "Understood. But we do have another possibility to explore first."

Christopher asked me, "Can you hold the listing until, say, two o'clock? I have a client who has a house in Palm Springs— he's out of town for a few months on a job assignment. I called him regarding Allison's 'situation,' and he said he might be willing to rent out his place while he's away. He arranged for his housekeeper to meet us there at one so we can check it out. Can you wait that long, Dante?" He gave me a soft, pleading, pretty-please smile.

"Sure." I dug out one of my Sunny Junket cards. "Just let me know as soon as you decide."

Christopher pocketed the card. "*Fab*-ulous."

Hmm.

Allison said to him, "What a relief—we've got options, so we're covered. With any luck, Lanford can drive out from LA tomorrow."

Jazz chortled. "Are you dropping clues, Allison? Is Lanford

the author's first name or last?"

"Neither." She folded her arms. "Lanford Endicott is not the author. He's the author's publicist. I guess you could say he's also her handler."

"*Her?*" asked Jazz.

Christopher nudged Allison's arm. "Go ahead. What's the difference? It's bound to come out eventually."

Allison remained silent for a moment, looking skeptical. Then she leaned forward, elbows to knees, saying to Blade, Jazz, and me, "For now, at least, this must remain strictly *entre nous*. Agreed?"

We all nodded, Jazz eagerly.

"My client—who needs seclusion to work on her next book— is none other than Maude Movay."

Blade and I exchanged a shrug, but Jazz let out a squeal. "Holy shit! Maude Movay's coming *here*? To write her next *book*? I can't believe it!" Pausing to catch her breath, she noticed that Blade and I shared none of her excitement. "What's the matter with you two—don't you fuckin' *read*?"

I mustered a weak smile. "I, uh ... I've heard the name."

Christopher laughed. "I'm with you, guys. Maude Movay has many devoted followers, but I'm not one of them."

Allison reminded him, "She's the queen of romance. Her 'Seven Sordid Sinns' series has sold millions—many times over —in fifty-nine languages, including, most recently, Oromo. It may not be literature, but it's lucrative."

Jazz countered, "I dunno if it's literature or not, but it's *great*. Cynthia Sinns—she's the hero, sorta—and she goes through all these adventures, and she's got all these men, but she's also got these *problems*. Like pride and greed and such."

Allison explained, "Each of the series installments takes

its title from one of the so-called deadly sins, starting with *Cynthia's Pride*, *Cynthia's Greed*, and making its way through *Lust*, *Envy*, *Gluttony*, and the most recent installment, *Cynthia's Wrath*. Which leaves only a seventh and final installment, not yet written: *Cynthia's Sloth*."

"Catchy," I said, not bothering to mask my sarcasm.

Christopher stifled a laugh, turning to look at me. His eyes seemed to twinkle. Was he flirting? Would Jazz kill me if I tried to find out?

"The title," conceded Allison, "is a challenge. But the titles in the series were set from the start, and the only one left is *Sloth*. To say it's 'highly anticipated' would be a gross understatement—Maude's readers have been *clamoring* for this one—so much so, we've landed a film deal for a streaming series tied to the book, with an option for multiple seasons. It's huge. The whole setup has a *lot* of moving parts with interdependent deadlines, and everything hinges on delivering a manuscript by the end of next month: March thirty-first. Terms of the contract were nailed down a half-year ago—but Maude hasn't written the first *sentence* yet."

Jazz asked, "What happens if she doesn't finish on time?"

"*Please*." Allison shuddered. "That is *not* an option. We need to get her sequestered out here—posthaste—so she can grind out the damn book."

"Mommy?" said Emma, wandering out from the studio. She wore a messy artist's smock over her pretty little dress—crisp yellow cotton with a pattern of pink and gray balloons. Her biracial parents had endowed her with a caramel complexion and wondering dark eyes. She had her mother's black hair, but unlike Jazz, who wore a short no-nonsense Afro, Emma had a lavish burst of curly braids that flopped over one shoulder.

Jazz said, "Yes, honey?"

"I'm firsty."

Through a grin, Jazz corrected: "Thirsty."

"Can I have some juice or something?"

"*May* I…"

Blade stood, telling Emma, "Of course you may, darlin'. Apple or cranberry?"

She considered this, looking stumped.

"Tell you what," said Blade, taking her hand, "let's try both." As he led her toward the kitchen, he asked, "How are things going in the art world this morning?"

"Not so good," she said thoughtfully. "I think I'm blocked. A dry spell, maybe."

With a chuckle, Blade suggested, "Juice might help."

"Yeah!"

After a quick lunch in downtown Palm Springs, I needed to check in at Sunny Junket's offices on Palm Canyon Drive, the city's main drag. I parked behind the building and decided to leave the top down on my vintage Karmann Ghia convertible. Built before I was born, now painstakingly restored, the car had been given to me by a grateful client. I'd been tempted to refuse the gift as too generous—but I wasn't stupid. The car was perfect for a warm spring day in the desert, and its classic styling fit right in with the town's retro-modern vibe.

Taking off my sunglasses, I strolled through the glass doors at the corner of the building. "Howdy, Gianna," I said to one of several clerks stationed at the front desk on that hopping Saturday afternoon.

She barely glanced away from her computer to look at me.

"Where's your uniform?"

The Sunny Junket "uniform" consisted of dad jeans and an acid-yellow polo embroidered with the company logo. I hated it. Gianna wore hers with sloppy indifference. I told her, "Not working today." I wore dressy black shorts and a raw linen shirt with Italian loafers and a year-round tan.

She gave me a puke-face and resumed typing something.

Stepping around the front desk, I said, "Have a *splendid* afternoon, girlfriend."

"Bite me."

When I arrived at my own desk and sat down to sort through some accumulated paperwork, my cell phone rang. The readout said FRIENDLY LAW OFFICES. I answered the call: "Hello, this is Dante."

"Hi, Dante. Christopher Friendly. Is the rental in Indian Wells still available?"

I laughed. "I expected to hear from you at two, but it's barely past one. You must've had a quick tour."

"Let's just say the esteemed Maude Movay would not have been pleased with the lodgings we just inspected. The house was a fright."

"Then let's talk business, Chris."

"Uh, *actually* ... it's Christopher."

Mm-hmm.

He continued, "But let me hand the phone to Allison. Maude is *her* client."

Within ten minutes, the deal was done—and Sunny Junket would soon be adding the illustrious Maude Movay to its roster of happy, satisfied guests. I noticed that the door to my boss's office was open, so I went to give him the news.

When I rapped on the doorjamb, Ben looked up from his computer, broke into a warm smile, and waved me in. As managing director, he was second-in-command at Sunny Junket, reporting directly to the owner of the company, who was never around. Ben had hired me about two years earlier, at a time when I was piecing my life back together and needed the job badly. Though I was a few years older than Ben, he seemed to take a paternal interest in me. He was nice. He was plump. He was from Wisconsin, I think, or maybe Minnesota. And he wore the dad jeans and yellow polo with pride.

Gesturing for me to sit in one of the two chairs in front of his desk, he asked, "What's up, Dante? You're not on the schedule today."

"It's about that new property in Indian Wells."

With a finger-snap, he said, "That's right—get the listing posted?"

"Didn't need to." After sharing all the details, I concluded, "So I think I should be there to provide our VIP Check-In service. Maude Movay—it's a party of three, actually—they plan to arrive at noon tomorrow."

"Of *course*," said Ben, standing, pacing, tickled. "Give them all the attention they want." Then he paused, asking, "And it was Jazz Friendly who set this up?"

"Indirectly, yes. She's the link."

"I'll have to thank her, maybe send her something." Ben was well acquainted with Jazz, having put her on retainer to handle occasional security and code-enforcement issues with unruly renters. He hooked his thumbs in his pockets and sputtered a quiet laugh.

"What?" I asked.

"Maude Movay—the queen of romance—sounds like the ideal guest."

Isandro Vieira walked from the car with me through the gate to the modest apartment complex where we each lived. The night sky glittered with stars, reflected on the surface of a round swimming pool centered in the shared courtyard. Strolling with his arm around my waist, Isandro hooked a finger through one of my belt loops, shook his curly dark hair aside, and looked up at me with deep brown eyes. Through the trace of a Brazilian accent, he asked, "Your place or mine?"

We had just returned from dinner—a Saturday night date, just the two of us, which had become something of a weekend ritual over the last several months. More often than not, the ritual did not end with a chaste peck under the porch light. "My place," I told him.

"My pleasure, *coração*." His simmering groan of anticipation reminded me of a purring cat. We paused outside the door to my apartment, one of six, as I fished for my keys.

"Yoo-*hoo*-oo," a woman's voice called to us. "Up for a nightcap, boys?"

I laughed. At thirty-three, Isandro was no kid, though he had an air of boyish playfulness. Me, not even close. But to our neighbor Zola Lorinsky, pushing eighty, we were both pups in our prime. Under my breath, I asked Isandro, "Can you wait?" (I knew from experience that once he reached a simmer, turning down the heat was iffy.)

"For Zola—of *course*." As he walked off in her direction, I stuffed the keys back into my pocket and followed. He called, "Hello there, Z-Doll. All's well?"

"Well enough, Isandro. Thank you for asking." Two doors down from my apartment, Zola lounged on the tastefully upholstered cushions of a wrought-iron settee. She held a tall cocktail in a frosted chimney glass—her usual Tom Collins, garnished with a cherry. Retired from a long career as an in-demand society decorator and now living alone in reduced circumstances, she still exuded style and flair. An array of flickering votive candles surrounded her, like a living shrine to this priestess of pizazz.

Stepping near, I leaned to kiss her cheek. "You're looking ravishing tonight, as always."

With a wry croak of a laugh, she said, "Don't I wish..." Then she raised a finger, tilted her head back, and took a long, noisy breath. She asked, "Isn't that divine? The citrus trees are in bloom already."

The end of February had turned warm, a mere hint of things to come. And throughout our neighborhood in south Palm Springs—throughout the entire Coachella Valley—fruit trees were gassing the night like cheap perfume. It made my eyes sting. My nose itched. But Zola loved it.

After drinking a healthy slug of her Tom Collins, she rattled the ice in the glass, extending it toward me. "Could you, love? You're the pro. And do mix a couple for yourselves."

"Gladly." Having once tended bar during an earlier—shall we say—"rough patch," I was plenty proficient at serving booze, even though liquor was not high on the list of my own vices.

When I returned to the patio from Zola's kitchen with the three cocktails, Isandro had joined her on the settee, where they gabbed, holding hands. Zola told me, "I'm trying to seduce your boyfriend."

"Good luck. I owe you big-time, but I don't owe you *that*."

"You don't owe me anything. It was only ... *curtains*." She dropped Isandro's hand and reached for the drink I offered her.

I sat facing them from an adjacent chair and passed the second glass to Isandro. After we took a moment to taste our drinks, I said to Zola, "Turns out, it was way more than curtains."

"Curtains?" said Isandro. "What'd I miss?"

"Last June," I said, "when I started doing some side work for Jazz Friendly, she'd just rented her office space downtown. A large window in the front reception room was decked out with awful plastic curtains left behind by the previous tenant—they looked like used shower curtains."

"Ghastly," affirmed Zola with a shudder.

"So Zola came to the rescue." I explained how she had once saved a bolt of fabric from a decorating job in Indian Wells—a huge house being built by a former ambassador and his wife. The fabric featured an oversize pattern of lush banana leaves, and Zola thought it would be a lively choice for Jazz's office. I told Isandro, "Then Zola made the curtains *herself*. They're gorgeous. But she wouldn't let me pay for them."

Zola shrugged, telling Isandro, "Dante was a friend in need."

"Indeed I was. Now—flash forward—the guesthouse at that same estate has just been added to Sunny Junket's luxury offerings, again thanks to Zola, who put me in touch with the ambassador's widow."

Zola breathed a gentle sigh. "Marjorie Payne and I are still friends, and I know it practically *killed* her—deciding to take in paying guests. Any takers yet, Dante?"

"In fact, yes. They'll arrive tomorrow, for a full month."

"Wonderful. I do hope you've found someone nice."

"Very." I paused. "Aren't you going to ask who it is?"

Zola and Isandro exchanged a quizzical glance. He asked, "Anyone we might know?"

"You might know the name," I teased. "But the booking is hush-hush."

"Spill it," Zola commanded.

I hesitated, but not long, before blurting, "It's *Maude Movay*. And a few hangers-on." Waiting for a reaction, I elaborated, "The author?"

"Uh, sorry," said Isandro. "If she hasn't published in Portuguese, I probably wouldn't know her."

Annoyed by this lack of enthusiasm, I pointed out, "She's been published in a *shitload* of languages—most recently Oromo."

Isandro grinned. "*Não falo oromo.*"

Zola swirled the drink in her hand. "Maude Movay. Unless I'm mistaken, she's a romance writer—women's books—something about the deadly sins?"

"Yes. Sordid Sinns, actually. And Movay needs to knuckle down—writer's block—because *Sloth* is due and there's a *streaming* deal at stake."

Zola eyed me blankly—as if I'd been speaking Oromo.

Isandro blew me a kiss. "If it's big deal for you, *querido*, it's a big deal for me. Glad it worked out."

"Ahhh," said Zola with a contented smile, "you boys are so *right* for each other."

Isandro and I shared a glance, as if weighing her words—and what they might imply about our future.

He and I had met as neighbors about two years earlier. He was then an emergency-room nurse working odd hours, and he sometimes returned home at dawn, when I was starting my day with coffee on the terrace. His apartment was across the pool from mine, and routine greetings eventually led to conversations, then drop-ins, then closed doors for an occasional quickie. But it wasn't until last autumn that we finally tried a dinner date and began exploring the possibilities for "us" beyond sex.

Just that morning, Jazz had referred to Isandro and me as "attached," and I had pushed back, telling her that we were merely "seeing each other."

And now—as he and I mulled Zola's proclamation that we were so *right* for each other—he broke into a noisy yawn, stood, and stretched, saying, "It's been a long day, Z-Doll. Will you excuse us?"

She nodded with a smile as Isandro reached for my hand.

She knew as well as I did that what he needed wasn't sleep—not yet.

CHAPTER
TWO

We woke the dog.

Mitzi the rat terrier lived in a neighbor's apartment that shared a common wall with my bedroom. Though I've never owned a dog, I have always—generally—liked them, so it gives me no pleasure to describe Mitzi as deranged. But she was. Maybe it's a terrier thing. Maybe she was inbred. Maybe she lacked training from her human, Mrs. Templeton. Whatever the root of Mitzi's derangement, it surfaced in a tantrum of barking whenever disturbed in the quiet of the night by Isandro's energetic, often vocal, lovemaking.

Despite the dog's small stature, with a bark better described as a yap, this did nothing to diminish the annoyance caused by her outbursts. What the yapping might have lacked in brute lung power was more than compensated for by its heightened, hysterical pitch and its frenzied zeal, producing an aural assault that easily penetrated not only cinder block, but also two layers of plasterboard.

This was no mere annoyance. This was a *distraction* at the very moment when I was trying to accommodate the immediate needs of a horny Brazilian.

Fortunately for Isandro, the uproar always gave him a laughing jag, which only stoked his carnal urgency, with the predictable outcome.

Me, not so much.

By dawn, therefore, I was itching for a reprise—Isandro was always ready—and Mitzi, recharged by a few hours' sleep, once again had something to bark about.

For the unchurched, Sunday mornings are meant for lolling, but it was not an option that day, the first of March, because I had to welcome Maude Movay and her retinue to the guesthouse in Indian Wells at noon. The drive would take at least half an hour, and I wanted to be there early enough to give the place a thorough spiffing, which meant I couldn't fritter away the morning in lazy noodling with Isandro. So I took him out to breakfast.

By nine thirty, we had showered, shaved, and dressed for the day as I drove him downtown to Huggamug, a coffeehouse that also served limited—that is, "artisanal"—breakfast and lunch offerings. When we walked through the door, I wondered if I might find Jazz Friendly at one of the back tables, huddled over some paperwork; her office was on the second floor of the building, where she worked alone at odd hours and sometimes preferred the stimulation of busier surroundings. But she was nowhere to be seen, probably engaged in some lazy noodling with Blade Wade at his loft.

Isandro and I didn't need to wait for a table. On weekday mornings, the place would be jammed, but not today—most of the party town was still sleeping off the antics of Saturday night. Over the explosive *whoosh* of an espresso machine, the barista called to us, "Anywhere you like—we'll be right with you."

A prime window table was open, but it was bombarded by a blinding shaft of sunlight that angled in from the street, so we chose a shadowy booth along the wall, where we could sit across from each other. "Please," I said to Isandro, gesturing for him to take the side of the table facing most of the room. "I want to show you off."

He hesitated, as if surprised by my words, eyeing me with a look of dreamy affection. Then he grinned, slicked back his hair over one ear, and slid into the booth.

When we were settled, a hunky college-age waiter appeared with menus. "Morning, guys. Something to start?" Chipper and earnest, he seemed familiar. I was hoping he'd do the spiel, introducing himself as our server, but he didn't. And I couldn't get a direct look at his face—because he was ogling Isandro.

"I'm Dante," I said. "Haven't we met?"

When he spun his head to look at me, his features hardened. He seemed all the more familiar, but I still couldn't place him. He didn't answer my question or tell me his name. Instead, he asked brusquely, "Coffee?"

Isandro claimed to like my coffee better than Huggamug's, and we'd had plenty at the apartment, so we both ordered French-style cocoa—thick, dark, and slightly bitter. To my way of thinking, that, paired with a fluffy croissant, qualified as "breakfast." But Isandro felt he needed protein (and in light of his overnight performance, I imagined he was running low), so we added quiche to our order—Florentine for him, Lorraine *pour moi*—plus a plate of slab bacon and lumpy, handcrafted sausage patties to share.

"Got it," mumbled the waiter, sounding annoyed as he turned and left.

Isandro and I both watched as he headed off to the kitchen. "Jesus," I said, "talk about a bad attitude."

"Great ass, though," said Isandro. He reached across the table and twiddled my fingers. "But yours is better."

Objectively, I agreed with him, but modesty prevented me from voicing it. So we sat, waiting for cocoa. Moments passed.

"*Coração*," he said, "have I ever told you how happy I am that we met?"

"Not in those exact words, but you've told me in many *other* ways." I smiled as my mind reeled with some of the steamier highlights of a friendship that had begun casually as sex buddies and had progressed to a relationship that now felt ... *comfortable.*

"Last night"—he spoke through a grin—"Zola said we were 'right for each other.' I think her years have brought wisdom." He arched his brows, as if to ask, Don't you agree?

Uh-oh. Again I was faced with a dilemma of my own making. Back in our sex-buddy days, *I* had been the one to suggest a dinner date, hoping we could just talk and get to know each other better, and when he declined because of his erratic nursing schedule in the emergency room, I felt jilted, certain that his interest in me ended at the bedroom door. But then he switched jobs, working for a gastroenterologist who never probed by night, and suddenly Isandro and I were dining—and "dating." And I was constantly tempted to tap the brakes.

The surly waiter delivered our cocoa and left, saving me from an awkward and uncertain conversation about my future with Isandro. Instead, we babbled about chocolate, cream, calories, fat—while indulging—and the waiter soon returned with a tray of plates that covered our table.

"Anything else?" His tone dared either of us to speak.

Surveying the bounty, I asked gingerly, "Maybe some water?"

He glared at me. I explained, "To help clear the palette—a bridge between the sweetness of the cocoa and the saltiness of the food."

He huffed off.

Isandro and I had begun to sample everything—loving the quiche, feeding each other bacon—when the waiter returned with water. He set two empty glasses on the table, but before filling them, he asked me, "Is anything all right here?"

I gave him a quizzical look. Had he misspoken? Was he trying to be funny? Or was he just being snarky? With an uncertain laugh, I said, "It's great, thanks."

"Enjoy." And he dumped the pitcher of ice water into my lap.

Isandro was even more upset than I was, unleashing a torrent of Portuguese as the waiter took off his apron, slapped it on an empty table, and walked out the front door, followed by the stares of everyone in the room. Horrified, the barista stepped in back to call out the manager, a hardworking woman of fifty or so who rushed to our table with profuse apologies.

"Who *was* that guy?" I asked while blotting my lap and the seat of the booth with a pile of towels brought by the barista.

The manager told me, "His name is Zane Smith. Been sorta moody lately—good riddance."

"He looked familiar."

Isandro asked, "You *know* him?"

"Guess not." With a laugh, I added, "I'd remember a name like *Zane*."

The manager comped everything and helped the barista pack up what was left of our meal.

I drove Isandro back to my apartment, where I could change clothes while he fed me more bacon and polished off what remained of both quiches.

"Try the sausage?" he asked.

"It's all yours, kiddo. Put that protein to good use."

Highway 111, the valley's main thoroughfare, felt deserted that morning, so it was an easy, pleasant drive from Palm Springs to Indian Wells—all the better in my jaunty Karmann Ghia, top down.

While technically a city—with a city hall and a city council—Indian Wells had no downtown, no library, no parks, no playgrounds. But it did have a world-class tennis garden, sprawling resorts, golf courses, country clubs, and banks.

And in this pretend city, fabled for lavish living amid enviable surroundings, few of its gated enclaves were as lavish or enviable as Vanguard Ridge, which contained within its walls the estate of the Honorable Grover Payne, Ambassador of the United States to the Kingdom of Norway, deceased.

When I drove up to the main gatehouse, the guard recognized me from my frequent visits during the prior week, while I was readying the Payne guesthouse for Sunny Junket's clients.

With a little salute, he pressed the magic fob that rolled back the gates, then asked through a squint, "Didn't they give you access to their private gate?"

"They did. But I wanted to make sure you were expecting Mrs. Payne's…*guests*."

He gave me a knowing nod. "Mr. Endicott, arriving at noon with two other…*guests*."

I returned the nod. The ambassador's widow had been insistent that her short-term renters never be referred to as such. And Lanford Endicott, Maude Movay's publicist and handler, had insisted there would be no record of Movay's presence.

Confident that the rules were understood, I drove slowly

through the gates. A scattering of cameras swiveled to watch me from various angles as I entered the hallowed grounds.

There was a championship golf course (ho-hum in these parts) with a vast edifice of a clubhouse, but the true allure of Vanguard Ridge was its community of estate-size housing, all of it custom-designed by name architects from the valley or the coast. The development had been fully occupied for at least twenty years, so these homes were not new, but many were now considered timeless. One of the larger estates, which loomed beyond the next curve of the winding cobbled roadway, had been built by the late ambassador—and decorated by my neighbor, Zola Lorinsky.

Most of the other houses were sleek and contemporary, but the Paynes had taken a different tack, choosing a style often described as Hollywood Regency. The design was opulent but playful, and while it was clearly meant to impress, it also felt comfortable and welcoming. Pink stucco walls were pierced by tall, slim windows, arched at the top—every one of them offering glimpses of Zola's fanciful curtains with their wild pattern of huge green banana leaves. White columns and poodle-clipped olive trees framed the entrance, where double doors of gleaming black enamel were tricked out with massive brass knockers and sunburst knobs the size of dinner plates.

And that was just the main house. It stood at the left edge of a large gravel motor court—very European—while across from it sat a many-doored garage disguised as a storybook stable. The grounds beyond were dominated by formal gardens and a flagstone terrace surrounding a swimming pool and its pool house. Nearby was the three-bedroom guesthouse. Having once lodged visiting royalty, it was now primped for the arrival of the queen of romance.

All of this was backdropped by the foothills of the Santa Rosa Mountains, dolloped just outside the Vanguard Ridge perimeter wall, which was broken only by the Paynes' private gate. Over the years, other residents had lobbied the club for such a convenience, but the ambassador alone had wielded sufficient pull to override the covenants committee.

The guesthouse had its own motor court with a fanciful trellised carport instead of a garage. I parked in front of the house, near its far end, leaving space for Maude Movay's party to pull up to the front door. After removing a large welcome basket and a folder of paperwork from the convertible, I carried them to the door and punched in the entry code. Mrs. Payne had resisted the installation of electronics, but she relented when Sunny Junket refused to represent the house if its security was limited to traditional locks with keys that could be lost or duplicated. Plus, the entry code could be changed for each new guest. With a beep, the new lock opened, and I stepped inside.

At a glance, I could tell that everything was in order for the guesthouse to receive its first *paying* guests. After a full week of preparation, nothing had been disturbed since Friday. Even the plush living-room carpet still looked freshly groomed, showing the tracks left by a heavy old Electrolux.

I walked through all the rooms and opened the curtains, which sported the same pattern of banana leaves as those in the main house—except, in these guest quarters, Zola had chosen a variation of the print that stripped away most of the color, leaving a subtle, more elegant pattern of beige leaves against unbleached linen. Beyond the windows at the back of the house, a smaller, private pool sparkled beneath the noontide sun.

After making my rounds of the bathrooms, flushing all the toilets, I returned to the living room and carried the welcome basket into the kitchen, where I arranged a few things on the granite countertop of the center island. I'd brought fresh fruit and packaged snacks. A box of dates from nearby Indio. Several bottles of wine. Two pounds of pricey coffee beans, regular and decaf. Bottled water, fizzy and still. Copies of Sunny Junket's contract and the city codes for short-term rentals. And a gadget like a garage opener, which controlled the private gate.

I had also brought a bottle of champagne—good stuff, French—its neck festooned with curly ribbons, one of which was attached to my business card. That went into the fridge, where I hoped Maude Movay would find it as a pleasant surprise the next morning when she went nosing for breakfast.

Closing my eyes, I took a deep breath, then slowly exhaled. All was ready. I could relax.

But when my eyes opened and drifted to the window, I choked at the sight of Agnetha Berg, the Payne estate's majordomo, chugging across the courtyard, heading toward the guesthouse in her ashen uniform, starched apron, and chunky black service shoes. Her head sprouted a pair of Nordic braids twisted into side buns, which brought to mind Princess Leia, except the hair was blond gone steely gray, and the woman herself would never be mistaken for a valorous young princess—perhaps a persnickety stepmother.

I heard her enter the front door. She called, "They are late."

Checking my watch, I moved from the kitchen to the living room. Annoyed by her carping, I said, "It's two minutes past twelve."

She tossed her hands. "Then they are late."

"For Christ's sake—they planned to arrive 'around noon.' It's not a *doctor's* appointment. It's Sunday morning, and they're coming here to unwind."

"It is *not* morning. They are *not* here. They are late."

"I'm *so* sorry you don't find them sufficiently prompt."

"No, Mr. O'Donnell, you are not sorry. You are sarcastic and ill-mannered. I do not appreciate your tone."

Her English had the stilted cadence and stunted syntax of a non-native speaker, and her accent still bore the haughty imprint of British tutoring. Although I didn't know the exact history of her journey from Norway to California with the ambassador, it must have been more than twenty years earlier, and in all that time, she had made little progress in assimilating the speech patterns of her adopted land. She still spoke with the precision of memorized language drills—and had seemingly skipped the chapter on contractions.

I said to her, "When they arrive, could you at least *attempt* a measure of civility? Whether you approve of them or not, Mrs. Payne has made the decision to rent this place, and it's my job— *our* job—to make sure they feel welcome and enjoy their stay. Got it?"

With a *harrumph*, she pulled a dustcloth from a big pocket in her apron, spun on her heel, and marched off to the dining room, where she gave the long mahogany table a last-minute polishing.

I stepped outside the front door for some fresh air—it was early spring in the desert, a perfect day that might later nudge eighty degrees. Full-blown beds of geraniums bordered the courtyard with mounds of pink and red. Mockingbirds with mating on their minds flitted from the trees and loop-de-looped as they warbled and sang. After marveling at this for a few minutes, I checked my watch and began to share Agnetha's impatience: Where were they?

Right on cue, two vehicles turned in from the street and

paused in the main motor court as if unsure of their bearings. When I gave them a wave, they drove slowly toward the guesthouse, crunching the gravel. A full-size BMW sedan, basic black, led a monster of a chrome-laden SUV, shocking pink—which looked very much at home amid the geraniums and the pink stucco walls. They came to a stop near the front door and cut their engines.

The queen of romance had arrived.

Or so I thought.

Agnetha Berg came out from the house and joined me on the stoop as the front doors of the BMW opened. Two men got out of the car, stretched, glanced around, and exchanged an approving nod. The passenger was several inches taller than the driver. With a look of casual sophistication, they both wore polos and linen slacks, badly rumpled by their time on the road.

I asked, "Mr. Endicott?"

"Yes." The taller man approached me with a smile, extending his hand. "Lanford Endicott—but Lanny's fine. And this is my husband, Guy Kirby."

Guy stepped over from the driver's side of the car, and I shook his hand as well. "Welcome to the Payne estate," I said. "I'm Dante O'Donnell, from Sunny Junket Vacation Rentals. And this is Agnetha, who works for Mrs. Payne."

She corrected me sharply, "I am Miss Berg."

Lanford turned to Guy with a comical *oops* expression. I sensed that Lanford was a few years older than me, probably in his mid-fifties, while Guy was younger, late forties maybe.

Through a stiff smile, I told Agnetha, "As you please, Miss Berg." I assured the men, "We're both at your service. Hope you'll enjoy your stay."

Lanford winked. "I'm sure we will."

Guy reminded his husband, "But we're here on a mission." Guy turned and explained to me, "It's not really a vacation for any of us. Lanny is Maude Movay's publicist; I'm her agent. And for the next month, we'll be her *constant* companions."

"Understood. I'm aware of the deadline. We're honored that Miss Movay chose to work on her next project here." I was watching the pink SUV, wondering when the queen of romance would emerge. Because of the darkly tinted windows and the sun's glare on the windshield, I couldn't see inside the vehicle, and I wondered if she had driven herself—or did she have a driver? That seemed unlikely, though, because Lanford had made the reservation for a party of three.

The driver's door cracked open about a foot, then paused while a man's voice spoke rapidly from inside.

Guy called over to the SUV, "Ramil! Come *on*."

A hand poked up from the door opening, bidding patience.

"*Move* it," yelled Lanford.

The door opened fully, and out he stepped.

Well, now.

I've always had a thing for short guys. And there stood quite the specimen, gabbing on his phone in a language that mystified me—it contained snippets of Spanish, but the speaker looked more Asian than Latino. Although his face struck me as both handsome *and* beautiful, there was nothing androgynous about his ripped physique. This guy was clearly no stranger to the gym. In fact, he was already dressed for his next workout, wearing cross-training shoes, spandex shorts that bunched above his thick thighs, and a muscle shirt that would've looked ridiculous on anyone else. Considerably younger than the rest of us, he could not have been thirty.

Reacting to something said over the phone, he let out a piercing laugh—a shriek that morphed into a giggle.

Guy told me, "That's Ramil Bagoyo. He may be a nutty Filipino—but he's *our* nutty Filipino."

Lanford added coyly, "He's our *constant* companion."

"Actually," explained Guy, "he's our trainer."

I got the picture: Ramil Bagoyo was their pet.

He tucked the phone into his tight shorts, which created a rectangular bulge in the stretched spandex as he walked over to us from the SUV. His smile grew wider with every step—and his eyes were trained squarely on *me*.

He stopped six inches in front of me and looked up into my eyes. His thick shock of jet-black hair gleamed iridescent in the sunlight. I blinked away the image of a raven as he touched my arm, telling me softly, "I'm Ramil. Are you single?" Then he broke into his crazy laugh.

Lanford and Guy gave each other a weary look, as if they'd seen this act before.

"Hi, Ramil...," I stammered, "... I'm Dante ... and this is Miss Berg."

The Filipino and the Norwegian exchanged a distasteful glance without speaking.

Was he waiting for me to answer his question: Was I single? He'd seemingly asked in jest, but more to the point, I didn't know what to tell him. And once again, I was unnerved by—feeling pressured by—the need to define my relationship with Isandro and to acknowledge the expectations it created.

"I'm a bit confused," I said, speaking not to Ramil, but to Lanford and Guy. "Where's Maude Movay?" By now I had concluded that she was not in the pink SUV, waiting patiently for someone to open the door for her.

Lanford rolled his eyes. "Oy. She had a last-minute ... 'thing' to take care of. She'll be driving out from LA later this afternoon."

Pointedly, Guy told his husband, "She *promised*, remember. She's *got* to get to work—no more delays."

"I know," said Lanford.

Ramil snickered, shaking his head.

Guy said, "So let's unload everything and get settled."

"*Just* a moment," said Agnetha.

All heads turned to her. I asked, "Yes?"

"Is the young man to stay?" Her eyes slid toward Ramil.

Lanford said with a shrug, "Of course."

Agnetha shook her head. "I think not. Three guests are expected. When Miss Movay arrives, there will be four."

I'd had enough of her nitpicking. "Now, *listen*, Agnetha—"

"Miss *Berg*," she reminded me.

"It doesn't *matter*," I insisted. "The carport fits three vehicles. That's what they're allowed—one vehicle per bedroom."

"Precisely," said Agnetha, clasping her hands tightly above her waist, like a stern nun of yore. "There are only three bedrooms—where is everyone to *sleep*?"

Lanford stepped up to her, speaking with restraint, "Do I really need to explain to you that my husband and I will *share* a bed?"

She glowered at him—and at Guy, the man who would share his bed.

I said to Lanford, "The double room will be plenty spacious for you. And I assume the main suite will go to Miss Movay. It has its own sitting room with a desk, plus a private terrace with mountain views—the perfect setup for some serious writing.

And that leaves the third bedroom for Ramil."

Agnetha sniffed. "It is barely a cramped cell." Addressing Ramil directly, she said, "You will not like it."

With a laugh, I assured Ramil, "You'll love it. Royalty has slept there—and I'll bet there were *no* complaints."

"Sounds good enough for me," he said, hands on hips, displaying biceps the size of coconuts. "Lemme start haulin' stuff inside." He moved to the back of the BMW and opened the trunk.

I didn't know if Ramil had been born in the Philippines or here in California, but he sounded like a bona-fide West Coast beach bum, with the laid-back swagger to match. No accent at all—unlike the Norwegian ice goddess.

"Miss Berg?" said Lanford, crossing his arms, studying her.

"Yes, sir?"

"It's ... *Agnetha* Berg, correct?"

She hesitated. "If you must know, yes, that is my given name."

He fingered his chin. "How do I know you?"

"I am certain you do not." Brusquely, she stepped around him to grab a few of the bags unloaded in the motor court, then carried them inside.

Guy came over to Lanford, asking, "What was that all about?"

"Not sure—but I need to look into something."

"Whatever it is, Lanny, it can wait. We need to get ready for Maude—and then *she* needs to get cracking."

"She does," Lanford agreed. Then he laughed. "But she has a tendency to come up with the *damnedest* excuses."

Guy wasn't laughing.

They had a *lot* of baggage.

Lanford and Guy had brought a full array of matching vintage Hartmann luggage—suitcases, carry-ons, and garment bags—which not only filled the BMW's trunk, but was piled to the ceiling in the back-seat compartment. The cavernous storage space of the pink SUV was loaded with Maude Movay's jaw-dropping collection of Vuitton, including the usual luggage and hand baggage, as well as hatboxes, purses, a sizable trunk, and four king-size pillows with satin covers. The back seat of the SUV contained Ramil Bagoyo's things—a few gym bags for his clothes, plus bulky canvas totes for equipment that had the muffled clang of iron. He'd also brought several rolled yoga mats and an assortment of hefty plastic jugs of powdered workout supplements—protein, creatine, nitric oxide, and such.

Granted, their visit was booked for an entire month, but they'd brought enough stuff to move in for good.

Agnetha and I helped trek all of this to the appropriate bedrooms, and the guests were duly impressed by their new lodgings. Within two minutes, Ramil had changed into a barely-there silver Speedo and padded out to the terrace, where he was blowing up a pool float—a flamingo that added another splash of pink to the blissful setting. Agnetha offered to unpack for Maude Movay and get her things put away in the suite. I wanted to review the paperwork with Lanford in the kitchen, and Guy went with us.

"Oh!" said Lanford, spotting the wine bottles on the center island. "Got a corkscrew, Dante? Grab an extra glass and join us."

One of the bottles was a dry rosé, which seemed appropriate for a Sunday afternoon, and moments later, we clinked as I toasted their arrival.

Guy, Maude's agent, was all business and didn't say much as he reviewed the terms of the contract and studied the city's rental regulations while Lanford and I gabbed. Then Guy interrupted us, mumbling, "I hope this is worth it—Maude better deliver." They were spending thousands per day here.

Lanford said, "Relax, sweets. It's only money." He swirled his wine, took another long sip, and swallowed. "Did I tell you? I heard from Nicole. She wants to see us while we're here— maybe dinner this week?" Then he turned to me. "Nicole is my niece. She and her husband live in Redlands. How far is that?"

I shrugged. "At least an hour."

Guy said, "Not so fast, Lanny. We need to see some progress on a manuscript before we start horsing around with social engagements."

Unconcerned, Lanford reminded him, "We've gotta *eat*. And so does Maude."

Guy started to reply, but then he noticed the gate opener, there on the countertop. Picking up the gadget, he asked, "What's this?"

I explained, "It's a clicker for the private gate, behind the guesthouse. If you're driving out, you can clip it to your visor and use it to get back in. Otherwise, I'd recommend leaving it in the house. Guests can phone you from the gate, and you can click it from here."

We heard the front door open and close. A woman's voice called, "Agnetha?"

"Coming, Mrs. Payne."

I told Lanford and Guy, "That's the owner, the ambassador's widow. You should meet her." And I led them out of the kitchen.

We arrived in the living room just as Agnetha Berg emerged from Maude Movay's suite and beelined toward the front hall, where Marjorie Payne waited near the door. Hanging above her, dwarfing her, was a fanciful oversize chandelier that could have been pilfered from a Bavarian palace. I knew that Mrs. Payne was in her mid-sixties, having been a young bride to the late ambassador, but the time since his passing had not been good to her. Despite her pampered circumstances, she looked older than her years, pale, and a bit shrunken. The floor of the entry hall was tiled with a pattern of huge squares of marble, alternating black and white. Standing at the center of a black square, Mrs. Payne brought to mind a chess piece—not a queen, but a frail white pawn.

Agnetha stepped into the front hall, asking sternly, "Yes, ma'am?"

Marjorie Payne seemed confused, as if she wasn't sure why she'd summoned Agnetha. She seemed all the more mystified by my presence. As for Lanford and Guy, their frozen silence spoke loud and clear—they were freaked, as if they'd strolled into a scene from a Bette Davis hag flick.

I moved a step or two closer. "Hello, Mrs. Payne. How kind of you to come over—*to greet your guests.*"

She blinked. Then smiled. "Dante, love—of course—won't you introduce us?"

I heard a soft but unmistakable sigh of relief from Lanford and Guy—we were all on firmer ground now. They moved with me toward the hall as Mrs. Payne stepped to meet us halfway. Agnetha followed her into the living room, where the five of us stood in a loose circle near a monumental stone sculpture of a nude Inca warrior, or perhaps he was a fertility god. Either way, he had plenty to brag about. At least ten feet tall, he rose above us toward the vaulted ceiling; if you didn't watch your step, he could poke you in the eye with his endowment. Lanford and Guy were transfixed.

Mrs. Payne said wryly, "You'll get accustomed to it, gentlemen. The ambassador acquired it on an impulse during a diplomatic mission to Peru. I hated it, so it was banished to the guesthouse. But now—I must admit—I hardly notice it."

With laughs and handshakes, Lanford and Guy introduced themselves to Mrs. Payne, who insisted they call her Marjorie. Agnetha watched stiffly as the three of them hugged. I was briefly distracted by the view through the French doors to the terrace, where Ramil was oiling himself for a sunbath. The bobbing flamingo seemed to be watching him as well.

Mrs. Payne asked, "And ... the lady ... your friend, the author? Are the accommodations to her liking?"

"I'm sure they *will* be," said Lanford. "Maude Movay was detained in Los Angeles, so she'll arrive later today."

"I look forward to meeting her. Meanwhile, Agnetha is at your service to help prepare for Miss Movay."

"Thank you," said Lanford.

Guy added, "She's been very conscientious."

"Actually," said Agnetha, "I just finished with Miss Movay's suite. All is ready."

"Splendid." Then Mrs. Payne frowned. "I suppose that means it's time for us to return to our ... *cleaning* project." Now that she mentioned it, she seemed oddly, unfashionably dressed and could easily have been mistaken for domestic help rather than the lady of the manor. Why was she helping Agnetha Berg with the housekeeping?

Agnetha checked her watch. "The day is slipping away, ma'am."

With a whimper, Mrs. Payne reminded her employee, "But it's *Sunday*. Why the rush?"

"Time is precious." Agnetha turned from us, marched out of the living room, crossed the front hall, and opened the door. "Come."

Mrs. Payne gave us a forlorn look—more resigned than pleading—then left with Agnetha, who closed the door behind them.

I stood there watching the door, scrutinizing it—as if, from the depths of its black lacquer, I might glean insights into the bizarre relationship between these two women. Finding none, I turned my attention back to the living room.

Guy was nosing around the Inca's phallus, about two feet long and thick as a baseball bat. "Marvelous craftsmanship," he muttered. "I wonder how they chiseled it from a single block of stone."

I joined the inspection. "I wonder how they *shipped* the damn thing—must weigh a couple tons. One false move, and *ouch*."

"You *two*," said Lanford with mock indignation, wagging a finger. "There's a mystery to be solved, here in the present, and it has nothing to do with *that* old thing."

Guy said, "You're absolutely right. The mystery we *must* solve is this: how to get Maude out here pronto, how to get her ass planted at her desk, and how to get a manuscript of *Cynthia's Sloth* finished in thirty days flat."

Lanford flicked a hand. "It'll happen, no worries. Meanwhile, there's a mystery *I* want to solve: What's the deal with Agnetha Berg? I sense a story here—and if I'm right, it's huge. But it needs some research first. Some digging."

With strained patience, Guy said, "*Focus*, Lanny. Focus on Maude. First things first."

I cleared my throat, then told Lanford, "If you want someone to do that digging *for* you, I know an investigator who could get all the background you need. Care to talk to her?"

Lanford grinned, nodded. "Set it up."

CHAPTER THREE

Monday morning, I planned to meet Jazz at her office, then ride to Indian Wells together, where she could interview Lanford Endicott about his research needs. But I wanted to catch up at my desk first, so I started the day at Sunny Junket, arriving shortly before eight.

"Where's your uniform?" asked Gianna from behind the reception counter as I walked through the door from the street. It was the busiest time of the year for us, and it seemed that everyone had come in early that day—the only vacant desk was mine. Gianna glanced at her computer. "You *are* working today, right?"

To my eye, she looked lousy in her baggy jeans and frumpy yellow polo with the Sunny Junket logo—a fat, cartoonish smiling sun that wore sunglasses while sunbathing on a rainbow-striped towel. Gag me. And everyone else in the room, wearing the same uniform, looked equally ridiculous. I told Gianna, "I'll be servicing top-end guests later, and in *their* world, that uniform just wouldn't cut it."

She chortled. "Tell that to Ben."

I looked over toward our supervisor's closed door. "Is he in?"

"Not yet."

"Let him know I need a minute. Okay?"

She gave her harlequin glasses a nudge with her middle finger as I stepped away from the reception area and went back to my desk.

I found a stack of files waiting for me, needing my attention, but I had grown curious about Maude Movay. Though I hadn't been familiar with her name—let alone her books—before Saturday morning, the last two days had provided something of a crash course in all things relating to the queen of romance. I now knew a good deal about her *oeuvre*, her deadlines, her finances, her lavish taste in luggage, and her cast of hangers-on. But because I'd assumed that I would meet her on Sunday—then didn't—I still had no idea what she looked like. I had no sense of how old she might be, or where she was from, or how she had risen to stardom in the bodice-ripping world of heaving breasts, quivering members, and breathless passions. In short, I had no mental picture of the woman.

But I did have a computer on my desk.

Before I'd even finished typing her name, my search filled the screen with links to everything from book reviews to fan blogs. First, though, I wanted to get a look at her, so I clicked on IMAGES, and the results were surprising—because there were so few.

I assumed that an international best-selling author would be pictured in all of the predictable settings: At work at her desk. At lunch with her editor. At readings and signings and conferences, globe-trotting to six continents. Gabbing and laughing with her legions of adoring readers. But no.

Instead, I found only some half-dozen headshots, the sort used on book covers. All of them appeared heavily retouched, to the point where they looked more like illustrations than photographs. I thought of those thumbnail pictures of Dear Abby, frozen and unreal. Maude Movay's photos made her look a bit like Betty Crocker—who never even existed—a corporate invention depicted over the years in Rockwellian brushstrokes invoking memories of everyone's mom or favorite aunt. Except, in Movay's pictures, she didn't come across as *quite* that wholesome. In fact, she could teach Betty Crocker a thing or two about selling the sizzle.

My internet search brought up these five or six images of Movay countless times in different sizes and contexts, suggesting that they were file photos, with no others available. I drew the obvious conclusion: all the pictures were outdated, and the real Maude Movay—the contemporary Maude Movay—was vain and aging.

There were no videos of her, and the handful of print interviews were basic Q&As, letter-perfect, probably conducted by email. Images running with the interviews were dominated by artwork from the book covers, accompanied by the same mug shots used on the jackets.

Turning to biographical entries, I found them sketchy at best, every one of them referring to Movay as "famously reclusive." Although she had received all of the highest awards honoring romance writers—some of them bestowed on her multiple times—she was shown in no press photos from the banquets where the awards were presented. Captions named others who "appeared on her behalf" to take home the gold. I recognized several pictures of Maude's agent, Guy Kirby, standing in for her. On other occasions, the awards were accepted by a woman identified as Maude's publisher.

Although I had meant to satisfy simple curiosity—okay,

nosiness—regarding one of Sunny Junket's guests, my digging had produced more questions than answers. Ample online speculation confirmed that I wasn't alone in my confusion. Which left me pondering what I'd be able to find out later that morning, when I would return to the Payne estate.

These thoughts were nipped when I looked away from the computer and saw my supervisor enter the building. Gianna immediately summoned him with a finger-wag and leaned across the reception desk to tell him something. He nodded, then began crossing the office in my direction. As usual, he wore the Sunny Junket uniform—and he suddenly seemed to be wearing it with an extra measure of pride.

I stood to greet him. "Good morning, Ben."

"Morning, Dante!" He flashed a broad smile, but I noticed a hint of concern in the pinch of his brows. Placing a hand on my shoulder, he asked, "You wanted to see me?"

"Yeah. Won't take a minute."

"C'mon." He waddled across the room through a maze of desks. Coworkers watched as I followed.

Entering his office, he switched on the lights; I closed the door behind us. He flumped into his chair and booted up his computer, gesturing for me to sit.

But instead, I approached his desk and remained standing. Spreading my arms, I asked, "How do I look?"

He laughed. "What's this about, Dante?"

Sharing the laugh, I said, "No, seriously—how do I look?"

"Well, *fine*. I mean, great! You're always presentable—*more* than presentable—on the job or off." He paused, then added awkwardly, "You've got a lot of style."

"Thank you, Ben." I sat. "But I wasn't fishing for compliments."

"Like heck."

"Okay, maybe I was, a little. But I was trying to make a point."

Ben grinned. "Gianna tells me you think the Sunny Junket uniform is the wrong look for our better clients."

"She's right. That's exactly what I think. I'm needed by Maude Movay's party again today, and trust me, these people are accustomed to a level of service not provided by guys in overalls."

Ben's eyes dropped to his lap. "These aren't 'overalls,' but I get what you're saying."

"Then, may I have your permission to dress as I feel is most appropriate for each day's tasks? When nothing special is happening, I'm back in the uniform."

"That sounds reasonable enough." Ben hesitated. "But…"

I asked, "But what?"

"The *others*. We have more than twenty people at Sunny Junket interacting with our guests, and they all wear the uniform. I'm not dense—I know some of them hate it. If I make an exception for you, they'll be asking about it."

I suggested, "Tell them I'm special?"

Ben rolled his eyes. "*Help* me with this."

With a soft laugh, I said, "Look. My job description is 'field inspector'—one of four at Sunny Junket. We already offer VIP Check-In service to our top-end clients, and I'm usually the one to provide that. While they're here, if they need assistance, I'm essentially their concierge. So why not make it official?"

Ben asked, "How?"

"Give me a promotion. Not necessarily a raise—unless you *want* to—but at least an actual title. How about: Field Inspector and Special-Clients Liaison?"

My boss had listened gravely. "That's a mouthful. But I *like* it."

Around ten o'clock, I left Sunny Junket, walking along North Palm Canyon Drive toward Huggamug's building, a block away, where Jazz Friendly had her offices on the second floor. Because we would be going to meet a potential client of hers, she didn't want to ride in my Karmann Ghia, which she described as projecting a certain carefree spirit of "fruitiness." Instead, she would do the driving—in her monster SUV, black, with fat tires and tinted windows, like something you'd see in a Secret Service motorcade. It had no badging at all, but it did have one of those fierce-looking matte-black grille guards bolted to the front. The very antithesis of fruity, it meant business, and it sat parked at the curb as I approached the coffeehouse.

I stepped from the sidewalk to a narrow path along the side of the building, which led back to a glass door next to a jumble of circuit-breaker panels and utility meters. Inside was a tiny lobby with a stairway leading up. There was also a joke of an elevator with its doors half open, dinging anemically; the fluorescent light within flickered yellow, on the verge of blackout. I took the stairs.

On the second floor, another glass door identified the offices of JAZZ FRIENDLY, PRIVATE INVESTIGATOR. I stepped into the reception room, where there was no secretary at the little desk, but there was a large window overlooking the street below—framed by damn nice curtains with a muted print of giant banana leaves. I called, "Jazz, it's me."

"Back here."

The stubby back hall led to either of two rooms—Jazz's working office on the street side, with a window, or the so-called conference room, which had no natural light. Jazz had switched on the ceiling lights, which alternated with acoustical tiles in a checkerboard pattern. She stood hunched over the "conference table," a battered folding banquet table, its top surface mottled with the crusty ring-shaped stains of paint cans.

Jazz looked up from a stack of mail she was sorting. "Hey, mister—looking good." With a laugh, she added, "Where's your clown shirt?" She had always derided the Sunny Junket uniform, goading me to stop wearing it, making it sound so simple.

Turns out, she was right. I told her, "I *think* I got promoted this morning. Ben says I can dress for the clients, not for the company."

She crossed her arms, studying me, allowing a smile of approval. She was no fashionista, but she had a sharp sense of personal style, appropriate to her work. Today, for meeting a prospective client, she took it up a notch, wearing a dark suit, nicely tailored for her lanky, athletic build, with a silvery blouse that had a simple band collar. No jewelry at all, but she sported a black shoulder holster, peeking out from the lapel of her jacket. Her short, tight Afro came across as both tough and professional.

I was wearing mostly black, a look I loved, not always right for the desert. But in early March, no problem. Unlike Jazz, I always wore at least *something* to add sparkle. Today it was a simple chain bracelet, polished titanium. A manly touch—as bracelets go.

Jazz showed me an envelope. "It's from Cooper Brant."

The name took a moment to click. "Aha. The architect."

"And the husband of Arcie Madera," said Jazz, referring to a detective with the Riverside County sheriff's department. Arcie had collaborated with Jazz—and by extension, with me—

on the investigation of an earlier series of murders. We'd met Cooper Brant when he and Arcie came to the opening of a gallery exhibit of works by Blade Wade.

I asked, "Didn't Cooper tell us he was a fan of Blade's paintings?"

Jazz nodded. "That's the point. Cooper just finished a commission for a new house in Palm Springs—it's a *big* deal—and his design includes a space intended for one of Blade's paintings." Jazz handed me the envelope. "There's a party next Sunday afternoon to show everything off. Blade got an invitation for him and a guest, and now, so did I. I'll have Emma that day, so if you can join us, we'll be a foursome. Wanna go?"

"Sure," I said while glancing over the invitation. "It's six days from now, but I doubt if I'll need to work that weekend." I slipped the invitation back into the envelope, then set it next to the stack of other mail. I must have grimaced.

"What's wrong?"

"Well ... this *table* ... this whole *room*. How can you expect clients to take you seriously?" The seating around the table consisted of vinyl-strapped aluminum lawn chairs.

Jazz shrugged. "Just starting out, Dante."

"That excuse may have worked last year, but it's wearing thin. I know you can't spend what you don't have, but you're getting established now. It might be time to set aside something to invest in *appearances*."

She took it all in, frowned, and turned to me. "You'll help, right?"

"Not with the loot—but anything else, just let me know."

She mouthed a silent "Thank you," then kicked at one of the lawn chairs, which toppled over and clattered shut on the floor.

She left the room, crossed the hall, and ducked into her office.

I waited for her in front, and when she emerged, she held a stack of several books in one arm.

"Let me guess," I said. "The first six of the 'Seven Sordid Sinns' series."

"Yup," she said, handing me the book on top, the most recent installment, *Cynthia's Wrath*. Jazz explained, "If I'm gonna meet the queen of romance, I'm gonna come away with a few autographs. They're hard to get—I've heard that Miss Movay is sorta reclusive."

"*Famously* reclusive," I said dryly.

When I flipped the book over, one of Movay's starched and ageless file photos stared up at me from the back of the jacket.

Riding down valley together in the black SUV, Jazz looked over from the driver's seat, asking me, "They said she'd be there *today*, right?"

"She was supposed to arrive late yesterday, so she ought to be there now."

"And the guy I'll be talking to—it's Miss Movay's agent, right?"

"Wrong. It's her agent's husband, Lanford Endicott. He describes himself as Movay's publicist and handler. But the reason he needs you has nothing to do with Movay. He's curious about the woman who runs the servant staff at the Payne estate. Her name is Agnetha Berg. She's Norwegian—and a pill."

"But why the background check?"

"Not a clue. Lanford Endicott will need to explain that."

A few minutes later, when we entered Indian Wells from Highway 111, I asked Jazz, "Ever been to Vanguard Ridge?"

She snorted. "Like most folks, I've driven *past* it, but let's just say they've never flagged me down and waved me in. The entrance—about a mile ahead on the right?"

"Yes, but I'll show you a shortcut. Turn at the next corner."

She slowed the vehicle. "*Here?*"

"This is it." It didn't look like an intersection, more like an unmarked driveway.

The two-lane service drive headed back toward the mountains, separating the grounds of Vanguard Ridge on one side from the neighboring club on the other side. It felt like driving through a tunnel, with high border plantings rising from both sides—hedges of ficus, oleander, and tamarisk, interspersed with stands of date palms.

I pointed to a clearing ahead. "Turn in—there."

The SUV swerved and came to a stop at a solid metal gate. A discreet sign informed us politely: PRIVATE ENTRANCE.

"La-di-da," said Jazz. There was no guard, no keypad, no intercom, no camera, no buzzer. She asked, "Now what?"

I explained coyly, "It helps if you know who to call." After punching a number into my phone, I waited a few moments, then responded, "Hi, Lanford. It's Dante O'Donnell. I have Jazz Friendly with me." And the gate rolled open on a track that disappeared in the bushes.

Jazz pulled forward and followed the narrow drive as it wound through the heavily planted grounds, then emerged into the motor court of the guesthouse. Stopping the vehicle, she muttered, "Sweet Jesus."

"My thought exactly." I'd been there many times already, but the moment of arrival never got old.

Jazz and I left her vehicle, and while walking toward the front door, I noticed the trellised carport and its three stalls. Two were occupied by the black BMW and the pink SUV; the third stall was vacant.

Lanford Endicott stepped out from the guesthouse and met us in the courtyard, extending his hand to me. "Welcome back, Dante. So this is Inspector Friendly, eh? Pleased to meet you." They shook hands.

"My pleasure. But please, Mr. Endicott, call me Jazz."

"Delighted—and I'm Lanny." Noting the stack of books cradled in Jazz's left arm, he asked, "You're a fan?"

"*Hell* yeah." Jazz beamed. "Hoping to get these signed, if Miss Movay doesn't mind. Hoping to *meet* her—I feel like I already know her through Cynthia Sinns."

Lanford reached to take the books from Jazz. "Let's leave these for Maude inside. I'm sure she'll be happy to sign them, but unfortunately, you'll have to meet her some other day."

I asked, "She's not here? Hasn't she arrived yet?"

"Oh, she *arrived*," Lanford assured me. "Later than planned, not till after dinner last night, but she's officially 'in residence' now, thank God. She managed to spend a good hour or so at her laptop this morning—it's a start—but then she insisted on running out for a few things. I think she just wanted to nose around. She's quite the minx—and *such* a procrastinator."

I laughed. "Good luck reining her in."

"Thanks, Dante. I'll need it." He heaved a dramatic sigh. "Now, then. Shall we?" And he led us over to the house. Jazz followed him through the front door, which I closed behind us.

In the living room, Lanford paused to let Jazz look around— the nude Inca caught her attention. The Filipino trainer caught *my* attention, just beyond the French doors, out on the pool terrace, directing Guy Kirby through an exercise routine. They had a few dumbbells and a weight bench, but I could tell it wasn't much of a workout, more like going through the motions.

When you employ a full-time, live-in trainer, if he's smart, he doesn't push too hard.

Lanford saw me watching, so he called out to the terrace, "Guy, Ramil, come in and say hi."

Ramil had already noticed me and bounded into the living room at a trot. Guy, who had been lying on the bench, concentrating on his presses, took a moment to sit up, orient himself, and follow Ramil indoors. Wearing gym duds, they both looked sweaty and sensual. Ramil was far more pumped than Guy, who was only an inch or two taller and quite a few years older, but it was easy to imagine them as a couple.

Ramil quickly introduced himself to Jazz, then turned to me with a look that went beyond friendly or flirtatious—he literally licked his lips. "*Dante.* You're *back.*"

"Nice to see you again, Ramil." I felt obliged to offer a chaste hug, which he leaned into with a low growl.

Jazz gave me a wry look—an accusation that I was thinking with my dick again. She'd developed an uncanny degree of insight.

Lanford said, "Jazz, this is my husband, Guy—we're both here to 'encourage' Maude to get her next book written on deadline."

Guy said, "And so far, we've got maybe a page or two. Good to meet you, Jazz. Hope you can help Lanny with his research project—because right now, he's got his hands full with Maude." Though spoken to Jazz, Guy's words seemed more directed to his husband.

Lanford told Guy, "I'm afraid we've got one more disruption on the horizon, but that should be it for a while."

"Christ. What's the 'disruption'?"

"Nicole phoned again this morning. She and Saxon want to drive over and meet us for dinner tomorrow."

I recalled that Nicole was Lanford's niece, living in Redlands. "*Lanny*," said Guy, "we *need* to knuckle down."

"Understood. So the sooner we get this out of the way, the better."

Exasperated, Guy tossed his arms. "I give up." And he left the room, returning to the pool terrace. Ramil followed him—but not before flashing me a smile.

Lanford shifted the stack of books from one arm to the other, saying, "Let's drop these off for Maude." Then he led us back to her suite.

I had seen it many times, but it was new to Jazz, and she was duly impressed. A housekeeper fussed with the bed, plumping pillows and straightening the dust ruffle; she was a woman I hadn't seen before, Latina and much younger than Agnetha Berg. Lanford greeted her as Nina, then stepped into the adjacent sitting room and set the stack of books on a graceful writing desk, where Maude Movay's laptop sat folded open, its screen darkened. Jazz went over to snoop, as if to absorb Movay's presence, but I was more interested in other details of the author's suite.

For instance, I was surprised to see that the Vuitton hatboxes that had been unloaded from the pink SUV contained not hats, but wigs. Four of them were displayed around the room, propped on white long-necked mannequin heads. Sinuous and featureless, the heads were meant to be glamorous, but to me they looked extraterrestrial. (Who could *sleep* with those things watching over the bed?) Movay also seemed to have an affection for Hermès scarves, with their equestrian motifs and autumnal palette of golds and browns. Each of the mannequins had a silk scarf pouffed around its neck; more scarves were draped over the arms of furniture.

Adjoining the bedroom was a sprawling bath outfitted with more marble and gilt than most churches. A glance through the doorway was all it took to discover that Maude Movay was not a fussy, tidy sort. Damp towels were strewn everywhere. The counter surrounding the sinks was covered with a haphazard array of cosmetics, pills, sponges, tweezers, brushes, and such, with wads of Kleenex plopped everywhere but in the waste-basket. The mirrored wall above the two gold clamshell-shaped sinks was splattered with toothpaste and smeared with God knows what. Nina had her work cut out for her.

"Um, excuse me," said Lanford, closing Maude's laptop. "I need to have a word with Guy. Back in a jiff." Then he walked out to the terrace and disappeared, leaving Jazz and me with Nina.

Jazz asked her, "Have you *met* her? Miss Movay?"

Nina grinned. "No, ma'am. She was gone when I got here this morning."

"Don't you just love her books?"

Nina hesitated. "Sorry. Never heard of her."

I laughed. "I'm with you, Nina. I'm Dante, by the way. And this is my friend, Jazz."

Nina stepped over to give each of us a quick handshake. "I'm Nina Rodriguez. I work for Mrs. Payne. She owns all this."

Jazz said, "It must be quite an experience, living here—what a setup."

"Oh, no, I don't *live* here. I'm just day help, working my way through college—psychology."

"Good field," said Jazz. "More and more crazies in the world."

"Yeah. *Tell* me." Nina laughed.

I asked, "So, the staff here—is it very big?"

"I hear it used to be huge, but not anymore. The only live-in is Agnetha. Everyone else is hired on an as-needed basis. Mostly maintenance guys."

"You like the job?"

"Well, *look* at this place—it beats waiting tables. And Mrs. Payne is really sweet—a little strange at times, but a good person, once you get to know her. Plus, she pays me."

I said, "But I assume you report to Agnetha. What do you think of *her*?"

"She's... I don't know... she's..."

"Well! It's all settled," said Lanford, returning from the terrace. "What say we adjourn to the kitchen? Don't know about you, but *I* could use a little something." And he shooed us out of the bedroom, leaving Nina to clean up Movay's mess.

As it was nearly noon, I wondered if Lanford's mention of "a little something" was a reference to lunch. But no, he needed a drink.

Waltzing us into the kitchen, he said to Jazz, "Ladies first. What'll it be—wine, perhaps a spritzer, or something *stronger*?"

Not even tempted, she replied, "Thanks, Lanny, water's fine."

"*Bor*-ing," he singsonged, "but your wish is my command."

Jazz and I seated ourselves on barstools at the center island while Lanford fussed at the sink, clearing a few breakfast dishes before drawing a glass of water from the tap. He turned to show me a smudged champagne glass bearing a lipstick print. "Maude said to thank you for the 'swell bottle of bubbly'—her words."

I laughed. "Did she have it for breakfast?"

"Nah. Got into it last night but didn't finish it. Want some?"

"Well... it's for *her*."

"She won't mind, won't even notice it's gone. If she does, I'll say it went flat and got dumped. But it's fine." He retrieved the half-full bottle from the fridge, removed its hefty chromed stopper, and poured the remaining champagne into two sparkling flutes. Then he brought all three glasses to the island and sat with us. "Cheers," he said.

We echoed the toast and drank.

"*So*, then," he said, setting down his glass, "I talked to Guy about tomorrow night. He's *really* ticked that my niece and her husband are intruding on our time, so I suggested that we host a simple little dinner here at the house—get them in and out and be done with it. Guy thought that sounded reasonable. Ramil will play houseboy, and maybe we can get that Agnetha creature to help with kitchen duties. Anyway, Ramil suggested we should invite *you*, Dante, and *I* think you should bring Jazz along, so she can watch that *horrid* Agnetha in action. How 'bout it?"

Jazz and I gave each other a quizzical look.

With a shrug, I told Lanford, "Sure…I guess."

Jazz said to me, "Shouldn't you bring *Isandro*? I mean, you guys are a thing, right?"

Here we go again, I thought. But she had a point. I said, "I'll ask him. Not sure if he's free."

Lanford said, "If he's free, let me know, and bring him. Either way, bring Jazz."

Jazz said, "Okay, count me in. But what's this about, Lanny? Why do you want me to see Agnetha 'in action'?" She took a notebook from her jacket, flipped it open, and clicked a ballpoint.

Lanford emptied his glass and sat back, gathering his thoughts.

"Before I joined Maude's team, I had a life of my own—as a writer. My background was in journalism, and I tried my hand at a few true-crime books, finding a measure of success. Just to be clear: I never got *near* Maude's league. So it was an easy decision—and lucrative—to sign on with her. As it happens, Guy is not only Maude's agent, but he was mine, too, when I was publishing. That's the connection that brought us all together. And now Guy and I are married, so we're truly committed to this enterprise."

"And that 'enterprise,'" I said, "is Maude Movay."

"Exactly. It's been fulfilling, and it's paid off. But still, sometimes, I get the itch to return to my roots as a writer, even if it's only a diversion while shepherding Maude's career. Then, yesterday, I came face to face with Agnetha Berg."

Jazz said, "And you want some digging—a background check on Agnetha. But why?"

Lanford leaned forward on his elbows, explaining, "When we arrived here, the moment I heard her name, it sounded familiar. I recalled a wire story—this was well over ten years ago, maybe twenty—about a man who died under suspicious circumstances in Palm Springs. He'd been married only briefly to a woman, a Norwegian immigrant, who I think was Agnetha Berg. The case went cold, but I'll bet this has the makings of a blockbuster—a blockbuster *I'd* like to write. Trouble is, I can't even *think* about a book of my own until Maude gets her next manuscript buttoned down. So I need some preliminary research."

"Easy," said Jazz. "But this sounds like basic internet stuff."

"To a degree, it is. And in fact, I did a good bit of it last night. This *is* the woman, I'm almost certain, but nothing was ever proven, and no charges were brought against her. The case files have been collecting dust for years, and there's not much documentation online that goes back that far."

I said, "Sounds interesting."

"It does," Jazz agreed. "But what's the rush? If the case has been cold for that long, nothing's gonna change during the next month."

"What *will* change," said Lanford, "is this: right now, I have daily access to Agnetha, and by extension, so do both of you. Once Maude meets her deadline—God willing—we're outta here. So I want you to get going on this, Jazz, while we're in a position to follow up on whatever you might find."

Jazz looked up from her notes. "As it happens, I used to be on the Palm Springs police force, and I still have friends there. Meaning, I have channels of communication you won't find on the internet."

"Sounds perfect," said Lanford.

I asked Jazz, "George?" He was a pal of hers when they worked together and had helped her with a previous case. He was a savvy, fit, and handsome Latino cop, a plainclothes detective I wouldn't mind seeing again.

Jazz nodded while giving me that wry look—she could guess what I was thinking. Then she told Lanford, "I'll need to review my fee schedule with you and the terms of payment. I can send those documents to your phone right now, and if you want to proceed, we can sign a memo of agreement."

Lanford pulled his phone from a pocket and set it on the counter. "Sure. Let's do it."

This was going to take a while, so I excused myself, got up, and set my glass of champagne near the sink—it *was* flat, despite Lanford's assurance and his fancy chrome cork. Then I strolled from the kitchen to the living room.

Out on the pool deck, Ramil was still "training" Guy. I watched through the open French doors while they went through several sets of bench presses using a pair of dumbbells that could not have weighed more than twenty pounds each. Guy grunted each time he lifted them, while Ramil squatted near Guy's head, assisting him by gently lifting his elbows. At the end of each set, Ramil said, "Good job." Nice work if you can get it.

The doorbell chimed.

I thought Nina might appear from Maude's suite to answer the door, but she probably hadn't heard the chime over the roar of the flamethrower needed to clean that bathroom. Ramil and Guy had just started a new set of presses. As the doorbell rang again, I called into the kitchen, "Want me to get that?"

"Please," said Lanford.

When I opened the door, an old fruitcake gave me a wink. "Hello there, handsome." He wore a gauzy white jumpsuit with a floppy-brimmed white sun hat and, on his feet, a pair of gold-strapped thongs. At his side was an oversize fuchsia weekender bag on wheels. "Could you let Miss Movay know that Bruce Tucker is here? To do her hair."

"Well, I wish Mrs. Payne had *told* me that I only needed to pick up Miss Movay's *wigs*—I wouldn't have bothered to pack up the whole damn *shop*." Bruce Tucker stomped one of his thongs, which made only the slightest thud on the thick carpet.

He stood in the living room, talking to Lanford, called in from the kitchen. The commotion had brought Guy in from the patio; Ramil stood near one of the open French doors, grinning, on the verge of laughter. Jazz and I kept our distance, watching from the front hall as Lanford tried to mollify the miffed hairdresser.

"I apologize for the confusion, Mr. Tucker," said Lanford. "It's my fault. When I asked Mrs. Payne if she could recommend someone, I guess I forgot to mention the wigs. Miss Movay will be *ever* so grateful if you can help her—Mrs. Payne says you're the best in the valley."

Flattery is everything, or at least it was for Bruce Tucker, whose little tantrum evaporated. Flopping a palm to his chest, he said, "I'll be *honored* to extend my services to Miss Movay. I'm such a huge fan." He leaned to unzip the top of his fuchsia bag, then pulled out a copy of *Cynthia's Wrath*. "Might I possibly get an autograph?"

Taking the book, Lanford said warmly, "Of *course*. I'm afraid Miss Movay is out at the moment, but I'll leave this for her to sign later. Now, let me go fetch those wigs for you." And he carried the book off to Maude's suite.

Guy said to Bruce, "I'm Miss Movay's agent. Can I assume you're looking forward to the *next* Cynthia Sinns installment?"

Bruce rolled his eyes dreamily. "Well, who *isn't*?"

Guy asked, "Don't you just *love* Cynthia—and Miss Movay—the way they always leave you wanting more?"

"You got that right." Bruce's mood took another turn and darkened. "Remember Darnell?"

"Ah, yes," said Guy. "Darnell was Cynthia's hairdresser."

Bruce said, "Precisely—he *was* Cynthia's hairdresser—till Miss Movay *killed* him. Darnell was the sweetest, funniest, most gorgeous hunk of a hair burner you'd ever wanna know. Then Miss Movay killed him *off*. How *could* she?"

"Uh …," said Guy, searching for the right words, "I imagine she was serving the greater needs of the plot—many writers are forced to disappoint their readers from time to time. Don't take it personally."

"How can I *not* take it personally? It makes me want to—"

"Here we go," said Lanford, returning to the living room with several wigs. Removed from the mannequin heads, they looked limp and ratty. One of them resembled a dead Pekingese. Lanford asked, "Can you have them back by Wednesday?"

Bruce took the wigs. "Day after tomorrow—sure. Can I meet Miss Movay then?"

"She should be here, and we'll have your autographed book."

Bruce's mood lifted again as he carefully tucked the wigs into his bag. "See you Wednesday." He turned and headed toward the door. His flip-flops slapped the marble floor of the front hall.

Jazz glanced at her phone and told me, "I need to check on something—meet you outside." Then she followed Bruce out the door, closing it behind her.

I asked Lanford, "Did you get everything settled with Jazz?"

He gave me a satisfied nod. "She's on the job—even as we speak, it seems."

I spent a minute or two with Lanford and Guy, making sure they were satisfied with their accommodations. Then they firmed up the logistics of Tuesday evening's dinner party, meant to be simple and brief: cocktails at six, dinner at six thirty or so, and "out the door by eight." They asked me to let them know if Isandro, referred to as my "friend," would be coming or not, and I assured them I'd have an answer by next morning.

Turning to leave, I noticed that Ramil had stepped farther

into the living room from the terrace. With a crooked smile, he told me, "Seeya tomorrow night."

I paused to eye him for a moment with a blank expression, liking what I saw, but thinking it best not to respond.

When I left the house and stepped into the motor court, Bruce Tucker had already departed. Jazz sat in her black SUV with the engine idling while she fiddled with her phone.

I hopped in. "And how's every little thing with your friend George?"

"I dunno—haven't reached out to him yet. I've been running the plates on that pink SUV. I assumed it belongs to Maude Movay, but guess what. The registered owner is Lanford Endicott."

Curious, I thought. "Well," I said, "he describes himself as Movay's handler. Maybe that's one of the things he handles."

"Maybe." Jazz set aside her phone and shifted into gear.

After work that evening, around five thirty, I drove back to my apartment complex. The sun would not set for another hour, and the sky was fully lit, but the south end of Palm Springs was already engulfed by the long blue shadow of the mountains. The day's end had turned chilly, and I was in my shirtsleeves, so after parking the Karmann Ghia, I went to my apartment and put on a sweater. Moments later, I returned to the patio, circled the pool, and rapped on Isandro's door. We had no specific plan that night, but I'd seen his car at the curb, and we often got together for a drink before deciding what to do about dinner.

"I recognized your knock," he said while opening the door.

We exchanged an easy kiss over the threshold. I suggested, "Put on a jacket. We can have a drink by the pool."

"Sure. Want to ask Z-Doll to join us?"

"Good idea." So I walked over to Zola's apartment while Isandro weighed the options for his wardrobe adjustment—a matter he never approached lightly.

I knocked twice, and Zola's windows were dark, so I returned to my own apartment and poured two glasses of wine. By the time I stepped out to the patio again, Isandro had come over, wearing not a jacket, but a basic charcoal V-neck sweater that looked a lot like mine. We arranged a couple of chairs and a small table near the edge of the pool, then relaxed, watching the sky turn orange as we sipped.

For a full minute or two, neither of us spoke. Then I said, "If you're free tomorrow night, would you like to join me at a dinner party in Indian Wells? It's just a client thing, no big deal, and Jazz will be there, too, doing some paid snooping for these folks. You're welcome to come, but it's kind of a long haul, there and back."

"You make it sound *very* enticing," he said with a sardonic chuckle. "But I have ... something happening tomorrow. Sorry."

"No problem. Just thought I'd ask."

"This is the author, right? Maude what's-her-name?"

"Yeah. But it's weird. I haven't actually seen her yet ... just 'her people.'"

Isandro chuckled again. "That *is* weird." Then we both went silent.

So. He had "something happening" tomorrow night. What did *that* mean? And why did he phrase it so evasively? I recognized the irony of my mixed emotions. Even though I had all but told him he wouldn't enjoy the dinner party, I felt jilted when he declined. On the other hand, I was relieved he wouldn't be there on the same turf with Ramil Bagoyo, a hot-as-hell little number who projected all the warning signs of forbidden fruit. What was I *thinking*?

A door opened behind us, and I turned in my chair to see Mrs. Templeton emerge from her apartment with Mitzi, the deranged rat terrier, on a leash. Isandro and I stood, looking twinsy in our matching sweaters as we greeted my neighbor: "Hello, Mrs. Templeton." "Nice time for a walk."

"Thank you, gentlemen," she said airily. "It's good to get out, and Mitzi *so* enjoys a little mingle with her friends."

As usual, the dog strained at the leash, darting toward the nearest victim's ankles—mine.

CHAPTER
FOUR

The next morning, I phoned Lanford to let him know that "my friend" would not be coming to dinner. Then I called Jazz, telling her, "It's just us tonight. Ride together?"

"Sure. Wanna drive?"

"If you're willing to take my car. You called it 'fruity.'"

"Won't matter with *that* crowd."

Lanford hoped to move things along that night and would not appreciate latecomers, so Jazz and I needed to be in Indian Wells by six sharp. To give us plenty of time for the drive, I told her, "I'll swing by your office at twenty past five."

"Got it. I'll be at the curb."

I offered to close the car's roof, but she said, "Nah, leave it open—nothin' messes with *this* hair." And we were off, heading down valley in the Karmann Ghia. Low-angled sunlight skimmed across the surrounding mountains, their slopes glowing deep orange against the jagged black crags.

As we left Palm Springs, I asked, "Talk to George today?"

She gave me a knowing look. "You seem a little obsessed with that topic."

I shrugged, eyes on the road. "Not obsessed. Just nosy."

She said, "I called him. Explained the situation. He sorta remembers the case and said he'd check the files."

Other than that, Jazz and I didn't talk much, enjoying the drive and the rush of air, which had barely cooled since the warm afternoon.

Shortly after crossing the city limits into Indian Wells, while approaching Vanguard Ridge, I decided to use the main gate, giving Jazz the full treatment, rather than slipping in through the back entrance. When I pulled up to the gatehouse, the guard recognized me, gave a thumbs-up, and pressed the button. "Well," said Jazz as the gate rolled back, "aren't *we* special?" Cameras swiveled to record our arrival, as if we were rock stars.

The Karmann Ghia crunched the gravel as we rolled into the motor court in front of the Paynes' guesthouse. It seemed we were first to arrive for the dinner party. The only other vehicles were the two parked in the carport—the black BMW and the pink SUV. As before, the third stall was empty, and I wondered if Maude Movay had slipped away again.

I parked, then checked my watch—three minutes till six. I said to Jazz, "Let's go in. Lanford won't mind if we're early."

When we rang the bell, Ramil Bagoyo opened the door to greet us. Though Lanford had told us Ramil would "play houseboy" that evening, he looked more like a butler, with black tux, white bowtie, and patent oxfords—but no gloves.

"Wow," said Jazz, "you clean up *nice*."

He certainly did.

He told us, "Guy and Lanford like me to dress up now and then." Grinning, he added, "... if you know what I mean."

When he walked us inside, I could see at a glance that Lanford's promised "simple little dinner" was nothing of the kind. The living room was resplendent with floral arrangements and candles that were not yet lit, awaiting sunset. The long mahogany table in the adjacent dining room was draped with white linen and bore more candles, more flowers. The table was set for nine, with four along both sides and the ninth looking like a seat of honor at one of the ends. Each setting included gold-rimmed china and enough sterling and crystal to service a five-course meal. I was well acquainted with the tableware provided with the rental, and this wasn't it—not even close. Where had they *gotten* all this since yesterday afternoon?

While driving from Palm Springs, Jazz and I had reviewed who was expected to be there that night: Lanford, Guy, and Maude. Lanford's niece and her husband, driving over from Redlands. Plus Jazz and me. That's seven at the table, but it was set for nine, so there were now two mystery guests. Ramil and presumably Agnetha Berg would be "the help."

But then Nina Rodriguez, the psychology student and part-time chambermaid, appeared from the kitchen wearing a frilly little black uniform with a lace-trimmed white apron, asking what we would like to drink. When she returned to the kitchen, I got a glimpse through the swinging door and saw Agnetha working at the stove, wearing her usual drab gray dress. So the help now numbered three.

This did not qualify as a "simple little dinner," even by royal standards. But when I had phoned Lanford that morning and asked what we should wear, he told me, "Whatever you're comfortable in—it's 'just us.'" Fortunately, I had not worn shorts or a T-shirt or Top-Siders. I looked reasonably dressy in basic black—silk shirt, slacks, and nice loafers—but it was no tux. As for Jazz, she always looked good. She wore her usual dark, mannish suit, glammed up for tonight with low pumps and a black blouse that was buttoned at the collar with a large iridescent pearl. She didn't bring her gun.

"Welcome!"

We turned at the sound of Lanford Endicott's lilting voice as he entered the living room from the bedroom hall. He wasn't wearing a tux, not exactly, but a wildly colorful dinner jacket—the fabric looked a bit like a Jackson Pollock splatter painting—with a silky mock turtleneck of peacock blue. He said, "You're prompt—I *love* that." Catching Ramil's eye, he mimed tippling a drink that he wanted.

Jazz said with a laugh, "I'm sorta blown away, Lanny. This is all so...*much*."

I asked him, "A simple little dinner—this is how you do it?"

"Always!" He reached for the glass Ramil brought him, apparently not his first. It looked like a brown martini with a cherry—a Manhattan or a Rob Roy, no doubt.

Dingdong.

"I'll get it," called Guy Kirby, shooting out from the bedroom hall and heading toward the front door. His getup was similar to Lanford's, but much more subdued. The jacket was a solid muted shade of mauve; the turtleneck, dove gray.

I heard the clack of the door's heavy hardware, then voices raised in greeting.

"Lanford," Guy called to his husband while escorting the arrivals into the living room, "the kids are here."

Lanford whisked over to his niece and her husband, bubbling pleasantries as he kissed each of them on both cheeks. They appeared to be around thirty years old. Lanford must have told them earlier, as he had told me, to wear whatever made them comfortable—and they had taken him at his word.

Nicole wore a loose-fitting sundress made of cotton with a faded, fussy granny print of little herbs and buds and arabesques. The shoes she wore to dinner were dirty white canvas high-top sneakers. Her long, straight honey-colored hair reached nearly to her waist and hadn't been washed in a while. She looked like a throwback to the hippie era that had disappeared while I was a kid, before she was born.

Her husband, a trim Asian man with glasses, wore a corduroy sport coat over a baby-blue polo, along with rumpled khaki pants and, sure enough, a pair of Top-Siders that resembled the pair I'd left at home. Overall, he gave the impression of being a bit nerdy and reserved, but he was clean. And he was damn cute—in an owlish, academic sort of way.

Lanford introduced Jazz and me to Nicole Endicott Chang and Saxon Chang.

I said, "And I understand you're from Redlands."

Nicole nodded. "I am *now*. I grew up in LA, but life has many journeys, and one of those paths led to *Redlands*, of all places, where I found Saxon at the university."

Jazz asked Saxon, "You teach?"

"A little," he said. "Mostly, I'm in research—neuroscience. I came to it by way of molecular biology." Though he had a trace of an accent, he spoke with complete fluency and ease.

Nicole grinned, telling Jazz and me, "He's a brainiac—gotta love him."

Saxon gave us a thin smile, as if uncomfortable with his wife's words.

Jazz asked Nicole, "Are you also at the university?"

She hemmed. "Off and on. I was doing some grad work when I met Saxon, then sorta soured on the program. Now I'm ... working in a shop, you could say. But it's not very interesting. What about *you* guys? I hear you're private eyes?"

I told Nicole, "Jazz is the private investigator; I just help out sometimes. I'm here because I arranged this rental for your uncle."

Nicole seemed far more interested in Jazz, asking her, "Then, why are *you* here?"

I noticed that Agnetha Berg had popped out from the kitchen and was fussing with something in the dining room, within earshot. I saw Lanford watching Agnetha as well. He told his niece, "That's why they call Jazz a *private* investigator—whatever she's doing here is none of your business, young lady." His admonishing words were tempered by a humorous tone.

Nicole shrugged it off. "Can I get a drink—or what?"

Lanford reminded her, "Magic words ..."

"All right, all right: *May* I get a drink, *please?*"

"Of *course,*" said Lanford brightly. With a finger-snap, he signaled for Ramil to take care of Nicole.

Saxon hadn't said much since noticing the ten-foot Inca warrior on the far side of the room. He took off his glasses, craned his neck, and blinked in the direction of the horizontal stone phallus, which seemed to defy gravity.

I told Saxon, "He was shipped here from Peru by the ambassador who built this estate."

"We named him Mr. Big," said Guy, taking Saxon over for a closer look.

Dingdong.

Nina skittered to the door, straightening her apron, while the rest of us drank, mingled, and gabbed. Assuming the chimes had signaled the arrival of our two mystery guests, I watched with curiosity as the couple entered the front hall. Then I nudged Jazz, directing her gaze to the door.

"Holy shit," she mumbled.

It was Jazz's ex-husband, Christopher Friendly, with his new law partner, Allison Harper, who was Maude Movay's longtime contract attorney.

Jazz pronged the fingers of one hand to her forehead. "I'm not quite...*processing* this."

I began to explain, "Allison Harper needed a place for her client—"

"I know the *connection*," said Jazz. "But isn't it weird? I just met this chick last Saturday, with Christopher. And now? Here they are again—together."

I reminded Jazz, "Maude is Allison's *client*."

"I get that. Fine. But what the fuck is *Christopher* doing here?"

I stated the obvious: "Allison must've invited him to come along."

"Uh-huh. And just *why* would she do that?"

I said firmly, "You are reading *far* too much into this."

Jazz broke into a huge, toothy smile as they approached. "Christopher ... and Allison ... what a delightful surprise!"

They returned the pleasantries, ordered drinks, and thanked me for finding "such splendid accommodations" for Maude Movay's writing retreat. Allison must have been accurately clued to the lavish plans for that evening's festivities, as she had worn a glamorous red cocktail dress that was a dead match for her striking, oversize eyeglasses. Christopher looked good, too, in a perfectly proper business suit.

He dropped out of our conversation for a minute or two when his attention drifted to Mr. Big—all of the guests eventually took turns marveling at and inspecting the stone warrior— but then Christopher snapped back to the moment, turning to ask us, "Where's Maude?"

The question kept popping up during cocktails, responded to with wondering shrugs from other guests and the staff—and with lame answers from the hosts.

Guy Kirby, clearly agitated by Maude's prolonged absence, could only speculate: "She must have been detained. She needed to go out briefly and said she'd be back by now. I'm sure she won't be long."

Lanford Endicott was nonchalant, telling us, "When she gets here, she gets here—that's just Maude being Maude."

By seven thirty, however, the queen of romance had not appeared, and we were finally herded into the dining room, where everyone took their seats—with the conspicuous exception of our esteemed hostess, missing from the head of the table. I could forget about Lanford's stated plan to get everyone "out the door by eight."

During the extended cocktail period, I had nursed a single glass of wine that I didn't finish, and Jazz had stuck to Perrier, but the others—to varying degrees—were already buzzed.

Working in tandem, Ramil and Nina efficiently served, then cleared, the first two courses—vichyssoise, followed by a shrimp salad. (It wasn't my imagination: Ramil made a point of brushing my shoulder each time he reached around me.) Since everyone was hungry, the conversation was limited and tended to focus on the food, with compliments to the chef. Agnetha made a brief appearance from the kitchen, accepting a polite smattering of applause. It was the first time Jazz had seen Agnetha, so she sat back to scribble notes.

After the wineglasses were topped up again, the main course was served, with Ramil and Nina circling the table with platters, offering a mixed grill of halibut, beef tenderloin, and dainty, frilled lamb chops. Once everyone sampled everything, settled back, and began to feel sated, the meal proceeded at a more leisurely pace—and the conversation became more pointed.

Allison Harper, the lawyer, said to Guy Kirby, the agent, "It's March third. How much of the new manuscript has Maude managed to write in three days?"

Guy deferred the question to his husband: "Well, Lanny? Is Maude on track?"

Lanford lifted the starched napkin from his lap and dabbed his lips. "She's, uh, writing ... making some progress ... but she hasn't quite found her pacing yet. It takes a while to build up a full head of steam, so to speak." He cleared his throat.

"And when will *that* be?" asked Allison.

"Very soon, I imagine."

"*Lanny*"—Allison persisted—"how much has she written? Exactly how many *pages*?"

Lanford whirled a hand. "Two or three? Probably *three*—she had a good afternoon."

Christopher told Allison, "Well, at least it's a start."

Allison said nothing, looking steamed. She reached for her wine and took a slug, gripping the glass so tightly, I thought she would snap the stem.

Christopher glanced over at me—and winked. Or was that a tic? Either way, I felt a rush of excitement, but I also wondered if Jazz had seen this. If she did, I'd be hearing about it.

She leaned near and said into my ear, "Is this some sorta *game*?"

Uh-oh. I asked, "What ...?"

Barely above a whisper, she said, "What if Maude Movay doesn't even exist?"

I took a deep breath, which I exhaled slowly before whispering to her, "That very question has crossed my mind. Hold that thought."

Jazz said aloud, "Lanny? I meant to ask if Miss Movay had a chance to sign my books yet."

He tossed his hands. "Sorry, Jazz. The day got away from us. As I mentioned, Maude was busy with her writing—tight deadline, you know."

With a tight smile, Jazz said, "Of course."

"Uncle Lanny?" said Nicole. "You really know how to do it, don't you?" Her speech was slurred, her meaning unclear. An uneasy hush fell over the room.

Lanford asked warily, "Sweetie? I know how to do...what?"

"How to *entertain*," she said with a loud, manic laugh, flinging her arms, one of them nearly smacking her husband. Saxon dodged her hand, which nicked his glasses, knocking them off. Allison Harper, who sat next to Saxon, removed the glasses from her lap and handed them back without comment.

"I *mean*," Nicole explained to the table, swinging her head to get a look at everyone, "Uncle Lanny is such a *role* model—always was. Just like me, he's a seeker of truth."

Lanford said softly, "That's probably enough, Nicole."

"But it's *true*," she assured us. "He's a seeker of truth—with the soul of a journalist—always so giving and generous. He's come to *my* rescue more than once!" Woozy, she turned to Lanford. "So thank you, uncle dearest. There's not a thing in this whole wide world to feel guilty about—not even the cash cow."

Lanford froze, mouth open, unable to speak.

Guy, Lanford's husband, spoke for him: "That's *enough*, Nicole—and totally unwarranted."

"Oops," she said, more giddy than repentant.

Saxon turned to his wife, eyeing her sternly, telling her flatly, "You need to shut up. Right now."

Lanford reached for the little silver bell that had been set at the unoccupied head of the table. He gave it a jingle.

Nina popped out from the kitchen. Seeing the grim faces, she squeaked, "Yes, sir?"

"Perhaps you could clear now. Dessert would be lovely."

Nina ducked back into the kitchen and returned momentarily with not only Ramil, but also Agnetha, who must have been alerted to the tense turn the meal had taken. No one spoke as they cleared the table and bussed everything away, out of sight behind the swinging door.

When Nina and Ramil returned to serve the plated desserts—a "pink fluff" concoction that had become quite the rage among the country-club set—it was past nine o'clock. Just as Agnetha stepped out from the kitchen with the coffee service, the doorbell sounded. *Dingdong.*

Agnetha set her tray on the sideboard cabinet.

Dingdong.

"Excuse me," she told us as she left for the living room.

Dingdong.

At the table, we strained to hear as the front door opened.

"... but you *said* you would finish by eight." It was Mrs. Payne, sounding distraught.

"... so sorry, ma'am, it could not be helped." Agnetha's voice grew louder as she followed Mrs. Payne, who now rushed into the dining room.

She halted as we all stared back at her. She was wearing exactly what she had worn on Sunday afternoon, looking oddly and unfashionably dressed. Her drab outfit resembled Agnetha's workaday attire—though she wore *much* better shoes, Ferragamo bow pumps.

Agnetha stepped next to her, explaining, "Your guests were just starting dessert. I should not be much longer."

Marjorie Payne looked bewildered. "*I* don't know these people."

I said, "Hello, Mrs. Payne."

"Oh! Dante. Of course. And the gentlemen, Lanford and Guy. And Nina—*my* Nina? What's *Nina* doing here?"

The young chambermaid reminded her, "You said I could help tonight, Mrs. Payne."

"Perhaps ... uh, perhaps I did. But it's getting late. And we have our project—our cleaning project—it needs tending to."

Agnetha said. "We shall get to it presently, ma'am. Both of us will help you."

From the table, Lanford spoke up: "Marjorie? I can't help but be concerned. What the blazes are you talking about? Cleaning—at *this* hour? And why would *you* be doing it?"

"This is special." Mrs. Payne smiled warmly and cast her eyes to the ceiling, as if seeing through the roof, directly into the heavens. "This ... is *death* cleaning."

Jazz was taking notes as Agnetha explained the Scandinavian tradition of tidying up during later life so that—when Valhalla beckons—you can slip away without worrying about leaving a mess for others to deal with. In other words, you yourself reap the benefits of dumping physical and emotional baggage in this life, and then, eventually, those you leave behind can remember you as wonderful and considerate, instead of a pain in the ass. It's a win-win. Or so goes the theory.

I said to Mrs. Payne, "Your dedication to this project is impressive, but I hope your sense of urgency doesn't spring from any ... 'issues' you're having."

She laughed. "Goodness *no*, Dante—I'm fit as a fiddle and bright as a bell."

That might have been pushing it.

Giggling, Nicole Endicott Chang plucked a bottle of wine from the table and sloshed some into her empty glass. When she set the bottle down, Saxon Chang placed it well out of her reach.

Guy Kirby said, "I'm a bit confused, Marjorie. When Lanford and I arrived on Sunday, Agnetha seemed to be driving the cleaning project, while you thought it could wait. Tonight, it's the other way around."

The ambassador's widow paused in thought, looking stumped. She turned to Agnetha with a quizzical expression, as if needing help with a response.

Agnetha explained to Guy, "Mrs. Payne's enthusiasm for the project waxes and wanes, one might say."

Mrs. Payne's eyes bugged. "Exactly!"

Agnetha gave Guy a sly nod, telling him, "... *exactly*."

Christopher Friendly suggested, "Waxes and wanes. Phases of the moon, perhaps?"

"Right," said Allison Harper, speaking low from the side of her mouth. "Looney Tunes."

Nina Rodriquez agreed to remain at the guesthouse to help Ramil with cleanup, and Agnetha walked Mrs. Payne back to the main house, where they could pack up and dispose of more of the widow's past.

Christopher mentioned to Jazz that their daughter Emma's babysitter was expecting him back soon, and he asked Allison if she was ready to leave. When the two lawyers got up from the table, Christopher thanked their hosts. But Allison did not—instead, she admonished Guy and Lanford, telling them, "Crack the damn whip and put Maude Movay to work for a change, if you can *find* her." Then Allison led Christopher out the front door.

The party was clearly over, and Saxon Chang was ready to leave. But when he and Nicole got up from the table, she needed to steady herself, gripping the back of the chair. "Christ," she said, "I think I'm gonna hurl."

Jazz leaned to tell me, "*Such* a charmer."

Nicole muttered, "… way too much booze."

With a hoot, Lanford asked her, "Booze—and what *else*?"

Saxon gave him a knowing nod. He told his wife, "C'mon. Let's get you home."

A gurgling, choking sound rose from her throat as she clapped a hand over her mouth.

Guy told Saxon, "I wouldn't recommend an hour's drive with her—unless you're planning to torch the car later."

Lanford agreed: "You kids stay here tonight."

Saxon whirled a hand. "I have a class in the morning."

Guy insisted, "You can get an early start tomorrow. Stay."

Nicole was whining something unintelligible. Saxon asked Guy, "Bathroom?"

He pointed. "Just down that hall."

When Saxon hustled Nicole out of the dining room, Nina and Ramil were at work in the kitchen, which left Jazz and me alone with our hosts.

With a pained sigh, Lanford told us, "I'm *so* sorry—what a fiasco."

"Nah," I lied, "it was fine."

"Food was great," said Jazz.

Lanford asked her, "Now that you've seen Agnetha, what do you think?"

"She's plenty strange. But look, it's getting late, and my source in Palm Springs hasn't gotten back to me yet. So let's save this discussion for later, okay?"

I suggested, "I'd like to come back tomorrow, when things are cleaned up, to make sure everything's in order. If Jazz has anything to report, she can come along. Maybe after lunch?"

Lanford and Guy exchanged a glance and a shrug. "Sure."

Jazz said, "I'll be here, one way or the other—because I plan to collect those signed books from Miss Movay. Can you tell her to expect me?" She grinned.

Lanford grinned. "Of course."

By the time we rolled back into Palm Springs, it was nearly ten o'clock. We hadn't said much during the drive—I still had the top down, and the noise of the wind made it difficult to compare notes. But we did voice our agreement on once crucial point: everything that had happened was consistent with our suspicion that Maude Movay did not really exist, and even if she did, it was fairly obvious that she had never set foot in the guesthouse at the Payne estate.

"Hey," said Jazz, "better slow down. Left turn ahead."

I gave her a curious look—I had assumed I was driving her back to her office to pick up her SUV. Then I realized that the left turn would lead to Blade Wade's studio, near the east end of town. "*Oh,*" I said, enlightened.

With a soft laugh, she said, "He asked me to drop by."

"Yes, ma'am."

And a minute later, I stopped at the curb in front of door H in the arty strip mall, which was dead quiet at that hour. As Jazz got out of the car, I lectured, "Home by midnight, young lady."

She chortled while crossing the pavement toward the door— and never looked back.

Returning to my apartment, I parked the Karmann Ghia on the street and closed its roof. When I walked through the gate to the pool terrace, I paused. I rarely went to bed that early, and neither did Isandro, so I decided to rap on his door—we could catch up on each other's day, maybe have a nightcap.

I knocked, then waited, then leaned to look through his window. His lights were on, drapes drawn. I knocked again and, a moment later, circled around the far end of the pool, walking back toward my apartment.

Along the way, I noticed Zola's door crack open. *"Psst."*

Stepping over to her door, I whispered, "If you're dressed, want a drink?"

With a loud croak of a laugh, she swung the door wide open— fully clothed, to my immense relief. She said, "I was just about to mix one for myself, but I'll let *you* do the honors."

Entering, I went over to her breakfast bar (never used for breakfast), where everything was set out for her usual Tom Collins—including two frosted chimney glasses. I picked up both, asking her, "Expecting company?"

"I happened to notice you over at Isandro's." She could always be depended on to peep a watchful eye through the curtains.

The night was too chilly for a frosty cocktail on the patio, so we settled in her living room, she on an Art Deco daybed, I in a butterfly sling chair (her taste for the classics was highly eclectic). We drank and gabbed. She gasped as I told her about Mrs. Payne's disturbing appearance at that evening's dinner party. And then, finally, I asked, "Have you, uh ... have you seen Isandro tonight?"

She nodded. "A man came over to pick him up. As soon as Isandro opened the door, they left, so he must have been expected. A handsome fellow—*tall* and handsome—familiar, too. I'm sure I've seen his picture. Many times, in fact. He might be a real-estate agent. He had big bleached hair and big bleached teeth."

"Don't they *all*?" There were dozens of agents fitting that description in Palm Springs.

Zola said, "He arrived at seven." So she was telling me they'd been out for three hours.

When we finished our nightcap, I didn't linger. Zola and I exchanged a parting peck. Then I headed home.

The breezy night had turned windy, and as I entered my apartment, a gust slammed the door behind me. I braced myself for the outburst of barking from Mitzi next door.

CHAPTER
FIVE

Wednesday morning, I called Lanford Endicott from my office, and he said Jazz and I would be welcome at the guesthouse
around one fifteen. Then I phoned Jazz, and we agreed to meet
for an early lunch, eleven thirty at Huggamug. We'd beat the
rush, leaving us plenty of time for the drive to Indian Wells.

Earlier that morning, while having coffee at home, I had my
front door open and saw Isandro leaving his apartment, walking
toward the gate to the street. He was alone, which answered at
least one point of curiosity. Greeting him from the doorway, I
asked, "Want some coffee?"

With one hand on the gate, he said, "Sorry, kinda rushed.
Can we catch up tonight?"

"Sure." And that was that.

So my morning at the office was distracted by thoughts of
Isandro: Where had he been the night before? Who was his
toothy blond companion? Where was he going early that morning? And why the need to "catch up tonight"?

These questions continued to nettle me as I walked the short
distance from Sunny Junket to Huggamug. But they evaporated as I stepped inside the coffeehouse and found Jazz waiting
for me, already seated—and gabbing with her old pal George,
the dreamy Latino detective from the Palm Springs police department.

"Dante!" said George, rising to greet me with a smile and a handshake. "Great to see you again—under happier circumstances." The last time we'd seen each other was the prior summer, shortly after someone tried to kill me. Today, he looked better than ever, wearing a well-tailored business suit, a polished leather shoulder holster under his jacket, a badge on his belt— and a wedding ring. Jazz had assured me, more than once, that George did not have a husband, but a wife and kids.

We exchanged a few pleasantries, then seated ourselves at the table with Jazz, who told me, "George has been looking into that case involving Agnetha Berg." Turning to George, she added, "Dante might like to hear this."

George nodded. "The files are eighteen years old, dating from just a year or two after Ambassador Payne assisted with Berg's immigration to California from Norway. She married a man in Palm Springs widely known to be gay, and his friends assumed it was a sham marriage—maybe even paid for—to fast-track her citizenship. Seems the two of them never even lived together; he ran a high-end antiques store here in Palm Springs, while she managed the estate's live-in staff down in Indian Wells. Then, mere months after Berg became a sworn citizen, hubby died under suspicious circumstances, leaving the widow a nice little parting gift."

I had to ask: "How did he die?"

"Forensic testing revealed plain old garden-variety arsenic poisoning, low doses administered over time, mimicking heart disease. Not very original, but highly effective."

Jazz asked, "And how much did Agnetha inherit?"

"About a hundred thousand—not a 'fortune,' but a substantial windfall for someone working as a servant. Berg was the main suspect all along. There was a big wrinkle, though: absolutely no evidence linking her to the crime. So the case went cold. I talked to two of the guys who worked on it, and they still think she got away with murder."

George couldn't stay for lunch, so he left after delivering his report, promising to stay in touch. While Jazz glanced over the menu, I perused the room, just checking—in case that moody waiter, Zane Smith, had somehow finagled to get his job back. But he was nowhere to be seen, and I managed to quell the sense memory of ice water in my lap.

Since dinner the night before had been over the top, both Jazz and I opted for simple lunches—a panzanella salad for her and a grilled chicken panini for me. Waiting for the food, we sipped iced tea.

Jazz sat back and gave me an odd look.

I asked, "What?"

"I assume I wasn't the only one who tussled with unanswered questions last night."

"No, you weren't." I could guess the various issues perplexing her about the dinner party, but she had no idea that my sleep had also been robbed by Isandro's unknown whereabouts.

"For starters," said Jazz, "Maude Movay. If she's a real person, where *is* she? And if she's *not* a real person, why all the games?"

I nodded. "Her rental house. Her deadline. Her empty place at the table. If it's all a hoax, what's the point?"

Jazz's fingernails rat-a-tatted the vintage Formica tabletop. "Item two: What's the deal with Lanford's niece, Nicole?"

I ticked off a few thoughts: "Charitably, I'd describe her as troubled. Bluntly, I'd say she's fucked-up. Obviously, there's a booze issue. Probably, there's also an issue with drugs. But I think there's even more to it. Her comments about the 'rescue' and the 'cash cow'—pretty damn weird."

"And that brings us," said Jazz, "to the *death* cleaning. Sounds a little strange at first, and then, after you think about it, sensible enough. But what's up with that creepy dynamic between Marjorie Payne and Agnetha Berg? It's like: Who's gaslighting *who*?"

I grinned. "Anything else on your mind?"

"Yes..."

A server dropped off our orders, and we each tried a bite, voicing little grunts of approval—but her salad looked better than my sandwich.

I prompted: "You were about to say something. I'm guessing it concerns your ex."

Jazz set down her fork. "Did you *see* him when he left with her?"

"Of course I did; I was sitting right next to you. And I saw Allison Harper lead Christopher out the door."

"Aha. Then you picked up on that. I mean, she works for *him*, remember. At the risk of sounding like a jealous bitch: he needs to watch out for *that* one." Jazz picked up her fork and stabbed a chunk of bell pepper—stabbed it hard.

I told her softly, "I'm sure Christopher can fend for himself. After all"—I tried not to laugh—"he survived *you*."

She glared at me—then sputtered with laughter.

"And you both have a smart, loving, *beautiful* daughter to show for it."

Jazz smiled. Her face seemed to glow as she thought of Emma, and she returned her attention to the salad, which she ate contentedly, forking it without stabbing it. Our conversation lapsed while we lunched, and when she finally spoke, her voice took me by surprise.

"You know," she said quietly, "when I was little, growing up in LA, I never had the things Emma has now—the preschool, the day care, the dresses, the parties, the ballet lessons, even the *art* lessons, from a guy like Blade Wade."

"And look what you've accomplished," I said. "You can be so proud of *everything*."

"No, Dante—not everything."

"Mistakes happen. Then you learn from them. I don't know much about your childhood—what you had or didn't have— but I *know* you had lots of love. You wouldn't be the person you are without it."

She shrugged. "Yeah, Mama was great, still is—gettin' older now, but doin' okay. We're sorta like sisters."

"And your dad? You've never mentioned him."

With her fork, Jazz slid a few remaining slices of cucumber to the side of her plate. "Papa...he tried, I guess. He's gone."

Changing the topic, she checked her watch. "We'd better get going."

Jazz drove.

When we arrived at the Payne estate's private entrance, I called Lanford Endicott's cell phone, which rang a few times before sending me to his voicemail. "Lanford," I said, "it's Dante. I'm at the back gate with Jazz. It's one fifteen."

We waited about a minute, thinking Lanford would either call back or open the gate. When he didn't, Jazz said, "Maybe he's on the crapper."

I laughed, blinking away the mental picture. "Let's go to the main entrance."

When Jazz pulled the black SUV up to the gatehouse on

Highway 111 and lowered her window, I leaned over from the passenger seat so the guard could see me.

"Good afternoon, Mr. O'Donnell."

"Hi there," I said. "Jazz Friendly and I are here to see Mr. Endicott."

"Yep." The guard nodded. "Right here on the list—he's expecting you." The gate began to roll back.

"So he is *here*, correct?"

"Far as I know. The other gentleman, Mr. Kirby, went out this morning with the younger man who's staying with them."

"Thanks," I said, and Jazz drove through the gate.

We followed the roadway to the Payne estate and parked in the smaller motor court, in front of the guesthouse. I noticed that only one of the carport's three stalls was occupied—by the pink SUV, which I now knew belonged to Lanford, not Maude Movay. The black BMW was gone, consistent with the guard's story that Guy had left with Ramil.

Jazz and I walked across the gravel courtyard and stepped up to the front door. I pressed the button and heard the chimes within the house. We waited. Jazz reached across me and jabbed the button. More chimes—then silence.

She said, "You know the code, right?"

I rang the chimes once more, waited a few seconds, then punched in the keypad code. The lock clicked open.

When we stepped into the entry hall and closed the door behind us, the silence of the house was emphatic—no voices, no patter of footsteps, no background music, no gurgle of plumbing, no drone of motors, not even the chilly whisper of air conditioning—just a pervasive quiet. The quiet of a crypt, one might say.

"*Lanford*," I called. "It's Dante and Jazz."

The lack of response was amplified by the ringing in my ears. On the far side of the living room, beyond the French doors, high in the sky, the midday sun tried to vaporize the flagstone terrace with a shrieking bolt of daylight—or so it seemed. And just inside the living room, not far from the entry hall, the Inca warrior stood proud and stoic as ever, but he looked a bit silly that day with a gaudy striped beach towel hung to dry from the chiseled knob of his phallus.

Stepping in from the front hall, we snooped around (the beach towel was bone-dry), then walked through the dining room and kitchen. I noted that everything was in order—perfectly so— and there was no need for Sunny Junket to provide additional clean-up services for the prior night's party.

Backtracking, Jazz and I returned to the living room and made our way, as if on tiptoe, toward the hall to the bedroom wing. Jazz lifted her hand, a command to pause.

In a churchy whisper, she suggested, "Try calling his cell again."

Good idea.

I pulled out my phone and tapped in Lanford's number. A moment later, we heard the ringing of a phone—distinctly— and it came from the suite of rooms supposedly occupied by the queen of romance.

We rushed down the hall.

And when we entered the bedroom, we saw Lanford Endicott slumped backward in the chair at Maude Movay's writing desk. His arms drooped lifelessly from both sides of the chair. His head lolled back from the top of the chair, with his eyes bugged open, aimed at the ceiling. A long silk Hermès scarf, knotted tightly behind his choked neck, dangled nearly to the floor. The ends of the scarf fluttered when we raced to Lanford, but his body remained dead still.

Unshaven and wearing a robe, Lanford had evidently been interrupted while working on something before he was ready to get cleaned up and dressed for the day. It was obvious that he was now beyond helping, so Jazz and I took a moment to assess the surroundings.

The bed was slept in and had not been made up that morning. The four white mannequin heads all had their wigs and scarves on; other scarves, as before, were scattered about the room.

On the desk was a stack of six of Maude Movay's novels, an assortment of pens and pads, Lanford's phone, and—directly in front of his body—a laptop computer with its screen raised but darkened.

I borrowed a ballpoint from Jazz and used its back end to tap the laptop's space bar, hoping it might waken the computer. It did. The word-processing file on the screen was headlined CYNTHIA'S SLOTH, but glancing through some of the text, I found that it was not the working draft of a novel; rather, it contained Lanford's random notes and recollections regarding Agnetha Berg.

"Hey," said Jazz, "look at this." With a tissue, she had nudged open the cover of one of the books on the desk. It was inscribed in a graceful script:

To Jazz Friendly, my dearest chum and most devoted reader.
Yours forever, Maude Movay.

PART TWO

BONGO BOYS

CHAPTER
SIX

Jazz closed the cover of the inscribed book.

I told her, "*That's* gotta be worth something—it's the last thing written by the so-called Maude Movay."

"Maybe," she said. "But for now, it's evidence." Jazz took a careful peek inside the five remaining books, confirming they were all hers, all with the same inscription.

Then she got on the phone to report what we'd found, placing the call directly to Arcie Madera, the detective we'd first encountered the prior summer. Several of the Coachella Valley's resort cities held contracts with the Riverside County sheriff's department for police services, and Arcie was stationed in nearby Palm Desert, abutting Indian Wells, so she was first on the scene. Jazz quickly told Arcie about Lanford Endicott's background and also explained why she and I were there.

Within five minutes of Arcie's arrival, she was joined by a complete response team—paramedics, a forensic pathologist, two photographers, and an investigating unit that included extra officers to assist with the collection of physical evidence.

Vanguard Ridge—wealthy, exclusive, and impeccable, with a long history of safety and contentment for the pampered, chosen few—was suddenly a zoo, a slapdash crime scene of brutish vehicles with flashers and sirens, not to mention the trampling

of jackbooted khaki-clad lawmen with their badges and barri-
cades and guns.

But Arcie Madera stood out in this crowd. A woman in a dark
suit and a white blouse, she'd risen through the ranks while earn-
ing the respect of her peers, a testament to her competence and
professionalism. Arcie was older than Jazz—about my age—but
they had bonded in a sort of sisterhood thing. One Latina, one
Black, they'd known firsthand the struggles of being underrep-
resented in the male-dominated ranks of crime-busting.

Amid the hubbub at the writing desk, Arcie told the pathologist, "I'm guessing this is just what it looks like. Murder. By
strangulation."

"Safe guess," he said, "at least at this point. Other than being
garroted by the scarf, no signs of a struggle. They didn't fight—
no flesh, blood, or hair under the victim's fingernails. He was
apparently taken by surprise from behind. Simple."

Arcie asked, "Time of death—a couple hours ago?"

"Yeah, something like that. I'll have a closer estimate after we
get him back to the lab. We'll run routine toxicology, but this
looks pretty straightforward."

Arcie and Jazz shared a meaningful glance.

I asked, "What?"

"Sometimes," said Jazz, "straightforward is straightforward.
Other times, it's a setup."

Arcie asked one of the deputies, "Any signs of intrusion?"

"No, Detective. The house was locked up tight. Everything
seems to be in order—except in here."

A gurney was rolled in. The pathologist gave directions for
moving the deceased from the chair, then draped the body.

"Detective Madera?" said another deputy, stepping into the

bedroom from the hall. "Two gentlemen just arrived—said they're staying here."

Arcie nodded to admit them. The gurney crew paused.

Looking ashen and panicky, Guy Kirby and Ramil Bagoyo stepped warily into the bedroom. "Oh, my *God*," said Guy, rushing forward. Ramil stood back, horrified.

Arcie introduced herself to Guy and, taking notes, asked for his name, which he mumbled. Then she said, "If you've been staying here, I assume you *know* the victim."

"He's my *husband*."

"I'm so sorry. My condolences, Mr. Kirby. When you last saw your husband, was he alive and well?"

"Of *course* he was. I wouldn't have left if I thought he was in any danger."

Arcie asked him, "When did you leave? And where did you go?"

With a stunned look, Guy turned to Jazz. "Jesus *Christ*—does she think *I* did this?"

Jazz assured him, "Just routine questions. The investigation is only beginning."

"Exactly," said Arcie. "We need to construct a complete timeline of everything that happened here today. So: When did you leave? And where did you go?"

Guy took a deep breath. "We left around ten thirty; they can probably give you the exact time at the front gate. Ramil went with me. He's employed as our physical trainer and our ... general assistant. We ran some errands, then went to lunch. But the *actual* reason we went out was to give Guy some time and space to himself, so he could focus. He's been under a tight deadline, ghostwriting a book."

The jig, it seemed, was up.

Arcie asked, "Do you have receipts or other records from the time you were away?"

"I think so. Yes." He took out his wallet and handed Arcie a wad of rumpled credit-card chits. "Gas. Lunch. And a little something for Ramil."

The hunky Filipino held out a wrist and flashed a shiny new bracelet.

"Wow," said Arcie, checking the jeweler's receipt. "Nice." And once again, she and Jazz exchanged a loaded glance.

Gesturing toward the messy bed, Jazz said to Guy, "Obviously, Maude Movay never slept here. So who did?"

"Until last night, no one. We mussed it up each morning so the chambermaid wouldn't get suspicious about Maude's absence."

I said, "By 'the chambermaid,' you mean Nina Rodriquez, right? But it doesn't look like she was here this morning."

Guy nodded. "We were told—by that harpy, Agnetha Berg—to phone the main house whenever we wanted rooms made up, and she'd send Nina over. So we had her make the beds on Monday morning, the day after we arrived, and again yesterday, Tuesday morning. Then we had the dinner party last night, which Nina helped serve, and she stayed late for cleanup, so I told her not to bother coming back this morning."

I asked, "Then why did you muss this bed today if there was no need to fool Nina?"

"The bed's a mess because Lanford and I *slept* in here last night." Guy turned to Arcie, explaining, "From the time we arrived on Sunday, it was understood that this suite, for the sake of appearances, would belong to Maude, who doesn't exist; her books were written by Lanford. So Lanford and I slept together in the main guest room, Ramil slept in the smaller guest room, and no one slept in here."

"Aha," said Jazz, "but *last* night, you ended up with a pair of extra guests."

"Exactly." Guy told Detective Madera, "Lanford's niece and her husband drove over from Redlands to have dinner here last evening. She got a bit drunk—well, totally *wasted*—and was unfit to travel, so they stayed overnight. Lanford and I gave them *our* guest room, and we slept in here."

I asked, "Didn't they wonder why you took Maude's bed? The story last night was: she missed dinner but would return later."

"Nicole and Saxon never went inside Maude's suite. They had no reason to think we had taken 'her' bed. But if we had given them *this* room, which was clearly set up for Maude—her clothes, toiletries, and desk things are here—they'd know we didn't expect her to return."

Arcie tapped her pen on her notes. "So, then ... you had unplanned overnight guests. And when did *they* leave today?"

"Early," said Guy. "Saxon had a class at the university. By the time Lanford and I got up, around eight, they'd already left for Redlands."

Ramil spoke up from across the room. "I didn't see them, either."

The gurney made a sharp ratcheting noise, reminding us of the task at hand. The pathologist asked Arcie, quietly, "Okay to proceed?"

Arcie turned to Guy. "Would you care to see him first? His condition is disturbing, but we'd appreciate a formal identification."

Guy nodded. Then he turned to Ramil, who stepped slowly to Guy's side and put an arm around him.

The pathologist drew back the sheet from the draped body, asking Guy, "Is this your husband, sir?"

"Yes." Guy sobbed. "Oh, Lanford—dear God, who could have done this to you?" The scarf had been removed, revealing the abrasions and bruising of the neck. Guy looked into Lanford's reddened eyes, which seemed to stare back at him from their swollen eyelids. "Was he ... *strangled*?"

"Yes, sir. I'm sorry."

Guy turned to Ramil and held him tight. With his chin on the younger man's shoulder, he blubbered, "What kind of *beast* would do this?"

"I don't know, sweetie. But they'll try to find out. I loved him, too."

"I know you did. Thank God you're here."

"Yes," said Ramil, stroking Guy's hair, "I'm here for you."

Jazz and I gave each other a look. Arcie took notes.

The body was bagged and removed by the medical team, accompanied by the pathologist. Shortly after, the photographers finished and were next to go. Eventually, the entire investigating unit packed up their gear and left the crime scene, leaving only Arcie with us.

She had more questions for Guy and Ramil, as well as Jazz and me, so we moved to the living room. Just as we settled in, we heard someone enter the house through the service door in the kitchen.

Arcie told Guy and Ramil, "Wait here." Then she and Jazz followed me, walking through the dining room and into the kitchen.

"Mrs. Payne," I said.

"Dante, all this *commotion*—I thought it would never end. I came over earlier, when everyone arrived, but they wouldn't let me in. And now, as they were leaving, they took someone out on a *stretcher*—covered up. Did someone … die?"

"I'm afraid so, Mrs. Payne."

Jazz told her, "It was Lanford Endicott. He didn't just die—he was killed."

Arcie stepped forward, "And that's why this is a police matter." She showed her badge and introduced herself to Mrs. Payne, then asked, "You're the owner of this property, correct?"

The ambassador's widow was so stunned by this news, she struggled to find words to answer Arcie's simple, direct question. She looked even more pallid than usual, and I wondered if she was feeling faint.

I helped her to a chair at the breakfast table, telling Arcie, "Yes, she's the owner. The estate was built by her late husband, Ambassador Grover Payne."

The service door swung open. "Ah, *there* you are," said Agnetha Berg—as though Mrs. Payne had not merely wandered off, but escaped. Stepping inside, closing the door, she asked brusquely, "And who is *this*?"

Arcie introduced herself; Agnetha reciprocated. While they ran through a series of background questions, Agnetha stood with her back to Jazz and me, as if we didn't exist.

When Arcie paused to update her notes, I jumped in, saying to Agnetha, "I understand there were no requests from the guests for housekeeping this morning. Other than right now, have you had occasion to enter the guesthouse anytime today?"

"No."

"And Nina Rodriguez?"

"No."

"And Mrs. Payne?"

"No. She has not left the main house today, not once—until now." Agnetha's eyes slid to her employer with a steely look of reprimand.

In turn, my eyes slid to Jazz. We shared a subtle grin, having caught Agnetha in an untruth. Mrs. Payne had already told us she came to the guesthouse earlier but was refused entry by the arriving emergency team.

If Arcie also noticed this inconsistency, she didn't let on. Instead, she thanked Agnetha for being so cooperative, then told Mrs. Payne, "I know how upset you must be by these awful developments. I might need to talk to you again later, but I promise it won't be so disruptive."

Mrs. Payne thanked the detective kindly, then got up from her chair and told Agnetha, "Take me home."

Without another word, the two women left by the back door and walked off toward the main house. I watched through the kitchen window, noting that Agnetha guided Mrs. Payne by clutching her arm with a death grip. When I looked back from the window, I saw that Arcie and Jazz had already returned to the living room.

As I joined them and sat down, Arcie was saying to Guy, "I don't mean to prolong this while you're still in shock, but I do need to ask: Can you think of anyone who might have wanted to harm your husband?"

Guy sat next to Ramil in the center of a long sofa looking out through the French doors. The serene view of the pool, with the mountains beyond, stood in stark contrast to the topic of murder. Guy held hands with Ramil, telling us, "Everyone *loved* Lanford. He was the 'fun' one. I was always the numbers guy, the planner, the one who kept everything in perspective and on track. People always said we were the perfect couple—we *com-*

plemented each other—and I knew what *that* meant: Lanford was witty and talented and charming. I was not."

Ramil hugged Guy's shoulders, telling him softly, "Don't be nuts."

Guy lifted Ramil's free hand and gave it a quick kiss. He told Arcie, "So, Detective, my answer to your question is 'no.' Lanford had no enemies, at least not in the many years I've known him, at least not until—*possibly*—last Sunday, when we arrived here."

I'd been wondering when someone would finally say it. So I said it: "Agnetha Berg. She and Lanford seemed to dislike each other the minute they met. He suspected there's something she wants to hide, and he was planning to write about it."

Jazz explained to Arcie how Lanford had hired her to find the dirt on Agnetha and how her friend George had been digging in the Palm Springs police files, concluding, "Lanford's suspicions appear to have some merit."

"And," I said, "he'd started writing. You'll find his notes on his laptop."

Nodding, Arcie looked up from her own notes. "We'll be sure to check that out. The laptop is secured in evidence—we took everything on the desk. Except your books, Jazz. I saw the inscriptions and thought you'd want those. But hold on to them in case something comes up."

"Great. Will do."

"Along similar lines," Arcie said to Guy, "I hope you'll remain accessible to the investigation for a while. Things are bound to develop, and I'm sure we'll be needing to see more of you—all in the interest of bringing your husband's killer to justice."

Guy looked uncomfortable with the tone of this request, and I couldn't blame him. He tossed his arms. "We were *planning* to be here a month—so Lanford could write Maude's next book, which is now a lost cause. I'd like to help you, Detective, by sticking around, but this place is crazy expensive, and pardon a blunt assessment, but the cash cow has departed." He then turned to ask me, "The terms of the rental contract—is there a penalty for canceling?"

"I'll double check, but I'm pretty sure that once you've moved in, you're on the hook for at least half. In other words, you'll be paying through the fifteenth whether you stay or not. So…"

"So…," Guy picked up the thought, "I guess we're here for a while."

"Cool," said Ramil, whose mourning was brief.

Arcie said flatly, "I think those arrangements are a *very* good idea." She passed one of her cards to Guy, who looked it over with a disgruntled sigh before sliding it into his shirt pocket.

Arcie then took out her phone and began typing briskly, without looking up. The rest of us looked at each other, as if wondering what, if anything, was next. Jazz cleared her throat.

"Sorry," said Arcie, still focused on her phone, still typing, "I need to get some of these details into my report while they're still fresh."

"Uh, Detective?" asked Guy. "Will the police report make any reference to Maude Movay? For whatever it's worth, I'd be grateful if she wasn't mentioned."

Arcie held up her phone, as if we could read her typing from several feet away. "No mention of her so far—just the facts—and since 'Maude Movay' is not, in fact, a *fact*, she won't appear in this initial report. That could change, though, if the investigation determines that the Movay angle is relevant to solving the murder."

Guy nodded. "Thank you. I'd like to keep that quiet until we assess how to roll out the news."

Jazz asked him, "Who's 'we'?"

"Maude Movay may not have existed as a person, but she represented a rather sprawling enterprise—her publishers and editors, her attorneys and accountants, her partners in the new film and TV deals, her heirs, and of course me, her agent."

Jazz said, "And don't forget her *readers*. How are *they* gonna feel? I'll tell you how: they'll feel screwed, like they've been *lied* to all along."

Slumping, Guy held his head with ten pronged fingers. "Jesus, don't remind me."

Jazz persisted: "They *won't* like it, and I say this on good authority because Miss Movay herself wrote that I was her 'dearest chum and most devoted reader.'" Jazz paused, then grinned, telling Guy, "I was thrilled—for about two seconds—cuz it was obvious I'd been suckered."

Arcie finished with her phone and began tucking things away in her briefcase. I asked her, "Okay if I go grab the signed books for Jazz?"

"Sure. But don't disturb anything else in there—still a crime scene."

As I got up and walked from the living room toward the bedrooms, Arcie was telling Jazz, "First thing I'll do is check the calls to and from Lanford's cell phone this morning. I've already assigned someone to check logs and videos from the gatehouse..."

As I entered the lavish bedroom suite—quiet, deserted, disheveled—where Maude Movay had never slept, my eye instantly shot to the elegant little writing desk where not a single word of *Cynthia's Sloth* had been written. The chair had been pushed out of the way, and it was now empty, but I had to blink away the lingering image of Lanford Endicott's lifeless body, strangled by one of Maude's scarves. Had he worn her scarf while sitting down to do her writing that day, or did his attacker simply make use of one of the many that were strewn about? I also wondered if Lanford ever wore one of the wigs to get into character as the great and reclusive Maude Movay—the "cash cow."

Guy Kirby had used that expression just a few minutes earlier. And the night before, Lanford's niece, Nicole Endicott Chang, had used those words as well. Were they all in on the joke? Had Nicole been fully aware that Maude Movay would not—could not—appear last night?

When I picked up the stack of six books belonging to Jazz, nothing remained atop the previously cluttered desk—except the dusty mess of now-revealed fingerprints, which struck me as a hopeless jumble.

Before leaving, I paused to survey the entire suite one last time, noticing something that had not previously seemed significant.

When I walked into the living room, everyone was standing as Arcie prepared to leave, and Jazz was explaining to her that the Payne estate had its own private entrance, a back gate without security or video.

Arcie rolled her eyes. "Well, *that's* a nice wrinkle."

"The wigs," I said. "When were they returned?"

Everyone turned to me. Arcie looked mystified by my question. I reminded the others, "When Jazz and I were here Monday afternoon, that old fruitcake of a hairdresser showed up, thinking he was called to give Maude Movay a hairdo, but he ended up leaving with three of her four wigs. Lanford wanted them returned today, and they're all back in the bedroom right now, on the mannequin heads. Were they delivered this morning?"

Guy said, "They must have been. When Lanford and I slept in there last night, I noticed the three bare mannequin heads—and thought they were freakish."

Arcie dug out her notes again. "Who was the hairdresser?"

Guy said, "I can't think of the name—Lanford set it up through Mrs. Payne."

Jazz snapped her fingers. "Wasn't it, uh...Bruce?"

"*Yes*," I said. "Bruce Tucker."

"Right," said Ramil. "That's him. If he showed up this morning, I never saw him."

Jazz said, "He had this nutty kinda love-hate thing for Maude. Left a book for her to sign. He said he hoped to meet her today."

"And the book," I said, "is gone. So he was here—probably after Guy and Ramil left, and before Jazz and I arrived."

"Got it. He's on the list," said Arcie. Looking up from her notebook, she told Guy, "But I'm confused. Why did you invent Maude in the first place? Why all the subterfuge?"

"By far," said Guy, "most romance readers are women, and it's conventional wisdom that a man's name on this stuff is risky. So, on a whim, Lanford came up with the Maude Movay byline for the first Cynthia Sinns book. He considered it a joke—presumably an open secret. But then, with that book's huge success, we understood that we had a *lot* riding on perpetuating the Maude myth. She took on a cult status, and we could *not* afford the risk of letting her readers feel betrayed or deceived. It worked for six books. But now..."

In the hush that settled over the room, Arcie jotted something, then closed her notebook. Picking up her briefcase, she said, "There's a lot to sort out here, and I want to get on it."

We followed her as she left the living room and crossed the front hall. When she opened the door, she turned back to say, "I'll be in touch, Jazz." She told Guy, "Again, Mr. Kirby, my condolences on the tragic loss of your husband. We'll do our best to figure this out. But meanwhile, I want you to let me know if you or Mr. Bagoyo have any plans to leave the valley." She gave him a curt little nod. Then she left, closing the door behind her.

The four of us stood in silence, listening as she went to her vehicle, started the engine, and drove out of the gravel courtyard.

"Jesus *Christ*," said Guy, "I need a drink…"

"Fabulous," said Ramil. "It seems like *hours* since lunch."

Guy asked Jazz and me, "Join us? The bar's always open—in the kitchen."

Incredulous, Jazz said, "After what's happened, aren't you guys *exhausted* by the shock of this?"

"Amazingly," said Guy, "it hasn't fully set in yet. I'll be a basket case tomorrow. Right now, I need a bit of assistance in processing this—and let's face it, booze *always* helps."

Jazz caught my eye. She'd been there, done that. She told Guy, "Water will be fine, thanks, unless you have some iced tea."

"Let's take a look," said Guy, turning to lead us from the front hall. As he moved into the living room, heading toward the dining room, he caught sight of the Inca warrior and stopped cold. "What the hell is *that*?" he asked, referring to the beach towel hanging from the phallus.

Ramil broke into shrieking laughter.

I asked them, "Didn't you notice it when you came in? It's pretty hard to *miss*."

Guy said, "When we got back from lunch, we were stunned by the police presence, and they walked us right through the house to the bedroom. I didn't really *see* anything."

Jazz said, "We assumed you or Lanford or Ramil hung it here."

Guy gave her a get-real look. "It's *hideous*. Do you honestly think one of *us* would be seen with that cheesy rag?"

He had a point. The towel looked old, faded, and ratty, with wide alternating circus stripes of red, blue, and yellow. Guy and Ramil, however, were smartly dressed in well-coordinated outfits in a limited palette of tasteful neutrals that ran the gamut from oatmeal to putty. Even Lanford's death robe was consistent with this look—a fuzzy mohair caftan the color of café au lait. No, the towel didn't seem to be theirs.

Guy reached up to snatch it from the cantaloupe-size knob of the phallus.

Jazz asked, "Was it maybe supplied with the guesthouse linens?"

I assured her, "No. Sunny Junket requires its properties to provide bath linens that are white or beige." Then I took out my phone, called the main house, got Agnetha, and described the towel to her, asking, "Did it come from over there?"

She answered with a derisive snort of a laugh and hung up.

"Ramil," said Guy, still holding the towel, "could you *please* mix our drinks?"

With a bow and scrape, Ramil led us all into the kitchen.

Guy tossed the towel onto the breakfast table while Ramil set up for drinks on the center island. Jazz and I sat on stools at the island, and Guy joined us, sitting on the opposite side of the granite countertop.

Ramil offered iced tea to Jazz, and I asked for some as well. Guy wanted "something stronger, please," and Ramil improvised a tropical punch with a bit of fruit juice and a *lot* of rum.

When we raised our glasses in Lanford's memory, Guy cried again, but softly. Ramil, sitting next to him, cooed comforting words. Between sips of our drinks, we spoke in platitudes about life and death, about crime and justice, about destiny and change.

Then Jazz spoke about her work. "Guy," she said, "I've barely begun the background check that Lanford hired me to do—on Agnetha Berg. The job isn't finished, but Lanford doesn't need it now. I've spent very little time on it, so I'm happy to forget it. In other words: no charge."

"Ah," said Guy, "thank you, Jazz. But frankly, the tangle of Lanford's unpaid bills is the least of my concerns right now."

Jazz nodded. "Of course. You need to mourn and heal first."

"Yes, I suppose I do, but that's not quite what I meant. My immediate concern is Detective Madera."

I told him, "Don't worry about Arcie Madera. She's smart and dedicated. She won't rest until Lanford's killer pays the price for this tragedy."

"The *problem*," said Guy, "is that Madera seems to think Ramil and I are involved in this. You heard all that bluster about not leaving town."

Jazz offered the stock reassurance: "Arcie just needs to eliminate all the usual 'persons of interest'—with spouses and lovers always topping the list—before she can get down to the finer points of naming serious suspects."

It was a nice little speech, doubtless what Guy needed to hear, but I had a hunch that Jazz considered both Guy and Ramil to be perfectly reasonable suspects. I sure did.

And it seemed that these thoughts had finally begun to gel for Ramil, too. He wasn't laughing, for a change, when he turned to ask Guy, "Uh, sweetie...?"

Guy patted Ramil's hand while speaking to Jazz: "I'm not a killer. But I'm not stupid, either, and I assume I'll need a lawyer, eventually. Right now, though, I need *you*, Jazz."

"For what?"

"That account Lanford set up with you? Keep it open. The best way to prevent either Ramil or me from being accused of killing Lanford is pretty simple. Just find the *real* killer first—meaning, of course, someone else."

Jazz told him, "I can't and won't try to subvert Arcie's investigation in any way. But I can conduct a parallel investigation on your behalf, and if you're lucky—and if you're honest with me—it *might* clear you. If the evidence points *back* to you, though, there's nothing more I can do to help."

He nodded. "Understood."

"Get some rest. I'd like to meet with both of you tomorrow at my office in Palm Springs. We can go over plans for the investigation and formalize an agreement."

Guy and Ramil exchanged contact details with Jazz and set up a time—eleven o'clock. With the drinks finished and the next meeting booked, we all stood.

I helped Ramil move a few things over to the sink. He ran the faucet and looked up into my eyes. "Will you be there tomorrow?"

"Maybe. I guess so."

Ramil whispered, "I hope so."

Jazz was standing near the breakfast table with Guy. He picked up the wadded beach towel and asked Jazz, "Can you toss this when you leave? The trash caddies are out by the carport."

She took it, asking with a grin, "Don't you want to *keep* it?"

He rolled his eyes. "Puh-*leeze*."

I joined Jazz, and Guy opened the kitchen's service door for us, which led out to the carport. Ramil joined Guy in a round of goodbyes with us. As we left, Guy closed the door, and I heard the click of the lock behind us.

Jazz stepped over to one of the trash caddies, glanced back at the kitchen windows, rattled the lid of the can, replaced it, and tucked the towel under her arm.

Walking next to her, approaching her SUV, I asked, "Evidence?"

"Probably not 'evidence,' not exactly. Arcie didn't think so, or she would've taken it. But who knows? It might be a clue."

When Jazz and I arrived back in Palm Springs after our ill-fated visit to the Payne estate, it was nearly four thirty. She dropped me at work, confirming I would join her for tomorrow's meeting at eleven. Then she gunned it as she tore away from the curb in her husky black SUV.

Walking through the doors to the Sunny Junket offices, I braced myself for Gianna's expected smart-mouthing—and she delivered.

"Nice of you to drop in, Mr. Special Clients Liaison."

"Not now, Gianna. It's been a rough day."

She laughed merrily. "Don't tell me. Another body in a swimming pool?"

"Nothing of the kind."

She seemed disappointed and went back to work on her computer.

I crossed the room to my desk and found the new nameplate with my new title—so the day was not a total loss.

Hump day. Some called it date night. To most, it was just Wednesday.

That particular Wednesday had indeed presented a midweek hump—in the form of a murdered guest at one of Sunny Junket's most exclusive properties. Worse yet, getting "over the hump" was not a simple matter of running out the clock and sliding downhill toward the weekend. This was a hump that would remain stubbornly lodged in the foreground for a while, and the investigation had barely begun.

But it would not resume until the following morning, which gave me an open evening—a *Wednesday* evening—for more enjoyable pursuits. Date night.

While sitting at my computer, glancing at and trashing a day's worth of emails, I pulled out my phone and called Isandro's cell number.

I asked him, "Still at the office?"

"Yeah, but it's dead here. Procedures are in the morning. Afternoons are just filing and follow-up. I'm heading home soon."

"Busy tonight?"

He laughed. "With *you*, I hope."

I suggested, "Let's go out for dinner—someplace nice."

"Great. Anywhere's fine. You pick it."

"Will do. I've been out most of the day and need to put in a couple hours at my desk, but why don't I swing over and pick you up at seven?"

"I'll be at the front gate—and I'll try to make myself pretty."

I assured him, "You're always pretty." Which was true. But yes, he definitely needed to ditch his office scrubs for our night out.

When I pulled up to the curb in front of our apartment complex, he was waiting at the gate, as promised. In the darkening twilight, he looked mysterious and seductive—yet utterly adorable.

Hopping into the convertible, he said, "Good evening, *coração*," and leaned over for a peck. As we drove off, he added, "You've had a long day."

"Uh…yeah, I have. Tell you about it over dinner."

"Where are we going?"

"Fusión," I said, pronouncing it "foo-see-*own*" with just a touch of a Spanish lisp.

"Nice." Laughing, he added, "Get a raise?"

"Doubt it. But I got a promotion." I told him about the new title. "Nothing much has *changed*—except, I can dress how I want."

He reached over to pat my knee.

The chic bistro was only a few minutes away, downtown on a quiet side street—the sort of place you need to "know about." I'd call it trendy, but it had opened more than twenty years ago, surviving the many ups and downs of what's in and what's out among the town's various fusion-style restaurants. Others were typically Asian or Mexican; this was Spanish.

The parking valet all but drooled over the Karmann Ghia, handed me a ticket, and told us, "Have a great evening, guys." We were both looking good, and even though I was nearly nineteen years older than Isandro, I didn't feel it. If the valet noticed this disparity at all, he seemed to fully approve of the pairing.

Inside, in the small entryway, a single stalk of pink ginger protruded from a tall glass cylinder on the hostess stand. Black-garbed and sunken-cheeked, the young lady greeted us with a hushed "Welcome to Fusión. So nice to see you again, Mr. O'Donnell." She ushered us in, passing through the tiny barroom—where a muscular bald man with a leather vest and nipple rings shook the bejesus out of someone's martini—and then we emerged into the main dining room.

We paused to take in our surroundings, which were starkly minimal, with black carpeting, black leather chairs with chrome frames, narrow-beamed spotlights aimed at each table, and eye-searing arrangements of red tropical flowers. The hostess seated us, placed menus before us, and disappeared.

We ordered drinks, we ordered dinner (*paella, croquetas de jamón*, sharing both), and then we talked.

I delivered my news: Maude Movay was not a real person, but a publishing enterprise, and the man who wrote her books, Lanford Endicott, who was renting the guesthouse in Indian Wells, had been murdered earlier that day.

"That's ... tragic," said Isandro. "And let me guess. Jazz has a new client."

I nodded. "Lanford's husband, Guy Kirby, hired Jazz to help clear him—*and* their Filipino houseboy—before the cops start making charges. I don't know if they were involved or not, but the circumstances are suspicious."

Isandro grinned. "So you're sidekicking again."

"Seems like it." After an awkward pause, I said, "This morning, when you were leaving your apartment, it was earlier than usual, and you said you were rushed and wanted to talk tonight. So...what's up?"

He paused. Poker-faced, he told me, "I saw another man last night."

Well, at least he was up-front about it. Deflated, I said, "I know. Zola saw you. She told me." I couldn't resist adding, "She said he had bleached hair and bleached teeth. She said he looked like one of our local dime-a-dozen real-estate hussies."

Isandro eyed me askance. "I doubt if Z-Doll said *that*."

I conceded, "I *might* have been reading between the lines."

"Mm-hmm." Then he chuckled. "But her observations were correct. I was with Krill Collie, who does in fact have bleached hair, bleached teeth, and a broker's license." Isandro reached for his wine and took a sip.

Warily I asked, "And the purpose of your hookup?"

He nearly choked, laughing. "Well, certainly not *sex*. With *Krill*?"

Relieved, but confused, I asked, "What, then?"

"Real estate, of course."

I blinked. "You're in the market?"

"Not really—or at least I wasn't." Isandro topped up our wineglasses, explaining, "I've known Krill awhile, had dinner a couple times—he probably wanted more, but that was *not* gonna happen. I guess I mentioned to him that my apartment was feeling small, my career was advancing, and he should keep me in mind if he came across something that semed right for me. Then I instantly forgot about it."

I picked up the thread: "And then he called."

"Right. Yesterday. He said he had a 'pocket listing,' not published yet, because the owner of one of the larger properties in the Old Las Palmas neighborhood was thinking of selling off an unused slice of the estate—but he wanted it handled discreetly."

I noted, "This sounds a bit like the ambassador's widow, renting out her guesthouse. I guess moneyed seniors are feeling the pinch of tough times."

Isandro shrugged. "Same sorta deal—except Denny's guy doesn't have a guesthouse, but a coach house, and he doesn't want to rent it, but sell it. On a whim, I went to see it last night."

"And?"

"Oh, *coração*, I never gave much thought to moving, but now it's hard to think of anything else. You should *see* this place. I think it was originally built for horses, like a barn, but no one has horses in that part of town anymore. So then it was used for cars—on the ground floor, of course—but upstairs, there's this big open space, nicely finished with a kitchen and bath.

Basically, it has the feel of one huge room."

"Like a loft," I said.

"Exactly. And it's fabulous—or could be."

"Sounds great. But what are they asking for it?"

He told me.

I weighed the sum in my mind for a moment. "The price is right—for *that* neighborhood. But is it right for *you*?" Although I knew nothing of Isandro's finances, it struck me as unlikely that he had the means to upgrade from our decidedly modest apartment complex to one of the toniest districts in town, even if the property amounted to a glorified garage.

He took a deep breath and exhaled a long sigh. "No," he said, "I could never swing it." Then his frown turned devilish. "Not on my own…"

Uh-oh.

He reached for my hand on the table. "But together, I'll bet we could make it work."

With a weak smile, I gave him a curious look, as if waiting for him to announce that he was just kidding.

Instead: "I know you weren't expecting that—you should see your *face*—and I know you'll need time to give it some thought. No pressure. But meanwhile, wouldn't you like to take a look at the place for yourself? I could set it up sometime."

I felt as if my mind had left my body as I said numbly, "Uh, sure… sometime."

And Isandro was on a roll, ordering dessert, crunching numbers, making plans.

Back at my apartment—it was always *my* apartment, after an evening out—Isandro laughed and gabbed as we lingered over a nightcap, sitting at the breakfast bar in my cramped cubby of a kitchen.

When I glanced at my watch, he said, "I know, I know—we both have to work tomorrow." He leaned to kiss me, speaking into my mouth, "Can I put you to bed?"

I knew what that meant. He was already unbuttoning my shirt.

I turned out the lights, and he led me into my bedroom, where we undressed each other in the dark—feeling our way, so to speak.

And before long, we were at it on the bed. Isandro was always ready and totally into it, but tonight he seemed not only impassioned, but thrilled and happy. Approaching his point of no return, he howled with delight.

And while this was happening, I was—God help me—conflicted. The flesh was more than willing, but my spirit was weak as I tussled with the implications of the damned coach house. All day, I'd been afraid Isandro was thinking of dumping me that night, and now I was terrified by the possibility of feathering a nest with him.

Compounding this confusion—what freaked and angered me, *again*—was the outburst from Mitzi on the other side of the wall.

CHAPTER
SEVEN

At the office on Thursday morning, I tried to focus more on my job and less on Isandro, the coach house, and the one-way ticket to happily ever after. All of that could wait, I decided, perhaps for quite a while, or maybe even for good.

My job at Sunny Junket—with or without the new title—had suddenly dovetailed with Jazz's private investigation of Lanford Endicott's death, so I gave myself some extra time for the meeting at Jazz's office, scheduled for eleven o'clock. Around ten thirty, while making the short walk along Palm Canyon Drive, I noticed a distinctive vehicle parked at the curb near the Huggamug building—not the flamboyant pink SUV registered to the late Lanford Endicott, but an unmarked sheriff's cruiser (fooling no one with its stripped-down trim, heavy-duty tires, and artlessly concealed flashers), which I recognized as belonging to Detective Arcie Madera. She was surely not there to hug a mug of coffee, but to visit Jazz.

I stepped inside the building's side door, climbed the stairs to the second floor, and entered Jazz's front office. "Just me," I called, closing the door behind me.

"Back here," Jazz called to me.

When I walked into the decrepit space that served as a conference room, I tried to avoid my usual wince so I could present

myself with a smile to Detective Madera, who was seated with
Jazz at the table.

"You're early," said Jazz. "Glad you're here. Arcie stopped by to
review some preliminaries."

After exchanging greetings with Arcie, I sat with them at the
god-awful banquet table.

Jazz said, "I've explained to Arcie that Guy Kirby plans to hire
me, and why."

Detective Madera told both of us, "And I have no problem
with that—the more heads working to solve this, the better.
But your purpose in doing this is not mine. You're working for
Kirby; I work for 'the people.' I'm fine with some reasonable
amount of sharing, but there's a line that can't be crossed—your
investigation cannot in any way *interfere* with mine."

"Understood," said Jazz. "Absolutely."

Arcie gave her a subtle, satisfied grin.

Jazz asked, "So then—for Dante's sake—can we back up?"

"Sure." Arcie flipped through the pages in a file folder she'd
brought, spread out on the table in front of her. "First, the medical examiner's initial findings: the victim died of asphyxiation,
which was the result of strangulation with the silk scarf found
at the scene, exactly as theorized yesterday. Routine toxicology
tests have now been ordered. Results take a while, but they're
not expected to reveal more than we already know. Long story
short: this was a homicide."

I asked, "Time of death?"

Arcie reminded us, "Yesterday, we were guessing the victim
had died a couple hours earlier, and testing bore that out. The
bedroom—the whole house—was closed-up and air-condi-
tioned, so the ambient temperature of the crime scene was high-

ly stable. Taking everything into account—body temperature, lividity, and such—the time of death has been pegged shortly before noon, between eleven thirty and twelve."

Jazz looked up from her own notes. "And that brings us to the entry-and-exit logs from the main gate."

Arcie nodded. "I must admit, the record-keeping at Vanguard Ridge is thorough and exacting, and over the years, it's really paid off—virtually no violent crime there."

I said, "No wonder they were so reluctant to let the ambassador build his private gate."

Jazz chortled. "Live and learn..."

"So here's what I've got," said Arcie. "Yesterday morning at seven fifteen, the Chang party of two, registered as guests of Lanford Endicott, exited through the main gate on Highway 111."

"Makes sense," I said. "That's Lanford's niece, Nicole, and her husband, Saxon. They're the ones who unexpectedly spent the night and needed to get back to Redlands."

Arcie continued, "Nina Rodriguez, a housekeeper employed as day help at the Payne estate, entered the gate about five minutes before ten o'clock."

Jazz scratched something on her notes. "Nina worked late at the dinner party the night before, so she was told to come in later than usual yesterday."

Arcie said, "And she apparently stayed all day, since the gate records supplied to me don't go beyond five o'clock. Then again, nothing's conclusive because they've got that *damned* back gate." Arcie quickly added, "Pardon my language."

"Don't mention it," said Jazz.

I gave her a look—in the time I'd known her, I'd never once seen her flinch at an expletive, let alone such a mild one.

Arcie said, "In addition to Nina, there's also Agnetha Berg

and Mrs. Payne, who were all at the main house during the day and had access to the guesthouse. So all of them had the *opportunity* to kill the victim. Strangulation with a silk scarf isn't difficult, once it's knotted, so all of them had the *means* to kill Lanford Endicott—even the rather feeble Mrs. Payne if she worked up an adrenaline surge, which can happen in a situation like that. But that leaves us with identifying a *motive*, and at the moment, the only one we know about is Agnetha's—her desire to keep details of her past hidden."

Jazz said, "And Lanford had hired me to go digging."

Arcie nodded. "I'll get back to that, but let's continue with the records from the main gate. Next, there's the hairdresser, Bruce Tucker. His visit was brief. He drove in at eleven fifteen and left at eleven thirty."

I noted, "Time enough to drop off three wigs and take his signed book. Also long enough to strangle a person—if sufficiently motivated—and let me tell you, he went through some whiplash mood swings during my brief encounter with him. Of particular interest, he had a little snit fit because Maude Movay had killed off one of his favorite characters in her books."

"Definitely worth looking into," said Arcie. "And the fact that he left at precisely eleven thirty is intriguing—that's right on the cusp of the period when the victim could have died."

Arcie paused.

Jazz asked, "And what about Guy Kirby?"

"I've been saving that one—your new client—for last."

That didn't sound good.

Arcie continued, "Guy Kirby drove Ramil Bagoyo through the main gate yesterday morning when they left at ten thirty. They returned at one forty-five, when they discovered what had happened at the house and our deputies brought them inside."

Jazz shrugged. "Nothing suspicious about that."

I reminded her, "The back gate. They knew about it, knew how to use it, and could have returned to the guesthouse undetected at the time Lanford was killed. They would have left the same way. Later, they could 'innocently' return through the front gate and stumble into the crime scene."

"And there was a plausible motive," said Arcie. "Their behavior yesterday suggested they had a love triangle, and two of the three might have gotten tired of sharing."

"*Except,*" I said, "their snazzy lifestyle was the result of Maude Movay's books, and they really *needed* Lanford to finish her next one—and quickly—or blow a huge deal. Why kill the cash cow?" That term was sounding more and more apt.

Arcie admitted, "Good question. So let's switch gears. Next, we have records of the victim's cell phone use from yesterday. He was very active. He placed or received more than twenty calls from the time he got up, around eight, until they tapered off to incoming calls, around eleven. Most of them appeared to be far-flung business calls—from LA, New York, even a couple from London."

Jazz said, "No wonder he couldn't get any writing done."

I suggested, "He could've just turned it *off.*"

"Eventually," said Arcie, "he did—it was still switched to DO NOT DISTURB when we managed to get into it, but that didn't prevent incoming calls from being logged and, in a few cases, going to voicemail."

Jazz said, "Let's hear about the calls that *weren't* routine business."

"Well," said Arcie, "for starters, he received two calls yesterday from Dante's phone, ID'd as a Palm Springs number. One was early, shortly after nine; the other was at one fifteen."

I explained, "The early call was to confirm that Lanford wanted Jazz and me to come and meet with him yesterday. He suggested one fifteen. The second call was from the Payne estate's private gate, asking Lanford to let us in. When he didn't answer, I left him a message, and we went around to the main gate."

Arcie nodded. "I heard your message." Tracing her finger down a list, she said, "There was also an incoming call from the Bruce Tucker Salon, Indian Wells, a minute or two after eleven o'clock. That would be consistent with his entry through the main gate at eleven fifteen—he was probably calling to check if he could bring the wigs over."

Jazz and I looked at each other and nodded. Arcie's reasoning made sense.

Arcie continued, "There were a number of calls that day from a cell phone identified as FRIENDLY LAW in Palm Springs. Calls placed after twelve went unanswered, of course. Then, around one thirty, the caller left a voicemail, identifying herself as Allison, who sounded worried about Lanford's whereabouts." Arcie turned to Jazz, asking, "'Friendly Law'—any connection?"

Jazz Friendly explained, "That's my ex-husband's law firm. One of his partners, Allison Harper, is the contract lawyer for the Maude Movay enterprise and had a lot to do with the huge deal for the next book. Allison is the one who wanted to seclude Lanford out here for a month to get the book written. And Dante set it up."

Arcie asked, "So Allison had good reason to be checking on Lanford, right?"

"You bet," I said. "The night before the murder, she and Jazz's ex were at the dinner party at the guesthouse. Allison's not exactly a...*pleasant* person, but she's—"

"She's a ballbuster," Jazz muttered.

"But," I continued, "she's clearly dedicated to her clients' best interests—she was *determined* to see Lanford finish that manuscript. He'd been making no progress, so it's no surprise she was riding him yesterday."

"I'll need to talk to her," said Arcie, making notes.

Jazz said dryly, "*Do* give her my best."

Arcie seemed amused by this. "Moving right along," she said, "Saxon Chang called from a Redlands number around nine, shortly after Dante's first call."

I said, "I'll bet he was phoning to let Lanford know they'd gotten home all right—and to apologize for Nicole's behavior the night before. She was really a mess."

"Sounds logical," said Arcie. "But then he phoned again just after ten thirty."

Jazz and I exchanged a quizzical look. She told Arcie, "That one is anyone's guess."

Arcie glanced over her list. "And that brings us to one more phone call that could qualify as significant. Lanford received it at eleven twenty that morning from an LA cell number belonging to Guy Kirby—your new client."

I interpreted Arcie's choice of words to mean that she found this suspicious. Jazz must have gotten the same vibe.

She said to Arcie, "Unless I'm mistaken, these overnight call reports only supply the information associated with each phone number, not the origin point of each call. But they *can* drill down to the specific cell tower, if it comes to that."

Arcie nodded. "Obviously, Guy Kirby wasn't calling from LA. He'd left the guesthouse with Ramil less than an hour earlier, and the receipts he gave me from their outing prove they didn't venture far from Indian Wells."

"In other words," said Jazz, "there's not much to read into this. Guy could've called for any number of reasons, like running late or whatever."

"Maybe." But Arcie didn't sound ready to cross anyone off her list.

I asked, "Any other phone calls?"

"No, none of the others look significant. And that brings us to the victim's laptop."

Jazz said, "I presume you saw Lanford's notes about Agnetha Berg."

"Indeed I did."

I told Arcie, "We only saw what was on the screen when I woke the laptop with its space bar. We didn't dig around or even scroll the screen."

She gave me a nod. "Thank you for leaving that to us. My team did plenty of digging, and we found that the file headlined CYNTHIA'S SLOTH contained no text for a novel. It consisted entirely of assorted ramblings about the mysterious demise of Berg's long-ago husband, including lengthy thoughts about the nature of their marriage, which Lanford considered a sham. Other files contained research notes; others still, copies of documents related to the case. To be honest, I think he might have been *on* to something—which makes his death all the more tragic."

I said, "It also points to a suspect and a motive."

"Yes. If we could place Berg in the guesthouse the morning of the murder—and so far, we can't—that would make a very strong case. If Berg actually *saw* what Lanford was working on, she might have been highly compelled to stop him." Arcie then looked at me. "What? You're frowning."

"Trouble is," I said, "after Lanford and Guy and Ramil moved in last Sunday, I don't think Agnetha was involved in their daily housekeeping."

"Right," said Jazz. "When we were there the next morning, we met the chambermaid, Nina, right there in Maude's suite. So she saw plenty, including—probably—the computer."

Arcie picked up the reasoning. "And then, Nina could have *reported* this to Agnetha. And then, who knows?"

After the three of us sat mulling this for a moment, Arcie checked her watch and packed up her files. "Plenty to do. Gotta run."

Jazz said, "Perfect timing. Guy and Ramil should arrive soon—actually, they're a few minutes late."

Arcie reminded her, "Do *not* strategize with them regarding how to answer my questions."

Jazz laughed. "I'm an investigator, Arcie—not a *lawyer.*"

Arcie shared the laugh, easily buying into Jazz's promise that she wouldn't coach her clients. As we strolled out to the front office, engaging in some parting gab, Jazz caught my eye ... and winked.

Mere seconds after Arcie left the building, we heard the downstairs door open again, signaling the arrival of Guy and Ramil. Surely they had crossed paths with the detective outside, and I wondered if they had stopped to acknowledge each other—or were they all on their phones?

Both Guy and Ramil were talking as they climbed the stairs, and not with each other. Jazz and I stood near the open door to her front office and gestured for them to step inside, which they did, glancing up from their phones to offer nods of greeting while not missing a beat of their separate conversations.

By the tone of it, Ramil was having fun with the receptionist at a day spa, making an appointment for a facial and mani-pedi later that afternoon. It seemed grieving agreed with him.

Guy, on the other hand, was agitated, and it soon became apparent he was speaking to his attorney. He told her, "If it's really that urgent, sure." Then he passed the phone to Jazz, asking, "Could you give Allison directions, please? The world will apparently *end* if she doesn't deliver certain documents into my hand—at *once*." Then he leaned near, confiding, "She's hysterical—so brace yourself."

Jazz took the phone. "Hello? Allison?"

While the girls talked logistics, the boys talked curtains.

Ramil had just pocketed his phone when he spotted the banana leaves with a shriek. "How *fabulous*—just like the guesthouse."

I bragged, "I'm *very* close with Mrs. Payne's decorator."

"Stunning," said Guy. "Most attractive. Have you been working with Jazz on the interiors?"

"Yes, in fact—off and on." (I couldn't *wait* for them to step into the conference room.)

With a purr, Ramil said seductively, "I like your style, Mr. Dante O'Donnell."

The buff Filipino was growing on me, but this was the wrong time to let on, so I said nothing, offering the slightest smile in response to his words.

Jazz returned Guy's phone. "Allison will be here in about ten minutes. I'd like to discuss a few things before she arrives. So if you don't mind ... this way, please." And she led everyone into the conference room.

As Guy entered, he said, "What the—?" but stopped himself.

Ramil couldn't control his reaction. He recoiled with a jolt and a piercing gasp, as if he'd been stabbed.

"This room is next," I told them. "It still needs a bit of work."

"We've been *so* busy," Jazz lied, "Dante hasn't had a spare minute to get to it. Please, have a seat." And she placed folders containing her proposal in front of each of us.

Opening her folder, Jazz told Guy, "This is essentially the same agreement I had with Lanford. You'll find a description of the services I can provide, along with the fee schedule and terms of payment." As she walked him through the details, Guy nodded while reading the text of the agreement. I followed along, turning the pages in my folder. Ramil picked at his nails.

Guy looked up. "Everything's fine, Jazz. Let's do it." He handed her a credit card.

She passed him a pen, and he signed several pages for her.

With that taken care of, Jazz opened another folder—her notes on the case. "First of all," she said, "let me again offer condolences. I know that Lanford's death has been a shock to both of you. We can't bring him back, but we *can* try to figure out what happened—and bring his killer to justice." She paused before continuing in a different vein, in a different tone:

"But we need to be completely honest with each other, and we need to work fast. Detective Madera is a highly skilled investigator, and she reminded me just this morning that she works for 'the people.' But she also cooperates with our district attorney, Peter Nadig, who's an elected politician—*and* a hotdog. He has a taste for headlines and convictions. So Detective Madera will be under pressure to name a guilty party so he can press charges and drag someone into court. In other words, we need to keep ahead of the game." Jazz fell silent and crossed her arms.

Guy cleared his throat. "Suffice it to say, you've captured our attention."

"Good. Let me ask you: Since we last saw each other yesterday, has anything come to your attention that you need to tell me?"

Gay and Ramil gave each other a meaningful look. Guy told us, "Cash is missing from the guesthouse. I discovered it this morning. Lanford kept his wallet in the guest room we were using—not in the Maude suite. It was still on the dresser with his keys when I got up today, and I thought I should put them away for safekeeping because he always carried a lot of cash. But it was empty. Credit cards and IDs were there, but the money was gone."

I asked, "How much?"

Guy shrugged. "Not sure. Lanford always had hundreds on him, maybe a thousand. And since we were going to be away from LA for so long, he also brought an envelope of cash he got at the bank before we left. That wasn't left sitting out. He kept it 'hidden'—not very well—in the top drawer with his socks. Found the envelope. Empty, of course. I'm guessing it came to several thousand dollars."

Jazz asked, "Any jewelry or other valuables missing?"

"Not that I'm aware of—just the cash."

Ramil reminded him, "What about the clicker?"

"*Oh*," said Guy. "It's not what you'd call 'valuable,' Jazz, but it's weird. When we were ready to leave the house for Palm Springs, I intended to use the private gate, so I thought I'd take the opener with me—to get back in. Couldn't find it."

Ramil said, "We'd been keeping it in the kitchen, on the center island, so we'd all know where to find it in case someone called from the back gate. But I tore the kitchen apart, and it's *not* there."

Guy said, "I'm guessing Lanford took it to Maude's desk when he settled there to do his writing yesterday. He was going to be alone at the house and must've wanted to save himself a few steps if anyone needed the gate opened."

"Makes sense," I said. "But if he took it to Maude's desk, it wasn't there when Jazz and I discovered his body—so the killer must've taken it."

Ramil asked, "But *why*? It wasn't worth anything. And you wouldn't need to *take* it to open the gate and leave."

Jazz explained, "You'd need to take it to *close* the gate after you left. The killer couldn't risk using the main gate if they didn't come in that way. And they wanted to make sure the back gate was closed—to cast suspicion on the 'insiders' at the estate."

I reminded her, "This all depends on whether the opener was, in fact, taken or not. It could still turn up somewhere."

Jazz told Guy and Ramil, "Keep looking—but this could be an important lead."

Guy nodded. "We were rushed this morning, trying to get here on time. We'll take another look."

Jazz said to him, "Arcie Madera has the log of calls to Lanford's phone yesterday morning, and it seems he got one from you at eleven twenty. Is that correct?"

"Not sure of the exact time, but yes, I did call him while Ramil and I were out. We'd finished a couple of errands and were nosing around for a place to have lunch. I asked Lanford if he wanted us to bring him something—so he could focus on his writing. He asked for a BLT."

"Did you get one for him?"

"Of course. But when we returned to the house and all the commotion with the police, we got out of the car and forgot about it."

Ramil said, "I remembered it this morning before we left, so I went out to the car and found it on the back seat."

"Yuck," I said. "Sitting in a black car—all afternoon—in the desert sun."

Guy said, "And Lanford always asked for heavy mayo. It wasn't pretty. I told Ramil to run it down the garbage disposal."

Jazz asked sternly, "Destroying evidence?" Then she chuckled. "Just kidding—sort of. You gave the lunch receipt to Arcie Madera, right?"

"Right. But I didn't take a close look at it—not sure if it was itemized."

Jazz made a note. "I'll tell her about it."

I asked Jazz, "The BLT would put Guy and Ramil in the clear, wouldn't it?"

"Maybe—unless our clients were *very* clever. There's no way to prove that Lanford actually asked them to get it for him."

"Oh."

Jazz said to Guy, "Lanford's phone logs show he had a lot of calls yesterday morning—more than twenty. Before you left the house with Ramil, did you happen to hear Lanford's half of any of those calls?"

Guy shook his head. "Lanford holed up in the Maude suite as soon as the morning coffee was ready. He took a carafe with him and closed the door. If he was talking on the phone, I never heard him."

Jazz turned to Ramil, who also shook his head.

I said, "Guy—and Ramil—this is a delicate topic, but it's bound to come up eventually because it's at the heart of Detective Madera's suspicions. So, if I may ask: Could your relationship with each other, and with Lanford, be described as a *ménage à trois*?"

They turned to each other, dumbfounded.

Then Guy turned to me, blurting, "Well, of *course*."

Ramil was laughing. "Did you really need to *ask*?"

"Apparently not," I admitted.

"Look," said Guy, "Lanford and I were never a 'traditional' couple—the hetero fantasy of marriage wasn't our thing. When Ramil eventually came along, he was just our personal trainer. That's how we met. Then things ... *evolved*. We all clicked. And we wanted to make it official—as far as the law would allow—so his employment status was upgraded to full-time live-in."

Ramil reached for Guy's hand, asking me, "Any other questions?"

I had plenty, wondering if their free-spirited arrangement included an openness to others outside the original triangle. The vibe I kept getting from Ramil seemed to say, *Anything goes*. But we were interrupted by a woman's voice from the front office.

"Yoo-hoo. Hello?"

"That's Allison Harper," said Guy.

I told the others, "Stay put. I'll get her."

Out in the reception room, the attorney responsible for the Maude Movay contracts looked like hell, as though she'd gotten little, if any, sleep the night before. But it wasn't just the fatigue that had taken a toll—the puffy red eyes behind her huge red glasses suggested a recent crying jag, and her twisted features made me wonder if she was on the verge of another. At Tuesday evening's dinner party, she'd shown tons of attitude and swagger. Today, she simply looked drained.

"Allison," I said, "please come in. Can I get you something— water, maybe?"

"No, thank you, Dante. Is Guy still here?"

"Of course. This way."

As we joined the others in back, the dismal state of the

conference room did not jolt her with dismay—she was *that* out of it.

She greeted Jazz with a limp handshake; Guy and Ramil pecked her damp cheeks. She set a tidy zippered portfolio on the table and flumped herself into an open chair, telling the world, "Christ, what a shitstorm."

Sounding sincere, Jazz told her, "I'm *really* sorry for your loss."

"You have *no* idea—thank you, Jazz. Lanford was a very dear, very old friend, as well as an important client. Burying him is bad enough, but blowing that deal—that *mother* of a book-and-film deal—I can't *begin* to process that." And she wept.

"I feel your pain," Guy assured her, sounding more pragmatic than grieved. Then he reminded her, "You were pretty tough on him Tuesday night."

She wiped snot from her lip. "I wish I could say I regret that, but he was blowing the goddamn deadline. The carrot wasn't working—time for the stick. You were his fucking *agent*. You had as much to gain, or lose, as I did. And you were right *there* with him. Why didn't you *pressure* him?"

Repressing evident anger, he said, "Short of writing it myself, I did everything I could."

With a shudder of disgust, Allison pulled herself together, opened the portfolio, and removed two file-size envelopes. "Here," she said. "This is a copy of the estate plan—we can deal with that soon enough. The other is more important—it's a draft of the press release and marketing strategy. We need decisions *fast*: How do we announce that Maude is dead? Or *not*? Thank God the local press hasn't gotten wind of this yet."

Jazz said, "The police report made no mention of the Maude Movay connection. By the time it found its way into the paper's 'Crime Blotter' column, it was just a suspicious death at a vacation rental in Indian Wells. No names yet—next of kin—blah, blah, blah."

"Good," said Allison. "And you're trying to keep Guy out of this, right?

"As much as possible, yes."

"Okay, then." Allison stood. "I'm late for another meeting."

We all stood.

"One more thing," said Jazz. "The book-and-film deal. That's part of the background of this case. Any chance I could get a look at the contract?"

Allison turned to Guy. "You're the agent. What do you think?"

"Fine by *me.*" He told Jazz, "I'd gladly let you read it, but my files are back in LA, and I don't think I can access a digital copy."

Allison said, "Not a problem, Jazz—I'll get the contract to you. And now, I *do* need to run."

When Allison left, Jazz covered a few remaining notes with Guy and Ramil. Several minutes later, they left as well.

Alone with Jazz, I asked, "What's next?"

"The hairdresser, Bruce Tucker. He's gay. You're gay."

I grinned. "I am *not* gonna sleep with him—even for a good cause."

Jazz laughed. "Just talk to him. Run him through the usual: what he saw, what he knows, what he thinks. Can you do it?"

"Not today. Probably tomorrow."

Back at the Sunny Junket office that afternoon, my phone warbled and showed an incoming call from Isandro. I connected, saying, "And how's every little thing in the madcap world of gastroenterology?"

"Never better. But let's talk about *you.*"

"What about me?"

"Would *you* like to see the coach house after work?"

I hesitated. "Is Krill Collie going to be there? He makes my skin crawl."

"Of course—it's his listing."

I niggled. "His *pocket* listing."

"C'mon," said Isandro. "Please?"

There would be no rest until I did this, so I agreed to meet him back at our apartment complex at five sharp. His first visit to the property had been in the evening, and he wanted to see it in full daylight.

When we turned from Palm Canyon Drive and entered the Old Las Palmas neighborhood, Isandro guided me through the labyrinth of streets that led back to the grand old estate that would soon be subdivided. It covered half a block, and the street where I parked the Karmann Ghia ran along the estate's rear privacy wall, broken only by a narrow driveway with a gate.

We walked from the car to the driveway, where the gate was open, and we entered the grounds. Parked to the side was a long white Mercedes sedan, obviously Krill Collie's—the vanity plates spelled a clumsy abbreviation of his name. The man himself stepped from around the corner of a small two-story building of Spanish-colonial style that resembled a barn, and despite my reluctance to come see it, I found it totally charming.

The broker also laid on the charm, to which Isandro was moderately receptive, but I couldn't even fake it. He had a pumped-up handshake to go with his pumped-up hair; I wiped my palm on my hip after we shook. "*Dante*," he gushed, "I was just thrilled to hear from Isandro that you wanted to come over for a look-see. Follow me ..."

When we walked around to the façade of the building—

whoa—I had not been prepared for anything nearly so sublime as the setting that opened before us.

The main house sat on the far side of an expansive brick-paved terrace that surrounded a pool. The house, like the coach house, was cream-colored stucco with a tile roof. Both buildings faced the pool through a loggia and colonnade on the ground floor. A pair of tiered fountains gurgled and pattered near opposite ends of the pool. Beneath a canopy of date palms, groupings of large terra-cotta pots overflowed with trailing vines and clusters of flowers—pink and white.

Krill explained, "Over the years, the stable, later a garage, also served as a pool house, providing a man-made view—a 'backdrop'—as seen from the main house. Fabulous, isn't it?"

I couldn't disagree. The garage doors were on the rear side of the building. On the front side, facing the pool, the ground-floor loggia contained lounge furniture and a fanciful stairway leading up to the second floor, which overhung the colonnade. Krill suggested, "Shall we take a look upstairs?"

Isandro reminded him, "That's why we're here." And up we went.

It's rare to step into a space and instantly think, *I could live here*. But this was one of those times. The overall plan appeared to be an exact square, with each side measuring some thirty-five or forty feet. Most of the area, in front, was an open space serving as living room, dining room, and a study with floor-to-ceiling bookcases. Closer to the back, an interior structure housed a galley kitchen, opening toward the front space; a bathroom, opening toward the sleeping area along the rear wall; and closets, laundry, and storage. Windows in the front space afforded elevated views of the manicured pool area, the main house, and—beyond the estate's perimeter plantings—the sunset-tinged mountains at the edge of the valley.

"It's perfect for two," said Krill.

Isandro shot me a grin.

After a loaded pause, I asked, "What's downstairs?"

"Let's go see," said Krill, leading us out of the loft and down to the loggia, where a passage door opened into the garage.

The space was immaculate—for a garage—though much less finished than the upstairs living quarters. Two generously wide spaces for vehicles were entered from conventional garage doors along the far wall. These doors were not centered, but tucked to one side, leaving nearly a third of the room for storage, a water heater, and junk—a place that was well suited, I thought, for a home gym.

While Isandro snooped around some of the items covered by drop cloths, I wandered into the parking area, which was empty. I asked Krill, "Just so I'm clear—these parking spaces are part of the deal, correct?"

"Yes, *absolutely*. The owner is a collector of vintage cars, and he built a separate facility to house those—as well as his day-to-day vehicles—on a lot adjacent to the estate." Under his breath, Krill confided, "It was a mighty expensive teardown, to put up a new *garage*."

Isandro said to me, "I bet you wouldn't mind getting your car off the street at night."

I didn't need to reply—he knew how I felt about the Kar-mann Ghia.

"Hey," said Isandro, "what's this?"

He had pulled back a drop cloth and found a classically modern Parsons dining table—a sleek rectangle big enough to seat eight, with a flawless black-lacquer finish, looking brand-new.

Krill told us, "The owner ordered it custom-built for upstairs, and when he got it, didn't like it. Thought it was too 'cold' for the space. So he replaced it with the more rustic table that's up there now. But if you two take the place, *you* get to decide. Everything on the premises is yours to keep and use—or haul away."

I knew exactly where the cold-as-business Parsons table would look just right.

Isandro and I went out for a drink and a pizza after leaving the coach house—not a celebration, but fuel, as there was plenty to talk about and even more to think about.

Isandro was ready to do it, period. He fiendishly enticed me by asking which garage stall I wanted.

Krill Collie, of course, had cautioned us to move at once: "This place won't last. But I know the owner would *love* to have a couple like you on the grounds."

As for me, I was ... interested. The place was great. The price was workable. The garage was a big plus. And even the Parsons table was a minor bonus. But it was the "couple" thing that threw me.

So when we drove back home and parked at the curb and walked through the gate to the courtyard at our apartment complex—which was suddenly looking *very* shabby—I knew that I needed some space and some time.

Isandro hooked a finger through my belt and pulled me close, asking, "Your place?"

I kissed him, then said, "Not tonight, kiddo. After the last couple days, I'm feeling whipped." Which was true.

"Of course, *coração*. Get some rest. We'll talk tomorrow."

"I'll look forward to it." Which was not true. But it left him satisfied as he strolled off to his apartment while I entered mine.

After closing the door, I sat on the love seat, feeling heavy and tired, then closed my eyes.

Within moments, a gentle rapping. *What does he want now?* I got up to answer the door.

"Good evening, Dante love. Am I intruding?"

"*Never*, Zola. Please come in." Closing the door after her, I asked, "What's up?"

"I wonder if I could possibly ask you a favor."

I grinned. "Try me."

"Marjorie Payne phoned me this afternoon."

"Ah. Then you've heard the news."

"Yes, how awful. Marjorie is beside herself, naturally. She says she just needs to 'spend some time with a dear old friend'— meaning *me*. So she asked me to lunch tomorrow at the estate. I'd like to go, I'd like to help, but..." She trailed off.

I asked, "Do you need a ride?"

She rolled her eyes. "Could you *possibly*? When I told Marjorie that I would need to find a driver—and that I might ask *you*—she said to invite you for lunch as well." From the side of her mouth, Zola added, "Careful, Dante. I think she likes you."

"I'll be happy to do that—if you promise to help me fend off Mrs. Payne."

With a croak of a laugh, Zola assured me, "*Count* on it. Now all I need to do is figure out what to wear—and how to put myself together. Marjorie is very la-di-da, you know."

I had a thought. "May I offer to book you a fresh hairdo—on the house?"

She gave me the strangest look. But she accepted.

CHAPTER
EIGHT

Early Friday morning, I phoned the Bruce Tucker Salon in Indian Wells. Assuming there would be no one there at that hour, I intended to leave a message, and at the sound of the beep, I did:

"Bruce, this is Dante O'Donnell. You might remember meeting me on Monday at the Payne estate. I'm taking a lady friend, Zola Lorinsky, to have lunch with Mrs. Payne today. The invitation was last-minute, and let's just say that Zola could use a wash and blowout before lunch. Could you *possibly* accommodate her?" And I left my number.

Shortly after nine, my phone rang. "Of course I remember *you*, Dante," said Bruce Tucker. "Things are a little crazy this morning, but since your friend Zola will be visiting Mrs. *Payne*, well ... I think you'd better bring her in."

I said, "We're expected for lunch at twelve thirty. Could you take Zola at eleven?"

"Eleven it is! Ta, Dante." And he rang off.

I asked Zola to be ready to leave by ten thirty, and she rapped on my door with two minutes to spare. She looked fabulous—stylish as ever, this priestess of pizazz. (And her hair looked just fine.) When I walked her out to my convertible, I offered to put the top up.

"Don't even *think* of it," she insisted, patting her purse. "And I brought a scarf for after the hairdo."

On our way into Indian Wells, I parked at the salon and then, suppressing a laugh, helped Zola out of the car.

"What?" she asked.

"Nothing, just a thought." The windy drive had given Bruce plenty to work with.

We found the salon to be a busy place that morning, heading into a weekend in high season. Hair dryers howled, stylists gabbed and laughed with their clients, and show tunes thumped in the background. When we checked in with the receptionist, he handed Zola a folded smock and directed her to a changing room, telling us, "Bruce is expecting you."

I took a seat near the front window, away from the fray, to wait and to get my bearings. I spotted Bruce at the farthest of four styling stations, working on a man's hair, although all the other clients were women. With Bruce hovering over him, fussing, it was hard to get a good look at the client, but then I caught a clear glimpse of him in the mirrored wall he was facing.

Unless I was mistaken, the young man was Liam Heimlich, who worked at the art gallery that represented Jazz's painter friend, Blade Wade.

Bruce gave Liam's hair a finishing brush-and-blow before handing him a mirror and twirling the chair for an all-around inspection. Liam responded with a thumbs-up, stood, and removed the smock he'd worn over his shirt. Bruce brought him up to the front desk, talking all the way—rather earnestly, it seemed. Liam gave a credit card to the receptionist. When he turned back to Bruce, he noticed me sitting near the window, and the surprise on his face prompted Bruce to take a look.

A moment later we were all standing together, greeting each other, asking how we all happened to know each other.

The connection between Bruce and Liam was a charity group they were both involved with, Safe Palms Community Center, which provided counseling services and a place to hang out for at-risk gay youth. Liam explained, "That's how I met Bruce—committee work on the annual fundraiser. And since the salon isn't far from the gallery in Palm Desert, well—*everyone* needs a decent stylist."

With mock umbrage, Bruce asked, "*Decent?*"

I laughed. "The way I hear it, Bruce is the best."

"*That's* more like it," he said.

I told Liam, "Great haircut. But I couldn't imagine what the two of you were *doing* together."

Bruce clicked his tongue. "Get your mind out of the gutter, Dante. I'm far too old for this moppet. Besides, this was more than a haircut. It was an informal brainstorming session."

Liam nodded. "We've got a problem—with the fundraiser. It's a charity drag show featuring a local lip-sync troupe in over-the-top costumes. It's a *big* deal."

"A gala," I suggested.

"Yes," said Bruce. "It sells out *months* in advance, and this year's gala—we prefer to call it an extravaganza—is a week from tomorrow night at Apockalippso Dance Bar in downtown Palm Springs."

"Sounds like fun. No more tickets, huh?"

"No, but that's a *good* thing. The *problem* is Darla Midnight."

Liam said, "In drag, she's the troupe's Black diva, and the show always builds to her big number. But she got into a pissing match with a couple other 'ladies' in the troupe and walked out on us at rehearsal last night—huge, hysterical screaming match.

Texted us from the airport this morning, on her way to God knows where, to visit a sister for a month. And the *others* say that if she decides to come back—and if we let her onstage—*they* won't go on."

"So we're down a diva," said Bruce. "She was going to impersonate Grace Jones singing 'La Vie en Rose.' Fabulous costume, fabulous hair—very androgynous, very Jean-Paul Goude. But, alas, *c'est la vie*. The show, as they say, must go on—and it will. But without Darla, it just won't be the same. We'll have a heap of disappointed donors on our hands that night."

Hmm.

The receptionist hung up his phone. "Bruce? Federico finished with your next client. Zola is washed and waiting for you."

Liam said, "That's my cue—gotta run." He opened the door, but paused. "Stay in *touch*, Dante." And he was gone.

I asked Bruce, "Can I introduce you to Zola?"

"Perfect. C'mon back." He led me to his station, where he pulled over a side chair for me.

Zola was already in the adjustable styling chair. A towel was wrapped around her wet hair, and she wore a silky purple smock embroidered in flourishes with the signature *Bruce*.

After I properly introduced them, Bruce said to Zola, "I hear you're on your way to Mrs. Payne's for lunch."

I had already coached her to play dumb about the murder, as I wasn't sure what, if anything, Bruce had heard about it. For that matter, I couldn't yet eliminate the possibility that Bruce himself was the killer.

Zola told him, "Marjorie and I have known each other forever—since she and the ambassador built the estate—and I think she just wanted to catch up."

"That *house*," said Bruce, combing and curling, "isn't it fabulous? I mean totally to-die-for."

After a tantalizing pause, Zola informed him, "I was the lead decorator. Thank you."

They launched into an excited discussion of the estate's various design elements, including—of *course*—the banana-leaf curtains, which gave me an opportunity to survey Bruce's work area, cluttered with the various implements and unguents of his trade.

Propped up on the counter, leaning against the mirrored wall but partially concealed by a towel that had been tossed aside, was a book. From what I could see, it looked like *Cynthia's Wrath*, sixth of the seven planned installments of Maude Movay's best-selling romance series. On Monday, when Bruce came to the guesthouse to pick up Maude's wigs, he had brought the book along and left it for her to sign.

"*No* one," said Zola, "and I mean *no* one, could do a hidden zipper like Lydia. I used her workroom for every pillow in that house."

"And they're still *there*!" said Bruce, flopping a hand to his bosom. "Talk about 'investment' decorating..."

Zola nodded gravely. "Sometimes, you do indeed get what you paid for. And trust me—Ambassador Grover Payne didn't hesitate to pay for the very best."

With a chortle, Bruce said into Zola's ear, but loudly enough to be heard over the chorus of hair dryers, "I understand the ambassador paid for more than *pillows*."

Zola tossed back her head for a hearty laugh.

"Ummm"—I leaned into the conversation from my chair—"are you saying the ambassador paid for...*women?*"

Zola and Bruce looked at each other, wide-eyed, then laughed with such gusto, they drew glances from everyone in the salon.

"Get real," said Bruce. "It's no secret that Grover Payne had a yen for men."

This... was news to me. (Though the Inca warrior should have been a clue.)

I asked Bruce, "Did Mrs. Payne tell you this?"

"God, *no*."

Zola added, "Marjorie *never* spoke of the matter—then or since. At the time, though, it was fairly hot gossip. It seemed *everyone* was in on it."

"For instance," said Bruce, "you know how they have that private entrance—back by the guesthouse?"

I nodded.

"Word is, that was built specifically for the ambassador's— shall we say—*assignations*. The men, the *boys*, could come and go at all hours without the rigmarole at the main gate, and without the records. The ambassador, too—he could slip in and out whenever the need arose."

Incredulous, I asked, "And Mrs. Payne never knew about this?"

"Marjorie isn't stupid," Zola assured me. "Surely, she must've known what was going on, but she never talked about it, not even in confidence to a trusted old friend—like me."

"Obviously," said Bruce, "she repressed it."

"Obviously," I agreed.

Bruce raised a pinky. "She's a lady through and through— there are things one simply does *not* discuss."

Zola said, "She may not discuss *that*, but get a few drinks in her, and she opens up about anything else." Zola turned to tell me, "Marjorie's a sucker for a Tom Collins. The ambassador never served them. I, however, did."

I wondered if Zola was telling me that our luncheon that afternoon might not be the yawn I had anticipated. Meanwhile, I needed to shift the focus away from Marjorie Payne and back to Bruce Tucker, who didn't know that my true purpose at the salon that morning had nothing to do with Zola's hair—and everything to do with Bruce's possible involvement in the demise of Lanford Endicott, a.k.a. Maude Movay.

While Bruce continued working his magic on Zola, I stood and moved to the mirror, fussing with the hair at my temples.

Bruce glanced over, offering, "Happy to give you a quick blowout before you leave—won't take a minute."

"I'm fine, but thanks for—" I stopped short, as if noticing the book. "Oh? What's this?"

He set his blow dryer back in its charging holster. Joining me at the countertop, he moved the towel and picked up the copy of *Cynthia's Wrath*, holding it like a precious object, a sacred text. With a happy little sigh, he said, "I've been showing it off."

"Why?" asked Zola.

"Because *she* signed it."

Bruce opened the book to its title page and presented it to Zola. After reading it, she handed it to me. Its inscription was familiar:

To Bruce Tucker, my dearest chum and most devoted reader.
Yours forever, Maude Movay.

I said to Bruce, "How lovely. Did you get to meet Miss Movay?"

He rolled his eyes. "I just *missed* her. I went back to the estate on Wednesday morning to deliver her three wigs, and—oops. Oh, dear." He glanced at Zola, then said to me, "I don't think anyone is supposed to *know* about the wigs."

Dismissing his concern, Zola mimed locking her mouth and throwing away the key.

"*Thank* you, love," he told her. Then he continued: "So when I went to deliver the wigs, I was hoping to meet Miss Movay and pick up the book, but when I got there, her manager-guy, Lanford something, said she was called out again—but she'd left the signed book for me on her desk. So he took me back to her bedroom, where she works, and I placed the three wigs on their stands—gave them all a primp, along with the fourth, which was already there."

"What time was this?" I asked.

"A little after eleven, I guess. I wasn't there long—gone by eleven thirty."

"Did you notice anything...*unusual*?"

With a snort of a laugh, Bruce said, "Lanford was dressed sorta weird—long mohair caftan—and around his neck, a silk scarf that I think was one of Maude's. He apologized for not being put-together by that hour. Said he had a rough night. If you ask me, he looked a bit fey—and I *know* whereof I speak."

"While you were there, did you talk to anyone else?"

He shrugged. "Not really. Said hi or something to a maid."

"Oh? Was she young, pretty, Latina?"

"Wrong on all three counts. She wasn't very pleasant. Snooty, in fact."

"Where exactly was she?"

"There in the bedroom—in Miss Movay's suite."

Then Bruce stepped back to the styling chair to give Zola's hair some finishing touches. He handed her a mirror and gave the chair a slow turn so she could check out what he'd done.

"You're a *genius*. If I thought you could be seduced, I'd ask you over."

He laughed. "Get in line, doll."

After Zola had changed out of her smock and returned from the dressing room, Bruce walked us to the front, where I gave the receptionist my credit card.

I thanked Bruce for taking us on such short notice, then asked him, "If you think of anything else regarding your visit with Lanford Endicott, could you give me a call?"

"Sure, glad to help. Poor guy. Hope you figure it out."

As we were leaving, he added, "Enjoy your luncheon. And give Mrs. Payne my best."

Helping Zola into the car, I said, "Don't forget to put on your scarf."

"Ah! Thank you, dah-ling." She snapped her purse open and pulled out a long silk scarf—Hermès, I noted, not unlike the one that had strangled Maude Movay's alter ego. Leaning to see herself in the rearview mirror, Zola hooded the scarf over her new do, then looped the ends around her neck. "Christ," she said, "I look like an old peasant in a babushka."

She did, sort of, even in a five-hundred-dollar Hermès. Thumping my door closed and starting the engine, I told her, "I'll remind you to take it off when we arrive."

We weren't going far, so I wasted no time comparing notes, asking her, "What do you think about Bruce's slipup?"

Zola turned to me, looking confused. "You don't like the hairdo? I'm quite pleased with it."

"It's *great*," I assured her. "The style's perfect for you. But there was a jarring inconsistency in what Bruce said about his Wednesday visit to the guesthouse—as if he was winging it and couldn't keep his story straight."

She tapped a finger on her chin, thinking. "As we were leaving ... yes ... there *was* something ..."

I recounted: "Bruce said he was 'glad to help' me. He referred to Lanford as a 'poor guy.' And he hoped I would 'figure it out.' To me, that implies that Bruce knows Lanford is dead, and he's aware I'm involved in an investigation."

Zola nodded. "And earlier, Bruce didn't seem to know that."

"Exactly. Bruce spoke of Maude Movay as a real person—who wears wigs and left a signed book for him. He spoke of Lanford as Maude's 'manager-guy,' alive and well while he was there. And I never said a *thing* to contradict any of that."

"Neither did I," said Zola.

"And yet, when we were leaving, he sounded totally in the loop."

Driving along Highway 111, heading toward the front gate at Vanguard Ridge, I pondered something else Bruce had said: he'd encountered a snooty "maid," surely Agnetha Berg, in Maude's bedroom on Wednesday sometime before eleven thirty. Wednesday afternoon, after Lanford was killed, Jazz and I were at the guesthouse when Agnetha came over from the main house, looking for Mrs. Payne. In the presence of Detective Madera, I questioned Agnetha about her whereabouts that day, and she said she had not entered the guesthouse anytime earlier. So: either Bruce or Agnetha had lied to me.

"Good afternoon, Mr. O'Donnell," said the guard at the gatehouse.

I told him, "My friend Zola Lorinsky and I are expected for lunch with Mrs. Payne."

"Indeed you are, sir. Have a pleasant afternoon." The gate rolled open.

We entered the grounds. While cruising slowly through the curves and manmade hills that led to the late ambassador's estate, Zola removed her scarf.

It seemed strange parking in the front motor court, rather than driving back to the guesthouse, as I had always done before. My Karmann Ghia was the only vehicle present at the main house; others were presumably garaged. Helping Zola out of the low convertible, I noticed that I couldn't see the guesthouse carport from there, so I had no idea if Guy, Ramil, or anyone else was on the premises that day.

While we walked from the car to the front door, Zola asked, "Have you been inside the house?"

"No—and I can't wait to see it."

She squeezed my hand.

One of the double doors cracked open while we were still in the courtyard, then it swung wide as we moved up to the stoop. "Welcome," said Nina Rodriguez with a smile, wearing the same frilly black uniform she had worn at Tuesday's dinner party. "Mrs. Payne has been *so* much looking forward to your visit today. Please—come in."

I had no clear understanding of the ranks and pecking order of "the help" in a household like this, but it surprised me—pleasantly—to find Nina performing these duties. I'd have guessed that Agnetha would answer the door, admitting us without cheer or warmth.

Inside, we walked through a main salon, an atrium of sorts, where the marble floor stepped up a foot or so at its center to contain a circular reflecting pool, replete with water lilies surrounding a pedestal. On it, in the glow of a skylight high above, stood a sculpture, a life-size bronze figure that looked like a Rodin—and probably was.

I turned to Zola with a blank expression of astonishment. She twitched her brows. And all around—the huge, riotous banana leaves of her curtains—framing tall, narrow, arched windows and their glimpses of fairways, mountains, and deep sapphire skies.

"You'll be lunching in the garden room," said Nina, leading us toward the back of the house, where we emerged into sunny, less formal surroundings, but lacking none of Zola's cherished wow factor. Here, her banana leaves felt truly at home, creating the feel of a jungle oasis in the desert. The oblong room had a round dining table in the middle, with views of a garden beyond, where actual banana plants grew; to the left of the table was a serving area, with sideboard and bar cart; to the right was a conversation area, with handsome stuffed furniture upholstered with—what else?—banana leaves.

Mrs. Payne rose from a settee when we entered, looking far more healthy, vivacious, and stylish than I'd ever seen her. "Zola!" she said, rushing to her old friend. "My God, it's been ... *years*, hasn't it?"

As they kissed cheeks, Zola said, "It does seem like years, Marjorie, but didn't we share a table at that library benefit just before Christmas?"

Looking confused, Mrs. Payne asked, "*Did* we?"

Through a soft smile, Zola reminded her, "It was not quite three months ago, when you first told me about your idea to welcome 'outside guests' to your guesthouse."

"Of course. Silly me. That's when you told me about *Dante*, so he could help." She turned to me. "You've been wonderful, Dante. I'm so pleased you could come with Zola today."

"My pleasure, Mrs. Payne. Your home is spectacular."

"And we know who to thank for *that*, don't we?"

Zola leaned into the conversation. "If you want to *thank* me, just hand me a drink." And she let out a bark of a laugh.

The party had begun.

Nina popped a champagne bottle, filled three glasses, and brought them over from the bar cart as Mrs. Payne, Zola, and I settled in the plump glazed-chintz armchairs. We skoaled to health, good cheer, and friendship—not all at once, but three times, which emptied the glasses quickly. Nina refilled them while Agnetha, in her lifeless gray uniform, appeared at the other end of the room with a trolley of serving dishes, which she set on the sideboard. Then she brought over a small silver tray bearing delicate little cheese puffs—hot and toasty. I hesitated, reminding myself that Agnetha might have poisoned her husband. But Mrs. Payne eagerly indulged in one of the puffs, so I did, too—perfect between sips of icy champagne.

Zola and Mrs. Payne did most of the talking, old chums catching up on their history of twenty-odd years, and it was often evident that Mrs. Payne's grasp of their shared timeline was contorted at best—Zola corrected her friend's lapses with patience and grace. "That was long *before* the ambassador's passing, Marjorie. You were still driving, remember?"

Mrs. Payne laughed. "Of course, Zola. You're absolutely right. And needless to say, I won't be driving *today*." She lifted her glass, and Nina came over with the bottle.

Sharing the laugh, Zola leaned near to tell me, "She hasn't driven in at *least* ten years."

Though Mrs. Payne was in her mid-sixties, considerably younger than Zola, she came across as older and enfeebled. If she'd quit driving during her fifties, these problems weren't recent.

Nina poured a last inch or two of champagne into Mrs.

Payne's glass. "Excuse me, ma'am," she said. "Should I open another bottle, or would you rather come to the table? Lunch is ready."

Sharing a glance and a nod with Zola, Mrs. Payne told Nina, "I suppose we'd better *eat* something—before the afternoon slips away." She tossed back the last of the champagne, set down her glass, and got up from her chair, looking a tad unstable.

"Let me help you," I said, rising and moving to her side.

Zola stood. "You can help us *both*, dear." She wasn't lit yet— she could hold her liquor better than I could—so I assumed her request sprang not from need, but from her reluctance to let Mrs. Payne hog my attentions. I obliged by offering Zola my arm.

Sandwiched between her and our hostess, I marched us slowly to the table.

Mrs. Payne took the chair with her back to the window, insisting that Zola and I should enjoy the view of the banana grove—a cockatoo or some such would have added a fanciful touch, but the only birds in sight were the ones in our bowls.

It was very much a "ladies' lunch," with a whole boned squab bathing in a consommé of its own juices, garnished with watercress and a spring bouquet of multicolored nasturtiums. The sterling flatware included a peculiar notched tool intended for a purpose unknown to me—a squab pick, perhaps?

"This is so delightful," said Mrs. Payne with a happy sigh, setting aside an uneaten nasturtium. She lifted the stem of her wineglass and took a generous sip of gewürztraminer. Setting it back on the table, she said to Agnetha, who stood at the sideboard, "I think we were wise to take a day off—it's time well spent."

Without emotion, Agnetha replied, "As you please, ma'am."

Zola asked her old friend, "You're taking a day off? From what?"

I watched Zola, who looked alarmed as she listened to Mrs. Payne tell her about the "special project," the cleaning project, the death cleaning.

Incredulous, Zola asked, "But why would you do *that*? Is something...*wrong*?"

Clearly, I thought, something was very wrong—but it had little to do with Mrs. Payne's physical health.

"Of *course* not, Zola. Nothing's wrong," said Mrs. Payne. Then she explained the basic concept and process of this Scandinavian practice—which by now I had heard more than once.

Agnetha piped in, "It is good, basic, common sense. Death cleaning lifts many burdens from the mind."

Zola turned to look at me while fussing with a lock of hair at her ear, which I think was meant to disguise the cuckoo sign.

Nina approached the table, asking Mrs. Payne, "Shall I clear, ma'am?"

The lady of the manor answered with a single nod. She said to Zola and me, "Hope you're in the mood for dessert—banana splits."

While I would charitably describe the appeal of the main course as esoteric at best, the themed dessert sounded dandy—and I was relieved she hadn't chosen bananas Foster, which I've always found more slimy than enjoyable.

Zola asked, "Will it have a cherry?"

"Three, in fact."

"Fabulous. And as long as you have the cherries, perhaps we could impose on Dante to concoct a Tom Collins—or three. No one does it better."

Agnetha looked aghast.

I said, "Happy to do it, but I'd hate to step on anyone's toes."

"Nonsense," said Mrs. Payne. "It sounds perfect, an old favorite of Zola's and mine—I *do* remember that!"

"Very well," said Agnetha. "I shall gather the ingredients and bring them to the bar."

"And I'll put dessert together," said Nina.

"Uh," said Zola as they were about to step out of the room, "if you don't have the traditional chimney glasses—just bring nice big tumblers."

While we waited and gabbed, Mrs. Payne finished off her glass of wine, sounding giddy and—not merely tipsy—but drunk.

Agnetha returned with her trolley, set up the bar for me, and left.

I excused myself and went to work. Moments later, Zola came over, set one of the three glasses next to the gin bottle, and told me, "Get her loaded—I want to know what's going on here." And she went back to the table.

When I finished putting the drinks together and was about to deliver them, my phone buzzed. It was a text from Jazz: "Call me. Important."

I took the drinks to the table. "Excuse me, ladies. I need to return a call. Please don't wait for me—enjoy."

They were drinking and laughing by the time I left the room.

Out in the atrium, the vast space echoed with the gentle patter of water that trickled near the feet of the bronze figure, who was bathing, I now realized, as if in a stream. Nina Rodriguez entered the atrium from a side hall, carrying a tray of banana splits toward the garden room, and then disappeared. I stepped into the shadows of a corner and placed a call to Jazz.

"Where are you?" she asked.

"At the Payne estate, finishing lunch—ever had squab?"

"No. Are you free tomorrow?"

"I can be, especially if it's related to Lanford Endicott—Sunny Junket's client."

"It is. I heard from Guy Kirby—*my* client. Their lawyer, Allison Harper, wants to meet at the guesthouse tomorrow morning to discuss details of Lanford's estate plan. This could be dull, but it *might* be interesting. I'll be there. You, too?"

"You bet."

After discussing logistics—we would drive separately—we then rang off.

When I emerged from the dark corner, I found Nina waiting for me. Her empty tray hung from one hand. "Mr. O'Donnell," she said, "do you have a minute?"

"Of course, Nina. What can I do for you?"

She seemed nervous, glancing furtively about the atrium, as if she didn't want to be seen with me. I led her back into the shadows, telling her softly, "I'll keep an eye out—so tell me what's on your mind."

She leaned near, speaking quietly: "As you know, I cleaned the master suite in the guesthouse on Monday and Tuesday mornings. The whole setup seemed weird to me—Mr. Endicott was always in there at the desk, and I never saw what's-her-name— Maude Movay. It was like they were just *pretending*, and Mr. Endicott really did the writing."

I nodded. "That's not public knowledge yet, but your suspicions were correct. There never was a real Maude Movay."

"At first," said Nina, "I thought this was funny—you know, *comical*. I know it's not polite to gossip about guests, but I did mention it to Agnetha, thinking she'd get a kick out of it. But she didn't. In fact, she looked sorta pissed."

"Pissed at *you*—for gossiping?"

"Not at all. She seemed disturbed by the whole situation. All she said was 'I had better look into this.'"

"Do you know if she did that?"

"She said nothing more about it. But she was back and forth to the guesthouse several times those days." Nina hesitated, then continued: "Wednesday morning, I arrived for work later than usual, around ten, because of the party the night before. Later that morning, Agnetha was away for a while—I assume she went to the guesthouse."

These details from Nina fit the sequence of events I had already pieced together—including Bruce Tucker's comment that he had seen Agnetha at the guesthouse on the morning of the murder.

When I thanked Nina for confiding in me, she turned to leave, but I said, "One more thing: Is there an opener for the back gate—a clicker—here at the main house?"

"Sure. And several spares—they have a way of disappearing."

I chuckled. "Yeah, I guess they do. Thank you, Nina."

She left with her tray, heading for the hall to the kitchen.

When I returned to the garden room, Zola and Mrs. Payne were well into their desserts and their cocktails, deep in conversation—they barely acknowledged me as I sat and joined them. Noticing that Mrs. Payne's Tom Collins was down to the ice, I asked, "Can I fix you another?"

"Yes, please. That would be lovely." Her speech was now badly slurred.

I said, "Tell you what. Just take mine—haven't touched it. Unlike you gals, I *will* be driving this afternoon." I got up, set the drink in front of Mrs. Payne, and removed her empty glass, which I took over to the bar cart.

Zola was telling her friend, "I'm sorry to hear that you've been feeling down lately."

"It's not *all* the time. It comes and goes. Believe it or not, the cleaning project does seem to help—keeps me occupied—but sometimes I wonder, What's the *point*?"

Sitting with them again, I said, "I can't help being concerned, Mrs. Payne. When did you start having these down feelings?"

She tossed her hands and flopped back in her chair, looking woozy.

Zola asked her, "Did this begin when the ambassador passed away? That's a *long* time ago, Marjorie."

The widow's head wobbled. Her eyes closed as an odd noise rose from her throat—it sounded a bit like snoring, then a brief choking before it morphed into a sad and desperate laugh. Her eyes bugged open. Speaking to us, but gazing into space, she said with a touch of fire, "Grover's death wasn't the problem. Grover *himself* was the problem."

Zola looked apprehensive but summoned a comforting tone: "I'm sure you don't mean that, Marjorie. Your years with the ambassador had to be—"

"They were a *nightmare*." Mrs. Payne spat the words while looking Zola in the eye. "Do you have *any* idea of what he did or who he really was?"

Zola brushed a tear from her cheek. "I'm so sorry, Marjorie. I've heard those stories. But he loved you. He showed you the world. He gave you all *this*. You'll always have those memories."

In no uncertain terms, Mrs. Payne informed Zola: "I loved him, once. But now I *hate* the memory of him. And I hate what he *did* to me."

CHAPTER
NINE

Mood swings could be dangerous for those afflicted with them—and dizzying for those trying to cope with the afflicted.

Zola had hoped to expose the root of Mrs. Payne's problems by getting her sauced. She expected to confirm a hunch that Mrs. Payne's decline was the result of Agnetha's creepy domination of the household. Instead, she discovered—as I did—that Mrs. Payne's distress, confusion, and unpredictable behavior stemmed from years of repressing the knowledge that her husband, the revered ambassador, had never genuinely, fully loved her. Rather, he had used her as a mask, a beard, an armpiece, enabling him to love others—*many* others, all men.

When Mrs. Payne erupted and finally spoke her truth, Zola was mortified by the ugliness of the scab she had picked. I, on the other hand, was simply shunned by Mrs. Payne, who now found it only too easy to equate my queerness with the predilections of the man who should never have married her.

Until that afternoon, my dealings with Mrs. Payne had always been cordial, and I would characterize her response to me as affectionate. Now, though, I was one of *them*, one of the he-devils that had tortured and humiliated her.

"I think you'd better *go*," she told me, trembling—and I hadn't even tasted my banana split.

I plucked one of the maraschino cherries from the ice cream, ate it, and flicked the stem onto the table as I stood. "Thank you for the extraordinary hospitality."

I turned, left the house, got into my car, started the engine, and waited.

Within a minute, Zola joined me—in tears.

That evening, I was in no mood for socializing—and certainly not interested in listening to Isandro harangue me about going halfsies on a new home and a future together. So when he called to remind me that we were planning to "talk" that night, I made a lame excuse and apologized, suggesting, "Maybe tomorrow, okay?"

Saturday morning, I drove from Palm Springs to Indian Wells, where there would be a ten o'clock meeting at the guesthouse to reveal details of Lanford Endicott's estate plan. Nearing Vanguard Ridge, I didn't even consider using the private gate —for starters, I didn't know if Guy or Ramil had managed to find or replace the lost clicker, but even if they had, it now seemed important to have all comings and goings recorded and accounted for.

So I continued along Highway 111 and turned in at the main entrance. The guard at the gatehouse didn't bother checking his list as he waved me through.

When I parked the Karmann Ghia in the courtyard of the guesthouse, I saw that Jazz had already arrived. Normally, a black SUV could have been anyone's, but not this one, with its fierce grille guard bolted to the front. Jazz and I had not ridden together because she'd taken her daughter, Emma, to early appointments that morning.

Two other vehicles were parked in the courtyard, a sleek silver Jaguar and an old Chevy hatchback, neither of which I recognized. Parked in the stalls of the carport, as expected, were Guy Kirby's big BMW sedan and the shocking-pink SUV Lanford had bought to perpetuate the myth of Maude Movay.

I walked through the motor court to the guesthouse and rang the bell. Ramil Bagoyo opened the door, greeting me with a sly grin. "I've been wondering where you were. C'mon in."

When I stepped into the front hall, Jazz spotted me from the living room and met me halfway. She carried a wineglass holding ice water. Ramil asked me, "What can I getcha?"

I'd previously seen him in a tuxedo, like a butler; I'd also seen him in workout clothes, like a gym bunny. But this morning's outfit landed nicely between those two extremes—tailored shorts with a dressy short-sleeved oxford shirt—baring just enough muscle to hint at the rest. I told him, "Know what? It's still early—water's fine."

"Sheesh," he muttered while traipsing off to the kitchen.

Jazz said, "Guess who's here."

I glanced into the living room. Guy was talking quietly with Allison Harper, the attorney, as I might have expected. Also talking to each other, but not expected, were Lanford's niece, Nicole Endicott Chang, and her husband, Saxon Chang. It seemed a fair guess that the Jaguar had been driven by Allison, impeccably dressed and coiffed for business, leaving the junky hatchback to the Changs.

I said to Jazz, "I wonder if Nicole had something to gain from her uncle's death."

Jazz shrugged. "I doubt if she just happened to drop by this morning. Guy probably invited her. That *could* mean she's an heir."

"Right," I said. "She's 'family,' and whether she's in the will or not, Guy must want her to get the news straight-up."

When Ramil returned with my water, Jazz and I moved into the living room. A small desk from one of the bedrooms had been brought out and set in front of the fireplace at the far end of the room, with chairs and a sofa turned to face it. I assumed this "staging" was arranged for a formal reading of Lanford's last wishes.

The lawyer—like Jazz and me—carried a glass of water. Guy, Ramil, and Saxon Chang each had white wine. Nicole, grieving niece of the deceased, slugged from a hefty highball glass containing a dark liquor that did not appear diluted much, if at all, with a mixer. She wore the same loose-fitting sundress and canvas high-tops she'd worn to Tuesday's dinner party. When she saw Ramil enter the room with Jazz and me, she waggled the nearly empty glass at him, needing more. As Ramil returned to the kitchen, I said to Jazz, "I hope Saxon is driving."

Guy stepped over to greet me. "Thanks for coming today, Dante. I'm sure you've seen enough of this place already, but Jazz thought it was important for you to be here."

"In spite of the sad circumstances, I'm glad to be included—maybe we'll gain some new insights. But I assume there'll be no surprises for *you* today."

He shook his head. "No, not at all. Lanford and I had our estate plans drawn up at the same time, and we're each other's successor trustee, so I'm feeling no suspense. The only unknown is...well, soon enough, so pay attention."

Jazz and I gave each other a look—these dry proceedings seemed suddenly more engaging.

Ramil returned with Nicole's fresh highball and handed it to her. Seeing this, Guy told everyone, "I think we can begin. If you could all take a seat and get comfortable by the fireplace, I'll ask our attorney, Allison Harper, to explain why we're here."

The quiet hubbub was quelled as everyone moved across the room. Guy and Ramil sat together on the small sofa directly in front of the desk. Nicole and Saxon took two chairs to the left of Guy. Jazz and I sat in the remaining two chairs, to the right of Ramil. Allison stepped behind the desk with a loose-leaf binder, at least two inches thick, and stood facing us with it.

"We're here today," she said, "to review some of the directives contained in the estate plan drawn up and filed by the late Lanford Endicott. These directives take the place of a more conventional last will and testament. Some parties with complex financial situations find it advantageous to create an estate plan, based on a so-called living trust—or revocable trust—for a variety of reasons, but mainly because this helps to avoid probate proceedings. Lanford Endicott is known as the grantor of this trust, and upon his death, the trust transitioned from revocable to *ir*-revocable."

Allison paused to ask, "Any questions at this point?"

Nicole gave a silly wave of her hand. "Do I need to stand?"

"Of course not. What's on your mind?"

"Well, I was wondering," said Nicole. "You said something about Uncle Lanny's 'complex financial situation.' Are you referring to the whole Maude thing?"

Allison hesitated. "What...do you mean?"

Nicole glanced at Guy, who did not react. She then said, "I *mean*, it was common knowledge, wasn't it? I always played along, but I thought it was an open secret: Maude Movay was just made up, like a pen name, and Uncle Lanny actually wrote the books. Right?"

Allison turned to Guy. Then all of us turned to Guy.

He stood to face us. "Uh...*yes*, in fact. You're right, Nicole. Lanny wrote all of those books, and he was working on another when he died. Maude Movay was not a person, but more of an enterprise—involving a lot of people and producing significant assets. To be honest, we're not sure about the future of this enterprise, or if there even *is* a future, but for now, it's really imperative that this discussion goes no farther than this room. Understood?"

"Yeah, yeah, yeah," said Nicole, bored by the details.

When Guy sat down again, Nicole said to Allison, "So cut to the chase. Who gets what?"

"Jesus *Christ*," said Guy, wagging his head.

Allison asked him, "Shall I read the distributions?"

He nodded.

Allison sat at the desk and opened the binder, then flipped through several tabs. Adjusting her big red glasses, she summarized: "With two exceptions, Lanford directed that, upon his death, the entirety of his estate shall be distributed outright and free of trust to his husband, Guy Kirby. This includes but is not limited to: all real property, tangible personal property, investment and banking accounts, rights to the books he authored, and their earnings."

Nicole leaned over to tell Guy, "Congratulations. I'm sure you earned it."

Guy clenched his jaw as Ramil reached to pat his knee.

Nicole raised her hand again, asking Allison, "Now, what about those 'exceptions' you mentioned."

"I was just getting to that." Allison flipped another tab in the binder. "Lanford further directed that, from his investment assets, a sum of five hundred thousand dollars shall be distributed to Ramil Bagoyo."

Nicole turned to look at him, rolling her eyes while emitting a low, breathy laugh. Guy reached for Ramil's hand and held it tenderly. Ramil bowed his head. He showed no signs of being surprised by this "news," so I assumed he'd already been told of Lanford's intentions—either by Lanford himself before his death, or afterward by Guy.

Allison said, "Lanford left a document of his own words to be read now: 'Ramil, you have brought love, excitement, and great pleasure to both Guy and me. In the years after we are gone, I hope this gift will serve as a reminder of our love and that it will help bring you happiness in whatever direction life may lead you. Our time together was treasured—more than you could ever know.'" Allison concluded, "These words were signed by Lanford Endicott in his own hand."

Ramil wept happy tears as Guy rocked him in his arms.

When their emotions had calmed, Allison said, "There's also a second distribution from Lanford's estate."

Nicole scooched forward, literally, to the edge of her seat. Another inch, I thought, and her ass would hit the floor. Her teeth pinched her lips, then she licked them while Allison flipped a page in the binder.

"Lanford further directed," said Allison, "that a duplicate sum of five hundred thousand dollars shall be distributed for the benefit of his niece, Nicole Endicott Chang."

"*Yes!*" shouted Nicole, forcefully flinging both arms toward the ceiling in a giant V for *victory*—and landing her ass on the floor. As she clumsily resumed her seat, she crowed to the hereafter, "Sweet fuckin' way to *go*, Uncle Lanny!"

Allison cleared her throat, informing Nicole dryly, "There's more."

"More? As in...*money*?"

"No. I'm referring to additional details and stipulations you may want to consider."

Nicole's brows pinched.

"Your uncle wrote the following: 'While this gift is made with the benefit and welfare of my niece in mind, the distribution itself shall be made outright and free of trust to her husband, Saxon Chang—"

"*Huh?*"

"I wasn't finished," said Allison. "Your uncle further writes: 'Nicole has had all the advantages of a privileged upbringing, including education and extensive travel, much of which I have paid for in the years since she squandered the resources left by her late parents, gone far too soon. Though intelligent and able, Nicole has wasted the prime of her life on substance abuse and addiction. I have paid generously for rehabilitation programs— once too often—and she has made no effort, let alone commitment, to rebuild a normal, productive life. Accordingly, this gift is made to Saxon. With any luck, it might give him some leverage to help straighten her out, but no restrictions are placed on his use of the funds.'"

In the dead hush of the room, Allison concluded, "This statement is signed by Lanford Endicott in his own hand."

Guy turned in his seat to face Saxon. There was no sarcasm in his tone: "Congratulations. You'll have your hands full."

Nicole screamed.

When Saxon turned and offered his arms to hold her, she smacked him, sending his glasses flying—again. She'd made a similar scene at Tuesday's dinner party.

There were documents to be signed—a lot of them—and many needed to be notarized. Allison suggested that Guy might want to follow her back to the Friendly Law Offices in Palm Springs, where they could take care of everything that afternoon, after lunch. Guy wanted to get it over with, so sometime after eleven, they headed out.

Nicole and Saxon Chang left solemnly, quietly, for their trip back to Redlands, which would surely be a tense drive. Nonetheless, as they walked out the door, I'd have sworn I saw a new bounce in Saxon's step.

Jazz was rushed—she needed to pick up Emma after a ballet lesson—so we took only a couple of minutes to compare notes. She reminded me, "We can pick this up again tomorrow." We had plans to attend a party on Sunday afternoon at a new house designed by architect Cooper Brant, the husband of Detective Arcie Madera—so there'd be ample time for updates all around.

When Jazz drove off, that left only Ramil and me at the guesthouse. I helped him put the furniture back where it belonged, and then we took the dirty glassware out to the kitchen, where he asked, "Are you hungry? Let's go to lunch somewhere—and *I'm* buying."

It seemed innocent enough—he had a windfall worth celebrating—why not? But in truth, I knew better than that.

Out in the courtyard, I said, "No point in taking separate cars. Want me to drive?"

Ramil laughed. "You mean, you don't want to take the pink beast?"

I stepped over to the passenger side of the Karmann Ghia and opened the door, telling him, "Get in."

"Yes, sir."

And we were off. We didn't need to go far, deciding on one of the huge resorts only a mile or two away, just off the highway. The biggest had multiple guest towers with hundreds and hundreds of rooms, a conference center, ballrooms, spa—even a water park, in addition to the obligatory golf course—and a variety of restaurants, where we could get a decent lunch. I left the car under the soaring entrance canopy, fetching the usual compliments from a valet whose uniform resembled a white tennis outfit with a matching white pith helmet.

The vast lobby, with its curved staircases, glass elevators, interior balconies, and milling crowd, felt faraway and anonymous. I said, "There's a quiet dining room on the second floor." And I led the way up an escalator.

Drinks first—it was nearly noon now—followed by pricey hotel salads with sprouts, papaya, and hefty chunks of chicken, no squab. We had chosen to sit on the same side of the table, next to each other on a long, cushy velvet banquette, looking out into the nearly empty dining room. Under the drape of the white linen tablecloth, we were free to explore the possibilities of touching—starting with an innocuous brush of ankles, which led to knees, then linked fingers, and eventually groping.

"The day we arrived at the guesthouse," Ramil reminded me, "out in the courtyard, the first thing I said to you: 'Are you single?' You never answered."

I grinned. "It's not as if I'm ... *married*."

Ramil pulled out his phone. "Let me just see if they have any rooms available."

Of course they did.

Saturday dinner dates with Isandro had become customary, and I had already put off our talk about buying a place together, so there was no gracious way to escape either the date or the talk that evening. When Isandro suggested we return to Fusión, where we had dined two days earlier, I wondered if he was anticipating something to celebrate—a retake, so to speak, with an ending more to his liking.

"Fine," I said.

It was a busy night, and we were lucky to get a table at all. The table we did get was small, near the kitchen door, conducive to neither a pleasant meal nor a serious conversation. The drinks were fine, though.

So I had begun to relax when Isandro set his fork and knife on his plate and mentioned, in a casual tone, "I got a call from Krill Collie today."

Here we go, I thought. I said, "Doesn't he sell real estate? What'd he want?"

Isandro smirked. "Quit your bluffing—you know what he wanted."

I nodded. "Look, kiddo. I know I'm taking too much time, thinking this over. But it's a big decision, and I'm just not sure. Sorry. Do you hate me?"

He touched my hand. "God, no. I don't *hate* you—I love you."

He said it so matter-of-factly, it could have been something he'd said many times before, but I was pretty sure this was a first. And now that he'd teed it up, I was faced with a timely opportunity to return the sentiment, which I probably felt—"love" has such a broad range of meanings and subtle shades of intensity— but I just couldn't say it.

Instead, I explained, "The coach house is fantastic. Of *course* I'd like to live there, assuming the finances would work. And if it's simply a matter of ... sharing space ... sharing a *bed* ... how could I say no? We've got *that* nailed."

He smiled, asking, "So ... that's *it*, right?"

"No, because now we're looking at *more* than sharing space or sharing a bed. It's a commitment—both financial and emotional. I've been *through* that before. It didn't work. The results were devastating for me and far worse for Anthony."

Isandro was well aware of my prior history with Anthony Gascogne, an ophthalmologist who'd been my "other half" for nearly thirty years, including several when we were married after moving from LA to Palm Springs. The marriage, the vows—*he* wanted that, a formal commitment intended to tie me down, a proposition I *never* bought into. And I still didn't (as evidenced that very afternoon in Indian Wells).

"*Coração*," said Isandro, "right now, this is simply about the coach house, not the bigger issue of 'us.' And with the coach house, timing is an issue."

"But there can be no coach house *without* 'us.' And I don't want to hurt you—by falling short of your expectations."

He settled back in his chair for a moment, closing his eyes as if evaluating the situation. Then he grinned. His eyes opened. He leaned near me with his elbows on the table. "Dante, I know you've been stressed this week—the murder at your rental and the investigation with Jazz. And I get it—the extra pressure of a real-estate deadline is something you don't need right now." He leaned closer. "But I know exactly what you *do* need right now. So take me back to your apartment."

Hmm. He didn't quite have the whole picture, including what had happened that afternoon, so he was wrong about what I *needed* that night. But I knew from experience that *he* needed it, and I owed him that much—if not a co-signed mortgage or a ring—so we took care of the check, and home we went.

When we stepped into my apartment and closed the door, I switched on a light, but Isandro switched it off, telling me, "Let's keep it dark." I could tell by the low quaver of his voice that his motor was already running. He undressed in a flash, signaling for me to wait, and then he helped take off my clothes.

We played a bit, standing there in the living room, but that was merely a greeting of sorts, a declaration of purpose. Nudging me toward the bedroom, he said, "We need to lie down."

And when we did, things got noisy—I heard wild, guttural things in Portuguese that I didn't understand and didn't ask him to translate. The whirl of that week's house hunting had clearly left him pent-up. Within a minute or two, the bed was thumping the wall and creaking as he reached a truly impressive climax—even by *his* standards.

He laughed and heaved while catching his breath, returning to planet Earth. Finally, a long, satisfied sigh.

I asked him, "Doesn't that *bother* you? That damned *dog*."

"Yeah, weird." But Mitzi hadn't bothered Isandro badly enough for him to lose focus. He rolled over for a full-body embrace and a deep kiss. "Your turn," he whispered. "Or did you come?"

No, I hadn't—and most likely wouldn't. There wasn't much to work with after Ramil had finished with me just a few hours earlier. I told Isandro, "Too much on my mind, I guess."

He sniggered. "Then I'll help you clear your thoughts." And he gave it a good shot. But ultimately—nothing.

"Sorry," I said. "I'm not very good company tonight."

"Shhh." He touched a finger to my lips. "You're the best company—*ever*." And he nuzzled in next to me, as if wishing me sweet dreams.

"Um, truth is, I think I'd rather be alone. Tonight, I mean. If you don't mind, kiddo."

In the dark, I felt him tense next to me. He said nothing. He was so still, he didn't even seem to be breathing. He remained that way for what seemed like *minutes*, and I was beginning to feel panicky when at last I felt him move.

He rolled over to the side of the bed, stood, walked straight into the living room, and switched on a light. By the time I got up and followed him, he was already dressed.

I said, "I'm really sorry." It was only nine thirty.

"Know what?" He opened the door. "This is the third night in a row you've 'dismissed' me."

I stepped forward, not sure what to say.

But he held up a hand, a barrier between us, telling me firmly, "I think we need some time off." And he walked out, yanking the door shut behind him.

He didn't slam it. But it was a sturdy, ominous thud—loud enough to trigger Mitzi again.

CHAPTER
TEN

Sunday afternoon, I planned to join Jazz and her daughter, Emma, along with Blade Wade, at the open house where one of Blade's paintings would be on display. When Jazz called that morning to confirm logistics, she told me, "We've got a little wrinkle. I just heard from Christopher."

To my mind, her ex-husband was hardly a wrinkle.

She continued, "He wants to meet today about a private school he has in mind for Emma—for *kindergarten*, in the *fall*."

"That's six months away. Why the hurry?"

"He says it's hard to get into—some parents apply when the kid is *born*, if you can believe it. But he thinks Emma might have an edge because she's biracial. *I* dunno. Anyway, he arranged for someone from the school to come to his office—this afternoon—to 'interview' Emma and meet the proud parents."

I asked, "You're on board with this?"

"Well ... sure. If Christopher can pull it off, and he's willing to pay for it, it'll be a wonderful opportunity for Emma. God knows, I never had a chance like that. So, yes, I need to be there, with Emma. He set it up for two o'clock, and the house party doesn't start till three. Shouldn't be a problem."

"Doesn't sound like a 'wrinkle' at all."

"Just this: I was planning to drive all of us to the party, but now, that would involve a lot of back-and-forth across town. So

I'd like to pick you up *before* the meeting at Christopher's, then pick up Blade afterward, on the way to the open house."

"Fine by me. Should I sit in on the meeting?"

"Sure, but bring a book—it'll be a bore."

I doubted I'd be bored. The purpose of the meeting sounded interesting enough, if a bit goofy, and I was more than happy to spend an hour watching Christopher Friendly in the role of a doting dad.

Even if the meeting proved dry as dirt, it would at least get me away from my apartment an hour early. My horribly botched evening with Isandro had left me feeling sick, sad, and confused. I wanted to make it right. But Isandro had clearly warned me that any groveling would not be well received and would need to wait.

Being stuck alone in my cramped apartment—with its constant reminder of what had happened there—felt like doing time in a cell. So, sure, I was happy to bust out, which might even help a delightful four-year-old get into a good school.

Jazz picked me up at the curb. "What's wrong with *you*?" she asked as I climbed into the SUV and shut the door.

Before answering, I turned to greet Emma, ensconced behind me in her safety seat, listening to music through a pair of pink headphones. Singing along softy, she twiddled her fingers at me.

Settling into my seat, feeling glum, I asked Jazz, "You mean, it shows?"

"Death warmed over." She pulled away from the curb, heading downtown.

"Didn't sleep well, I guess. Had a rough night—with Isandro."

She shot me a concerned glance. "Uh-oh."

"He'll get over it," I told her, but my words were based on little more than wishful thinking.

"Wanna tell me about it?"

I hesitated. "Not now, okay?"

She nodded, eyes on the road.

I had never been to Christopher Friendly's law office, which was located in a large low-slung building along a wide boulevard that led to the airport, not far from city hall. Jazz parked behind the building, where a sizable lot contained only a few cars.

Jazz lifted Emma from the safety seat and plunked her on the asphalt. "Let's go see Daddy," she said, locking the SUV and leading us through a back entrance to the building.

On a Sunday afternoon, the office complex was quiet and felt deserted, with the interior hallways barely lit by security lighting. Crossing a central lobby, which glared with sunlight from its glass walls, we took the stairs to the second floor, where a tasteful sign welcomed us: FRIENDLY LAW OFFICES, PC. Big windows looked from the hallway into a spacious but darkened reception room.

Jazz tried the door, which was unlocked. Emma and I followed her inside, where she led us past numerous empty cubicles to a lit hallway with doors to the partners' individual offices. "Here we are," she said, taking us into Christopher's suite, where another dark reception room—with two secretaries' desks—led to yet another hallway. A shaft of sunlight and the patter of pleasant conversation spilled from an open door.

"Hope we're not late," Jazz said brightly as we entered a stately conference room. Panoramic mountain view, massive bookcases, plush wool carpeting, executive-style leather chairs, elliptical granite table—the contrast to the equivalent space upstairs from Huggamug could not have been more pronounced.

"Right on time," Christopher told Jazz, standing.

A matronly woman also stood to meet us. Sixty-something,

nicely dressed in a navy silk suit, with a kindly face and a twinkle in her eyes, she was introduced as Patricia Cubbins, director of Gilded Palms School for the Gifted.

Mrs. Cubbins hunkered down to greet Emma at eye level. "I've been hearing *so* much about you, dear. You've been study-ing ballet already?"

Emma nodded.

"And is it true—did you really make this painting—all by yourself?" The first of the girl's paintings, executed in crayon and turpentine on canvas, under the patient guidance of Blade Wade, had been framed by her father and was now propped on a brass easel there in the conference room.

With an eager nod, Emma explained, "It was fun! But my lat-er work is a little more moody. I'm still exploring."

"That's perfectly *splendid*, Emma. How *very* precocious."

Emma gave Mrs. Cubbins a wary look.

Jazz and Christopher gave each other a sly nod.

Then Christopher suggested, "Shall we all sit down?"

Mrs. Cubbins and Emma sat next to each other at one end of the table, where various forms and documents were spread about. They began with a series of inkblot tests (Emma aced them, if the jolly burbles from Mrs. Cubbins were any indica-tion). Then the woman began asking the child questions, taking notes.

Jazz and Christopher sat nearby, facing each other over the table, hanging on every word.

I sat at the far end, losing interest. After several minutes, feel-ing thirsty, I quietly excused myself and stepped out to the hall.

Glancing in both directions, I spotted a drinking fountain I'd noticed earlier. My footfalls were muffled by the thick carpet as I moved down the hall toward it. The fountain's condenser was running as I drank, then switched off with a clunk. In the quiet, I heard a woman talking on the phone. The familiar voice came from an open doorway not far from where I stood. When I moved closer, the placard next to the door confirmed the woman's identity: V. ALLISON HARPER, PARTNER.

She was saying, "... so I'll be looking into it. Nothing definite, but I think we *might* have a chance to save the series." She paused to listen. Then: "Sure thing, Guy. I'll let you know. Bye, now." I heard her set down the phone. She took a deep breath and exhaled. Then papers rustled as she got back to work.

When I rapped on the doorjamb, she looked up, startled.

"Sorry," I said with a soft laugh, "didn't mean to sneak up on you."

She smiled. "No problem at all, Dante. I knew Christopher was expecting Jazz and Emma, but he didn't mention you were coming."

"I sorta tagged along. The esteemed Mrs. Cubbins has begun the inquisition. I got bored."

Allison chuckled. "Can't say I blame you. If you care to hang out, have a seat."

"Thanks." I stepped in from the hall. Her single-room office bore no resemblance to the suite enjoyed by Christopher, who owned the firm. She had a window with a slice of a view, and her desk had a couple of upholstered guest chairs, but there was no reception area, no secretary. As I sat, I asked, "Are you sure I'm not disturbing you? If you're working on a Sunday, I assume you're busy."

She shrugged. "I'm *always* busy. And after what happened to Lanford, it's been nonstop. But a little breather won't kill me—and might even do some good."

At the front edge of her desk, a stack of business cards was angled in a small bin, ready for the taking. I took one. Turning it in my fingers, I noticed the full name again: V. ALLISON HARPER. "Just curious," I said. "May I ask what the V stands for?"

She rolled her eyes. "Let's just say it stands for a name I've never liked. Allison is my *middle* name, but I've used it since grade school."

Since she chose not to tell me, I had to wonder: Veronica? Victoria? Vidalia? (No, that last one's an onion.)

Small-talking, she told me, "Christopher wanted to spend some time here today—easier to get things done without all the usual commotion—so I decided to come in as well."

While she spoke, sitting there behind her desk, I thought that something looked different about her. Same distinctive red eye-glasses, same clothes, but what was amiss? Her hair, I realized—it was always "just so," but today it could have used one of Bruce Tucker's magical blowouts.

I studied her again: same glasses, same clothes ... same *clothes*? She was wearing the same outfit she'd worn to the guesthouse yesterday, when she announced the distributions from Lanford's estate. She'd driven to that meeting in a silver Jaguar—a car that, today, was *not* among the few I'd seen parked behind the law offices.

Adding it up: she went out with Christopher Friendly last evening, spent the night with him, and then came to the office with him this morning. Lucky her. But I was certain Jazz wouldn't react as I did.

Allison was saying, "It was a bitch of a week, not only losing one of my top clients, to *murder*, but also losing the book-and-film deal. It just—*poof*—evaporated with Lanford's death. All the *work* I did, piecing that deal together, wasted. The loss of future profits is incalculable. And trust me, I had a stake in this, so I'm feeling the sting myself."

"I'm really sorry." How else could I respond? I hoped she wasn't winding herself into another crying jag, as she'd done in Jazz's office on Thursday.

She grinned. "But," she said, "after the initial shock wore off, I started making a few phone calls—having some conversations with a few of the right people—and if I'm right, we *might* have a shot at resurrecting this deal."

"How?"

She flipped her hands. "A ghostwriter. In effect, 'Maude' already had one—Lanford. So get her another. Any hack who's familiar with the books could write this crap. Same characters, new plot—it's a *romance* series, not rocket science. The only downside is, getting a new writer up to speed will cause production delays, but that's *way* better than scrapping the whole damn deal."

I asked, "Have you mentioned this to Guy Kirby?" I knew, of course, that she'd just told him about it on the phone.

Allison nodded. "He thinks it's worth a try. He asked me to check out the idea with Maude's publisher, her production company, and their lawyers. But the *problem* is Guy himself."

"How so?"

"The *murder*," said Allison. "Guy is the agent of record on this deal—for the entire Maude enterprise—and now, with Lanford's death, he also holds all rights to the series itself. But with Guy under suspicion of Lanford's murder, that creates a legal thicket of uncertainty that *no* investor would buy into. Bottom line: we need to get Guy in the clear, not only for his own sake, but to save the whole Maude franchise."

When I returned to Christopher Friendly's conference room,

Mrs. Cubbins was packing up her papers and preparing to leave. "I'll need to present this to the admissions committee," she said, "but I'm confident we can look forward to welcoming this *darling* child into the Gilded Palms community. Thank you *so* much, Mr. Friendly, for bringing Emma to our attention."

"And thank *you*," said Christopher, "for taking time to come over on a Sunday."

"Time well spent," she warbled, "time well spent." Turning to Jazz, she said, "And *Mrs.* Friendly—such a pleasure to meet you as well."

Jazz opened her mouth to correct Mrs. Cubbins, but Christopher motioned frantically from behind the woman that Jazz should zip it while Mrs. Cubbins continued, "Your beautiful family represents the very model of our Gilded Palms philosophy: *Fidelity. Tradition. Truth.*"

She took a moment to bask in the glory of her own words. Then she grabbed her satchel of papers, waggled her wrist in a queenly adieu, and left.

Out in the SUV, Jazz pulled away from the office building, telling Emma, "Put your headphones on, honey." I knew from experience that this signaled a conversation not meant for tender ears.

When Emma began to hum, Jazz pounded the steering wheel; the SUV swerved. "Can you fucking *believe* it?" she asked me.

"Uh, which part?"

"Christopher—he wants that dried-up old biddy to think I'm still his goddamn *wife*. And that bullshit about *fidelity* and *tradition*. Does he really think it's right to put Emma in a school that's stuck in some Victorian delusion?"

I reminded her, "Your situation—and my situation—may not

be entirely conventional, but lots of people are still content with the mortgage, the dog, the PTA, and the wife."

"I know that. And for them, Gilded Palms might be just dandy. But I'm not thrilled with the idea of indoctrinating Emma with so-called values that demean her own family—as well as her friends, meaning *you*, Dante."

Couldn't argue with that, so I shut up.

Jazz seemed to calm down as we neared Blade Wade's neighborhood. Glancing over from the wheel, she asked, "Can you text him? Let him know we're almost there."

"Sure."

When we pulled into the parking lot at the arty mall where Blade had his studio, we found him waiting outside his door. As Jazz stopped at the curb, I said, "I'll get in back with Emma."

After a round of greetings, we settled in and buckled up, with Blade in front with Jazz. Her tone turned cheery as she said to him, "Big day, huh?"

He downplayed it: "Just another painting on some rich guy's wall."

I piped in: "It's bound to be *great* exposure—beyond the usual gallery crowd."

Blade nodded, turning to me. "Good point, Dante."

We drove out to the north edge of town, within sight of the windmill fields. When we arrived at the gated development, situated on the rugged slopes of an alluvial fan, Jazz showed her invitation to the guard, who directed us to a line of vehicles attended by parking valets—it was apparently a *big* party.

And with good reason. The house was truly, literally, a jaw-dropper; at first sight, we stopped and gaped. The architect, Cooper Brant, had created a contemporary multileveled masterpiece in a surreal geological setting that would surely

find its way into future megabucks movies. The primary building material was rusted steel, sharp and angular, complemented
by chunky stonework and impossible expanses of seamless glass.

Cooper stood near the entrance with the owner, a Mr. Quimpton, greeting guests. When Cooper spotted Blade Wade, he
immediately introduced him to the owner, who fawned over
the artist and ushered us all inside to see the installation of
Blade's painting.

Seeing it in such magnificent surroundings, Blade wiped away
a tear or two as a photographer from *ArchitecAmerica* snapped
the moment. We were all a bit misty-eyed as Cooper's wife, Arcie Madera, stepped over to greet Jazz, saying, "Let's talk." With
Emma in tow, Jazz walked out to one of the terraces with the
detective.

Blade was getting the royal treatment from the gaggle surrounding Cooper and Mr. Quimpton, which left me suddenly
alone in the crowd.

And that's when I spotted Liam Heimlich, which at first
surprised me—I'd seen him only two days earlier at the Bruce
Tucker Salon—but then it clicked: Liam worked at the Heimlich Gallery, which represented Blade Wade, so of *course* he'd
be here.

He rushed over to me. "Mr. *O'Donnell*," he said, "such a pleasure, running into *you* again." His flirtatious tone made it clear—
once more—that he was undaunted by our age difference.

"First," I said, "you can knock it off with the 'Mr. O'Donnell.'"

He winked. "You got it, Dante. I *adore* being on a first-name
basis. We really should get together for drinks—or *whatever*—
sometime soon, don't you think?"

I'd tussled with his come-ons before and had always resisted, but I was still tempted. "Liam," I said, "you're an attractive

young guy, and I'm highly flattered by your interest, but ... I dunno."

"You're still single, right?"

I hesitated. "Yes..." Then I choked. "Jesus Christ!"

Alarmed, Liam asked, "*What?*"

"Over there." I jerked my head toward the far side of the terrace, across the swimming pool, where the catering crew was passing trays of appetizers. "That *waiter*—let's just say we've 'met' before." It was the studly but sulky college-age kid who had dumped ice water in my lap at Huggamug. And now, he'd noticed me with Liam and was staring right at us.

Liam laughed. "Are you talking about *Zane?*"

"Exactly. Zane Smith. You *know* him?"

"*Dante*," said Liam, as if I were dense, "don't you remember? Last year, when you came to Blade's big exhibit at the gallery, Zane was parking cars—and I told you that he and I were involved."

I did remember: Zane's name was never mentioned that evening, but Liam indicated they were dating, and I thought they made a good couple.

For that matter, I *still* thought they'd make a good couple. "But," I asked Liam, "you're no longer seeing him?"

"Uh, *no*—not after last Saturday, a week ago."

I must have looked confused—because I was.

Liam explained, "Last Saturday morning, I went over to Blade's studio with some gallery business, and then you arrived to discuss rentals with Jazz. I hadn't seen you in half a *year*, and pow, you were back on my mind again. That evening, when Zane and I were together, I guess I couldn't stop gushing about *you*. Zane can be a bit moody. The night ended early when he left mad, and I haven't seen him since. Till now."

I nodded, enlightened: it would have been the very next morning, while I was at Huggamug with Isandro, when Zane seemed to recognize me, turned sour, and dumped the pitcher of water on me. It still pissed me off, but now, at least, it was less baffling.

While recounting this to Liam, my eye was drawn to the house, where I saw Christopher Friendly emerge with Allison Harper—practically arm in arm—strutting out to the terrace to take in the view. Jazz had just finished her confab with Detective Madera and was walking in my direction, holding Emma's hand, when she, too, noticed the arrival. Her pace quickened, slowed only by Emma's inability to keep up.

Simultaneously, Christopher and Allison froze, grasping the situation. They turned to exchange a few words, but there was clearly no escape, so they feigned looks of happy surprise as they strode forward to meet us.

Jazz's tone was snippy: "*Well*. Small world."

Christopher said brightly, "You didn't mention you were coming here."

"Neither did *you*."

He explained, "Mr. Quimpton is my *client*—I've had this on the calendar for weeks. That's why I booked Mrs. Cubbins for two o'clock."

Jazz assured him, "And she's a *whole* nother topic."

Blade Wade appeared from the house and, sensing trouble, hustled over to us, suggesting to Jazz, "Maybe I could show Emma around."

Jazz gave him Emma's hand as if passing him a leash. Blade said to the girl while leading her away, "Let me know what you think of my new painting, and be honest—I can take it." Emma laughed as they entered the house.

Earlier, before leaving the law office, I had mentioned to Jazz and Christopher that I'd run into Allison Harper "in the hall" and that she'd struck on an idea to save the Maude Movay deal. Hoping to keep things civil during our current encounter at the open house, I asked Christopher, "Has Allison filled you in—about the possibility of a ghostwriter?"

"*Yes*"—he readily took the bait—"and it sounds promising."

Allison added, "And we *really* need your help with this, Jazz." What a pro—the sucking-up managed to mollify Jazz's frosty reaction to Allison's unexpected arrival.

With more curiosity than pique, Jazz asked, "How could I possibly help with *that*?"

"Not with the deal or the ghostwriter," Allison explained, "but with Guy Kirby. He's your client, and we need to get him off the hook. If Guy remains under suspicion of Lanford's murder, any hopes for a new Movay deal are sunk. I hate to sound mercenary, but it's my job."

Intrigued, Jazz said, "Tell me more."

While Allison gave Jazz the details, Liam, who was still standing next to me, asked quietly, "Should I leave? This sounds like none of my business."

"No, stay. There's something I want to ask you about."

"Gladly." He shifted his weight; his arm brushed mine.

Jazz said to Allison, "Dante and I are exploring a number of leads, and any one of these possible suspects could put Guy in the clear. But I just talked to Arcie Madera, the sheriff's detective on the case, and she let me know that the DA is *already* putting the pressure on her—he's just itching to indict Guy Kirby."

Allison said, "I understand—the inheritance alone would put him at the top of anyone's list."

"But there *are* others with possible motives," said Jazz. "For starters, the head servant at the Payne estate, Agnetha Berg, has some dark secrets that she didn't want Lanford writing about. Also, according to Dante, Mrs. Payne herself is half loony with a suppressed hatred of gay men. Closer to home, Lanford and Guy's houseboy, Ramil, got a half-million bucks from the estate, and by all appearances, he was aware of this bequest in advance. There's also that little 'family matter' of Lanford's druggie niece, Nicole, who was expecting a windfall of her own, but didn't get it—and Guy told me that a significant amount of cash was stolen from Lanford, funds that any addict would find useful."

Christopher asked Allison, "When you were setting up the estate plan, was Nicole discussed?"

Allison nodded. "Extensively. That's why Lanford added a written statement explaining his decision to give the money to Saxon Chang instead of Nicole. Both Lanford and Guy took part in those discussions, since their estate plans were set up reciprocally."

I asked her, "By any chance, did Saxon Chang know about this? When the distributions were announced yesterday, his reaction was hard to read."

"He *is* rather opaque," said Allison. "One might even describe him as inscrutable. To answer your question: I do believe he knew about the bequest in advance."

Jazz tossed her arms. "And there you go—still another suspect we hadn't even considered."

I said, "That's not the last of them." Turning to Liam, I asked, "Can I count on you to keep this to yourself?"

Doe-eyed, Liam gave me an eager nod. Had I asked him to cross his heart, I'm sure he would have.

I told the others, as well as Liam, "There's a hairdresser, Bruce

Tucker, who was brought in by Lanford to style some of the wigs supposedly used by Maude. He displayed some weird behavior the day he picked them up—regarding a character Maude killed off in a previous book. Then, when I talked to him at his salon on Friday morning, right after Liam had an appointment with him, he gave me an inconsistent story regarding his return of the wigs on Wednesday. Point is, he was at the guesthouse around the time Lanford died, so he had an opportunity to commit the crime, but I'm not sure—*yet*—about a motive."

Liam had listened to this, looking astonished.

The others were intrigued. Jazz asked, "So how do we follow up with this guy?"

I paused, grinning. "Jazz," I asked, "have you ever been on-stage?"

She gave me a weird look. "*High* school...yeah."

"And what do you think of Grace Jones?"

Hands on hips: "Whataya *think* I think? Best ever."

"I've noticed you share a similar sense of style—and bearing."

Liam's eyes bugged. "Oh. My. God."

"So?" she asked.

So I told her about the charity drag show next Saturday at Apockalippso—about the problem with their Black diva who was supposed to sing the big number—about the need to save the show with a last-minute replacement for Darla Midnight—about the possibility of a surprise appearance by a new drag sensation, Lady Jasmine, belting out "La Vie en Rose" à la Grace Jones. I concluded by asking Jazz, "How's your French?"

"Not bad—back in school—but rusty now."

Liam assured her, "You don't need to actually *sing* it—just lip-sync."

Jazz asked us, "And what, exactly, would be the point of all this?"

Liam said, "You'd be saving the show and helping at-risk gay youth."

"*And*," I said, "you'd be going undercover in a tight-knit drag troupe to sniff out what's going on with Bruce Tucker. He'll do your hair."

Liam added, "He does hair and makeup for the whole show."

Crossing her arms, Jazz looked me in the eye. "Let me get this straight. No more than an hour ago, my ex-husband wanted me to pose as his wife, and now *you're* asking me to pose as a gay man—impersonating a woman—pretending to sing in French?"

I shrugged. "It's a tad bizarre, I admit."

Allison said to Christopher, "Hold on. What's this about Jazz posing as your wife?" I noticed that the delivery of her question carried a defensive lilt of territoriality.

Christopher told her, "We'll talk about it later."

Jazz was still eyeing me. "Seriously? This sounds *nuts*."

I borrowed Christopher's line: "We'll talk about it later." But something told me she was already on board.

She turned to look up at the house. Cooper Brant, the architect, had reconnected with his wife, Arcie Madera, the sheriff's detective. As they stepped out to the terrace, Jazz waved for them to join us.

Liam already knew Cooper, but not Arcie. Christopher and Allison, the lawyers, already knew Arcie, but not Cooper. When the introductions were complete, Liam excused himself and made his way around the pool, where Zane Smith was now pouring drinks.

Jazz told Arcie the key points of new information we had on

two potential suspects in the murder case—Saxon Chang and Bruce Tucker. She added, "Dante and I will get to work on it."

"Good," said Arcie. "But remember—Peter Nadig is getting antsy."

Christopher and Allison exchanged a concerned glance—they needed no explanation that Peter Nadig was the hotdog DA.

Arcie said to her husband, "Sorry, Coop. No more shop talk, I promise."

Cooper Brant mused, "Ah, but the law never rests..."

Allison Harper told Arcie, "I admire your taste in men. My brother's an architect."

"Really?" said Cooper. "Is his practice around here?"

"He used to work in LA—so did I—but he's in Wisconsin now. Brody Norris."

"Of *course*. We've met once or twice. Love his work."

"And in case you're wondering," said Allison, "he's a Norris and I'm a Harper because *he* got Mom's last name and *I* got Dad's. Our parents were a bit—one might say—free-spirited."

"Good for them," said Cooper. "So you're *from* LA?"

"Born there, and later worked there, but Brody and I spent much of our childhood in Idyllwild—great place for a kid to grow up."

Arcie said, "And a lot *cooler* in the mountains."

"That's for sure. Hard to believe it's so near—and so different. Dad's long gone now, but Inez is still up there. They named the place Zenithgate—sort of a rustic retreat from the big bad city."

Cooper noticed that Mr. Quimpton, host of the open house, was waving him over to meet someone. "Time to move on," he said. "A pleasure talking with all of you." Then he and Arcie left us.

Christopher asked Allison, "Wanna see the rest of the house?"

"Sure." She told Jazz and me, "I'm glad we had time to talk. Let's stay in touch, and if we all put our heads together, we just might prove that Guy Kirby's not a killer."

As they began to step away, Jazz said, "Allison? I'd still love to get a look at that contract for Maude's book-and-film deal."

Allison pulled out her phone and typed a note. "Sorry, Jazz, too much on my mind lately—you'll have it tomorrow."

When Jazz and I went looking for Blade Wade and little Emma, we found them in the new home's quiet library, away from the bustle and flow of guests, who were still arriving. On the table in the middle of the room, Blade had gathered several oversize art books and opened them to photos of paintings that Emma studied intently. He was telling her, "When Claude Monet came along, everything changed. He had a whole new way of seeing things. His impressionist paintings opened the door to modernism."

"And they're pretty!" said Emma.

"Yes, sweetie, they certainly are."

Jazz said, "And I was afraid she'd get bored here…"

After Blade and Emma finished with the books, the four of us did a last turn through the house, congratulating the owner again and saying our goodbyes. Then we made our way out front and down to the curb, where the valet crew helped people into and out of cars.

When Jazz's SUV appeared, she helped settle Emma into her safety seat, then she walked around the vehicle and hopped in behind the wheel, with Blade next to her. I opened a rear door, and as I was climbing in to sit next to Emma, I noticed the arrival of a long white Mercedes behind us. The plates left no doubt—it was Krill Collie. When the doors opened, he got out from behind the wheel, and his passenger was none other than his new friend and client, Isandro Vieira. Absorbed in chatter, they didn't see me as we pulled away.

The back-seat area of the SUV was laden with Emma's clutter. Moving a few books and stuffed animals so I could sit more comfortably, I found, in the footwell beneath Emma, a rolled-up beach towel, old and faded, with red, blue, and yellow stripes. It was the towel that had been left hanging from the Inca statue on the day Lanford was murdered. Guy Kirby threw it out that afternoon, and Jazz took it.

I picked it up and set it beside me on the back seat. As we drove down from the party to the valley floor and began the journey home through Palm Springs, I thought that the four of us felt something like a family. Jazz, Blade, Emma, and I— we were nothing like the conventional families with children at Gilded Palms School for the Gifted, but we were nonetheless a *chosen* family.

Mulling this, I fiddled with the edge of the towel at my side. My finger traced over a small tag sewn into the seam. I lifted it for a look.

Worn and faded, it was barely legible: HARRIS.

CHAPTER
ELEVEN

The investigation had been hogging a lot of my time—and forcing me to juggle my schedule at Sunny Junket—so the next four days, Monday through Thursday, I was making up missed shifts at the office. My evenings were free, but Isandro was still out of the picture, and I was at a loss to guess when he might be open to having a calm and honest heart-to-heart. That, of course, would be only a first step toward reconciliation, and I recognized that the future of "us" was iffy.

So I spent those free evenings with Jazz, either at her apartment or at her office.

When we were at her apartment, we rehearsed her Lady Jasmine routine. (My prediction proved correct: although she had dismissed the whole idea as nuts, she couldn't resist—and eagerly recruited my help in polishing her act.) Liam convinced Bruce Tucker to take a chance on slipping an unknown drag queen into the show, keeping him in the dark regarding Lady Jasmine's true identity and the purpose of our subterfuge. Liam borrowed the costume and wig, delivering them to Jazz for rehearsal. She already had the recording of "La Vie en Rose," and I found a video of Grace Jones performing it, so we got busy. Jazz worked on the words and nailed the lip-sync. I gave her the moves.

On the evenings when we were at her office above Huggamug,

she worked on the Lanford Endicott murder from her computer and phone. I worked on the seemingly hopeless transformation of that god-awful conference room, where two coats of fresh paint worked wonders. Since the room had no windows, any attempt to make it appear sunny was sure to fail, so I took the opposite tack and went dark—chocolate brown—setting it off with crisp white enamel trim. Jazz was so thrilled, she agreed to pop for new carpeting, installed the next day. Which left the table and chairs. I had a particular Parsons table in mind, but there was little chance of getting it. As for the chairs, anything would be an improvement, so I went online and found some inexpensive knockoffs of the Thonet bentwood side chair—a classic often seen in restaurants—and Jazz ordered eight.

During that week's daylight hours at my *other* office—Sunny Junket—I spent my time sparring with Gianna, answering phones, running out on service calls, and stuck at my desk, feigning work. Thursday morning, while playing on my computer, I recalled finding that beach towel in the back of Jazz's SUV. The tag sewn into its hem had borne a single word: HARRIS.

The name meant nothing to me, but I assumed it identified either the manufacturer or the retailer of the towel. A quick internet search turned up no maker of towels named Harris. But then, a search for "Harris Company" turned up a Southern California chain of department stores, now defunct, that had been based in San Bernardino—which borders Redlands, where a Harris branch store had been in operation for over thirty years.

I phoned Jazz. "Guess what."

"Um, Darla Midnight came crawling back? And my Saturday night just opened up?"

"Not even close. Remember that striped towel you took from

the Payne guesthouse? While I was in your SUV the other night, I noticed that the towel has a tiny label." After explaining the details of my internet search, I concluded, "So that ratty towel, found at the crime scene, probably came from Redlands—home of Nicole and Saxon."

"When did the Harris store close?"

"The Harris brand and all of its stores disappeared more than ten years ago. The towel itself is obviously old. If it does belong to either Nicole or Saxon, I doubt if they bought it new. It looks like junk, and it could've ended up in a secondhand store. Judging from the way Nicole dresses, she knows her way around thrift shops."

"Yeah"—Jazz breathed a sigh—"if she has any 'real' money, it supports her bad habits."

"So," I said, "today's my last day stuck in the office for a while. Should we plan a little outing to Redlands?"

"Tomorrow morning. I'll swing by your apartment at ten."

Friday morning, the dawn lingered with a high cover of thin clouds, unusual for the middle of March in the desert. On a day when I was not due at the office, I would normally take my coffee out to the pool and wake up with the rising sun, but it was too chilly for that ritual, so I stayed inside. I didn't even open the door—another morning ritual—which not only helped cool the apartment during hotter weather, but also gave me a view of the patio, where I could keep an eye on comings and goings. When I had first gotten to know Isandro, back when he worked a night shift as an emergency-room nurse, it was my open door at dawn that had invited our initial conversations as he came home and walked through the gate from the street.

But this morning my door wasn't open, and he wouldn't be walking through the gate at dawn anymore, and besides—we weren't talking.

Right around ten, I got a text from Jazz—she was turning onto my street—so I grabbed my wallet, my phone, and a jacket, as Redlands would likely be ten degrees cooler.

When she stopped at the curb, I got in. While greeting each other, she drove us off, heading north toward the freeway. Not much else was said until we merged onto the 10 and began cruising west to Redlands, still at least a half hour away. "You're kinda quiet," she said.

"You, too."

"I *mean*, you've seemed sorta withdrawn all week. What's wrong?" When I didn't respond, she asked, "Having 'man problems'?"

"Ughh." I muttered, "It's Isandro. He asked me to buy a house with him."

The vehicle swerved as she turned to face me. "And this is a *problem*? If you ask me, congratulations are in order."

"First," I pointed out, "I did *not* ask you. And second, I didn't show quite enough enthusiasm for his idea, and now he won't talk to me."

Eyes on the road, she said, "I don't blame him."

"Thank you."

She gripped the wheel; her knuckles blanched. I could hear the short, angry exhales of her breathing. Without looking at me, she asked, "What the hell's the matter with you, Dante?"

I tried explaining: "Isandro found this great little place. He can't afford it on his own, so he wants 'us' to buy it." Needlessly I added, "Which means, he wants us to live together."

"And what's wrong with *that*? You've known him long enough—it's not like he was some one-night stand who suddenly went dreamy on you."

"Of course not. And truth is, we're comfortable together. Compatible. But the setup he's suggesting doesn't sound like we'd just be roommates—or joint investors. There's an implied emotional commitment. There's an implied knot to be tied."

"In other words," said Jazz, "you're thinking with your dick again."

I turned in my seat to face her. "So what? That's no crime. At least I'm honest about it."

A weary moan seemed to drain her anger. She glanced over to tell me, "Isandro is a great guy. He's nice."

"Maybe too nice—maybe that's the problem."

She smirked. "How could that possibly be a problem?"

"I *mean*: he's too nice to hurt."

Jazz had gotten Nicole and Saxon's address from Guy Kirby, who knew where they lived but had never been there. He also found, in his late husband Lanford's address book, information about a head shop where Nicole supposedly worked, as well as Saxon's office at the university.

As we left the freeway, entering Redlands, Jazz said, "No telling what sort of work schedules they have, so let's try the house first."

The address took us to a street just a few blocks from campus, which had the crowded, unkempt appearance of student residences—long, bland two-story apartment buildings—and small houses that were probably occupied by grad students and untenured faculty. Nothing suggested permanence or pride of ownership in these lodgings.

The Saxons had a dismal little house with a patchy lawn and a couple of potted dead geraniums on the steps at the front door. The carport, which looked ready to collapse, was empty.

"As long as we're here," said Jazz, "let's give it a try." Before getting out of the SUV, she retrieved a zippered canvas tote bag from the back seat.

When we stepped up to the door, we found that the doorbell didn't work—the button was stuck solid—so Jazz rapped on the screen door, which rattled as she knocked.

We were about to leave when the inner door cracked open. "Oh … it's you," Nicole said, sounding groggy. She opened the door wider, looking as if she'd been sleeping—at eleven in the morning. "What do you want?"

"May we come in?" asked Jazz.

Lifelessly, Nicole replied, "Sure," while pushing the screen door open. She wore a stained and flimsy seersucker bathrobe, hastily cinched. It looked like some stranger's hand-me-down. As we entered, she said, "Pardon the mess."

Mess? The Changs' living room wasn't merely untidy. It didn't look as if it was simply overdue for its weekly dusting. It wasn't just slightly disarrayed by the forgotten smudgy glass or two that hadn't been returned to the kitchen last night.

No, the Changs' living room was the sort of "mess" more aptly described as a dump, a war zone, a disaster area, or a gar-den-variety hellhole. The slits of sunlight angling in from drawn curtains were sufficient to reveal dirty furniture, dirty laundry, dirty dishes, dirty ashtrays, and a shiny new virtual-reality head-set, which sat on the low table within reach of a sagging old sofa that served as Nicole's sodden nest.

I said, "Hope we didn't wake you."

Wobbly on her bare feet, she held a hand to her forehead.

"What time is it?"

"Way too late for breakfast," said Jazz. "Shall we call in some lunch: Anchovy pizza? Tex-Mex burritos? Squid lo mein?"

Nicole clapped her other hand over her mouth and rushed from the room, gagging. While she retched and flushed, I flung all the curtains open. When she returned—"Jesus"—she recoiled at the light. Then she sat down and reached for her hightop Chucks, sprawled on the floor like downed guinea pigs. Each shoe burped as she jerked them over her feet. "There," she said. She was put together for her day.

Jazz removed a wadded pair of ripped and frayed jeans from the seat of a side chair and dropped it. The heavy Western-style belt buckle hit the floor with a sharp smack. Jazz sat, placing in her lap the canvas tote she'd brought. She told Nicole, "Dante and I were out this way, so we thought we'd return something you left at your uncle's place."

Nicole gave Jazz a skeptical look, as if she was joking. "Really?"

"Yes, really," I said, clearing another chair. Sitting, I explained, "You stayed at the guesthouse the night after the dinner party, leaving on the day Lanford died. Did you have time for a swim?"

Nicole lolled her head back. "I have *no* idea what you're talking about."

Jazz unzipped her bag. "We're talking about this." She pulled out the striped towel, held it up for a good look, then set it aside with the tote.

"Sorry," said Nicole. "You must be mistaken."

I said, "We *know* it's yours"—a leap of logic, lacking firm proof, but the bluff worked.

"Um, well," she said, "that *might* be one of ours. Saxon must've picked it up somewhere—before my time."

"Here's the thing," said Jazz. "The day Lanford was killed, we found the towel there at the guesthouse—hung up to dry. So it seems one of you must've taken a swim that day."

Nicole countered, "But we didn't know we were going to stay the night before. Why would we bring a *towel*? I certainly didn't. Maybe Saxon brought it along. Maybe he took a swim before we left that morning—but I didn't see him do it. Maybe I was in the shower."

I said, "You both left the guesthouse shortly after seven, driving back to Redlands, right?"

"Right. Saxon has a lab at nine, three mornings a week— Monday, Wednesday, Friday. He was up *way* before I was that day; I left there half asleep. So if he used the pool and left the towel, it's news to me. Ask him."

"We just might do that," said Jazz. "But we have every reason to believe the towel wasn't hung up to dry until well after seven. When it was found, it was really conspicuous, and no one in the house had noticed it earlier."

"Then why are we even *discussing* it?" said Nicole. "Saxon and I left around seven, period."

I told her, "Because we think you might've gone back—later that morning."

"*What?* That's nuts. I was here—on this couch—sick as fuck all day."

Jazz pulled a paper from her tote (I was guessing it was a grocery list or any old piece of junk mail). Glancing over it, she told Nicole, "These phone logs show that Lanford Endicott got a call from your number later that morning at nine, then again at ten thirty. Did you return to Indian Wells to see him?"

"*No.* I was right here. Lanford's phone and mine—both accounts are in his name because he pays the bills. So if you want to know what happened: talk to *him*."

Nicole wanted the towel back. Jazz wouldn't give it to her. The towel was now known to be physical evidence, and Jazz would be handing it over to Arcie Madera. But first, we needed to pay Saxon Chang a visit.

The grounds of the university were groomed, tidy, and green, but the overcast sky and first spits of drizzle gave the campus a dreary feel that day, and I was glad I'd brought a jacket. It was shortly before noon as Jazz cruised around, searching for the science building. There was virtually no traffic, but I assumed that would change fast when classes let out in a few minutes.

Jazz found the building and drove around to the back of it, where there was parking for faculty and visitors. Getting out of the SUV, I shrugged into my jacket while Jazz grabbed her tote bag and locked up. We were parked a couple of rows back and walked over to the side of the building to avoid the rain. The parking nearest the sidewalk was reserved for faculty.

I pointed to the sign in front of one of the reserved spaces: CHANG. Parked there was not the old Chevy hatchback we'd seen six days earlier, when Saxon and Nicole had attended the reading of Lanford Endicott's bequests. The woeful Chevy had already been replaced with a sporty little Lexus—brand new— bearing temporary plates from the dealer.

Dryly, Jazz noted, "Seems things are looking up in the Chang household."

"Forget the car," I said. "First thing *I'd* do—hire a maid."

Jazz laughed heartily as we ducked out of the rain.

In the building's lobby, we checked a directory and found the office number for SAXON CHANG, PhD, BIOCHEMISTRY. While climbing the stairs to the second floor, we heard the chimes of a carillon—noon—followed by the scurry of feet from the other side of the building, where classes and labs were located.

Ahead, the long corridor between rows of doors was quiet. As we got our bearings with the numbers, it seemed that Saxon's office would be about halfway down, on the left. When we were almost there, the door opened, and Saxon stepped out into the hall, turning to lock it.

"Mr. Chang?" called Jazz.

He looked our way, smiling blankly as we approached. Then, with a blink of recognition, said, "My gosh—Jazz and *Dante*? Correct?"

This led me to believe that Nicole had not phoned to alert him. Or: she had indeed called him, and he was now playing dumb. He opened his office door, asking, "Care to come inside?"

We followed him in. Jazz said, "I hope we're not keeping you from something. We should've called first." But Jazz *never* called first when checking on possible wrongdoers, allowing them no time to strategize.

He said, "Just going out for lunch, but that can wait. What can I do for you?"

Jazz began speaking, but we were interrupted by the sound of high heels snapping at the terrazzo floor in the hall, approaching the open door.

A woman's voice said, "I found an umbrella, Saxon." Then she stepped into the doorway. "Oh—sorry, Dr. Chang. I didn't realize you had people with you." She was young, pretty, and professional-looking, probably not a student, but a colleague.

Saxon said, "No problem, Brittany. Go ahead and tell the others to start without me—I may or may not catch up. Okay?"

"Sure," she said brightly—but looking disappointed. She gave Jazz and me a polite nod and a smile, but no introductions were made, and she left.

As the peck of her heels receded down the hall, Saxon closed the door, explaining, "It's a Friday thing, a group lunch. There's more drinking than I'd like, so I'm glad to miss it."

I wasn't so sure, though. On the credenza behind his desk, a framed photo of Brittany sat among a small collection of other people's pictures—all of them Asian, presumably Saxon's family—and his wife hadn't made the cut. So I found it doubtful that Saxon's "Friday thing" had anything to do with a group lunch.

He asked us to sit. Jazz and I took the two chairs flanking a small table with neat stacks of magazines that had the dry look of scientific journals. Saxon pulled his chair around from the back of his desk, facing us.

Jazz told him, "An hour or so ago, we dropped in on Nicole."

Wryly, he asked, "Were you able to wake her up?"

"It took some doing, but we managed to have a talk."

Jazz and Saxon continued in this vein, exchanging comments about the squalor of the house he shared with Nicole. While listening, I noted that Saxon's office was the very antithesis of his home environment. Here in his private domain, everything was just so—the stuff on his desk was arranged as if measured on a grid. Dr. Chang was no mad professor, working among teetering stacks of timeworn books, sharing week-old crusts of sandwiches with whatever happened to crawl in under the door. Instead, everything was in its proper place, organized not only with precision and purpose, but with an eye for aesthetics. I saw no dust, no fingerprints, no bent paperclips, no scraps of paper or crumpled tissues in the wastebasket. The place even *smelled* proactively clean, like Lysol or Pine-Sol. A bit sterile, maybe, but hey—sterile beats filthy any day.

Jazz told Saxon, "She threw up when I mentioned food."

"For Nicole," he said, "food isn't sustenance. It helps her keep down the liquor."

Finally, I interrupted them, asking Saxon point-blank, "How can you *live* like that?"

He hesitated. Shrugged. "I *can't*, of course. The worse she gets, the more I stay away. My refuge is *here*. I've *slept* here more than once—on the floor."

Jazz said, "Your wife is clearly, seriously troubled. Can I assume you've sought remedies with her?"

"Constantly. When we got married, there were promises she would get straightened out. I trusted her, but it was wishful thinking. She got worse and worse. We've tried talking about it. We've tried counseling and therapy. We've tried interventions. And yes, we've even tried several stints in rehab—at Betty Ford, no less—so she's been given every chance. You heard the lawyer read Lanford's statement about it on Saturday, in the distributions from his trust. Bottom line: we've *all* tried helping Nicole."

I asked, "Now what?"

"That's totally up to her. Nicole's uncle has provided me with the means to help her, but you heard the terms—I'm not *obligated* to do that. And I will *not* waste a fortune on a lost cause. I'm giving her one more chance to pull it together—just one— and if she doesn't, she's on her own. Then it's time to pull *my* life together again."

Jazz asked, "Did you discuss any of this with Lanford before he died?"

"Sure. At length—with Lanford, together with his husband,

Guy. All of this was nailed down while they were putting together their estate plans."

I said, "Knowing this, did you ever lord it over Nicole—in the sense of nudging her toward rehabilitation?"

"Maybe I should have, but no. Lanford was very specific that Nicole was not to get the news until after he was gone. God's honest truth—I think he was afraid of her."

Jazz and I glanced at each other, mulling this for a moment. She opened her tote and took out the striped beach towel. "Saxon," she said, "do you know how I happen to have this?"

With a befuddled laugh, he said, "Not a clue."

"It does belong to you and Nicole, right?"

"Right. It's Nicole's—I think it's *awful*. She picked it up somewhere, cheap." His expression turned quizzical. "So ... why *do* you happen to have it?"

Jazz told Saxon how, when, and where the towel was found. "This would seem to suggest," she said, "that either you or Nicole returned to Indian Wells from Redlands that day. According to Nicole, after arriving home early that morning, she was sick in bed all day. She says that if anyone drove back to the guesthouse with the towel—it was you."

Saxon had stepped over to his desk and called something up on his computer. "Do you know what time Lanford was killed?"

Jazz told him, "Between eleven thirty and noon."

Saxon tapped a key, and his printer warmed up, preparing to print something.

He told us, "On Monday, Wednesday, and Friday mornings, I teach two-hour lab sessions at nine; that's why we left Indian Wells so early that Wednesday. After that, I normally hold office hours—except on Wednesdays. That's when I give a combined weekly lecture to some sixty students—at eleven o'clock."

He took three pages from the printer and passed them to us. "That's the roster for the lecture, with names and contacts. Ask anyone on that list what I was doing when Lanford was killed."

While Jazz drove us back to Palm Springs, I phoned a few names on the roster, pretending to be a teaching assistant, re-checking attendance from March fourth because "we got our records mixed up." They readily bought into it. When each claimed to have been there, I said, "Just to verify—can you tell me, roughly, what Dr. Chang covered in his lecture that day?" Their responses made it evident that both they and he were there. After four of these calls, Jazz told me, "That's plenty."

That evening, with the drag show just twenty-four hours away, the regular troupe was having its final dress rehearsal—costumes, makeup, lights, music—at Apockalippso. But we couldn't risk having Bruce Tucker or anyone else figure out the true identity of Lady Jasmine prior to the show, so Jazz and I practiced again at her apartment.

The extended recording of the song she would lip-sync was nearly eight minutes long, including instrumental sections that needed to be filled with something like dancing, which we re-stricted to artful movement and posing. We had already spent many hours on these eight minutes, and we would spend several more in this last rehearsal, as Jazz proved herself a perfection-ist—and an absolute natural in the fierce persona of a vinyl-clad Grace Jones. At times, she didn't even need to fake it, adding her own voice to the song's cries and yowls.

When we took a break, she checked her phone and returned a call from Blade Wade. After greeting him, she said, "Yeah, he's here," then she switched the phone to speaker.

"Dante?" said Blade with a laugh. "How's it goin' there? She gonna pull this off?"

"Just *wait* till you see this," I told him. "You won't *believe* the debut of Lady Jasmine."

"Sounds like we'll need to celebrate."

Jazz said, "Hold on, now—this could totally bomb."

I told both of them, "I doubt that."

Blade said, "Then it's settled: Jazz, I'm throwing you a party after the show."

"Sweets," she said, "I'll be exhausted. And these things run late."

"Sunday then. Brunch at my place. Noon."

Jazz agreed, saying she should be able to handle that. When she hung up, I told her, "Okay, then—once more from the top."

She adjusted her wig, picked up her riding crop, and closed her eyes as the music began.

Saturday morning, I slept later than usual, not scheduled to work that day. With the drag show now only twelve hours away, I was probably more nervous *for* Jazz than she herself was about the performance. But I knew she was well prepared—there was nothing more I could do to help. She was *ready* for this.

(Except, I kept fretting, what about the unforeseen? What if she was stricken at the last minute by paralyzing stage fright? What if the lighting or sound guys, having never rehearsed with her, screwed up the cues? Or what if she was exposed as— gasp—a *real* woman?)

Coffee wouldn't calm these thoughts, but without it, my day would be doomed to sluggish inertia, so I brewed a stiff pot of arabica and took a mug out to the terrace, where I sat overlooking the pool. I'd missed the chilly dawn, so the morning sun felt warm on my face as I glanced across the water to Isandro's door.

Tonight would mark a full week since we'd spoken—a full week since he'd left my apartment, feeling "dismissed" and wanting "time off." I had not handled this well, before or since the walkout. His feelings were justified, and I was trying to accommodate his need for some distance, but I had no idea how long he wanted this to last.

I wasn't playing chicken, daring him to blink. Quite the opposite—I wanted to approach him, to make things right, to find a way forward, if that was still possible, but I was afraid he'd feel annoyed and disrespected if I violated our time-out.

Or was I being too cautious? For all I knew, he might have been waiting, at that very moment, for me to make the first move.

Emboldened by these thoughts, I set down my coffee, got up from my chair, and walked around the pool to knock on Isandro's door. What would I say when he answered? If he answered. And he did not.

Had he gone out earlier? He didn't work on Saturdays, but there were always errands to run. Or was he, in fact, in there? Had he seen me by the pool and decided not to answer my knock? I tried again.

When I gave up and turned back, I saw Zola standing in her open doorway. Even from across the pool, I saw a sadness in her face as she gave me a shrug.

I rushed over. We kissed cheeks. I asked, "Have you seen Isandro? Lately?"

With an uncertain wobble of her head, Zola told me, "I did

see him yesterday—he came and went a few times—unusual for a weekday. But then, later on, I didn't notice him in the evening, when we often say hello. When it got dark, his lights didn't go on. It seems he was away for the night."

"Ah." I nodded, finding the situation only marginally better than my theory that he might have been inside, brooding in a pique of adolescent grievance, refusing to talk to me.

Zola's features brightened some as she told me, "I phoned Marjorie Payne."

"I hope she's feeling better."

"A week ago," said Zola, "when we all had lunch, Marjorie's behavior toward you was deplorable, so I've been angry—but also concerned, about *her*."

I nodded. "Clearly, she's not well. And I don't think Agnetha Berg is helping matters." I could have added, but didn't, that I wondered if Agnetha might be an active danger to Mrs. Payne. Was Agnetha setting her up for a fleecing? Or worse?

Zola touched my arm. "So I called her on Monday—had a long talk. I insisted she get a full evaluation from her doctor. And I told her, 'Have *Nina* drive you, not Agnetha.'"

"Did she agree to do it?"

"Nina took her in on Thursday. Ran some tests. No word yet."

CHAPTER
TWELVE

Although the drag extravaganza at Apockalippso Dance Bar in downtown Palm Springs had been sold out for weeks, the addition of Lady Jasmine as a headline attraction entitled her to one of the "house tables" in the audience that had been held back for major contributors and other VIPs. Jazz herself wouldn't need one of the six seats, but Blade Wade and I would, which left room for four others we could invite to join us that Saturday night.

Because the underlying purpose of getting Jazz into the show was to help solve the mystery of Lanford Endicott's death, it made sense that we should invite Arcie Madera, the sheriff's detective on the case, and Allison Harper, lawyer for the deceased. In turn, Arcie invited her husband, architect Cooper Brant, and Allison invited her law partner, Christopher Friendly, who would of course get a kick out of seeing Jazz, his ex, in the show. In a spirit of further conviviality, Blade Wade had also invited this foursome to attend the next day's brunch he was planning in celebration of Jazz's debut. Everyone had accepted.

Apockalippso was more of a cabaret space than a bar, located in a strip mall at the edge of downtown. Because Jazz could not risk revealing key aspects of her anatomy by changing into costume with the rest of the troupe, she was already dressed as Lady Jasmine—sans wig or makeup—when I drove her to the club in her SUV and parked behind the building near the rear entrance. Twilight was fading to the dark of night at seven o'clock, an hour before the public would be admitted. We gathered Jazz's things from the vehicle—wig, props, garment bags, and a few personal items, including a dog-eared paperback copy of Maude Movay's last published work, *Cynthia's Wrath*.

Stepping through the door, we entered the vortex of nervous backstage energy. A long makeshift dressing table with mirrors and lights was set up along the far wall, where a row of hysterical drag queens awaited the ministrations of Bruce Tucker, working his way down the line, setting hair and correcting makeup.

Away from the dressing table, Liam Heimlich spotted us at once, checking his watch with a look of relief. He wore clamdiggers, sandals, and a striped T-shirt, red and white. His normally clean-shaven baby face had been penciled with a thin, scruffy beard. Stepping over to us, he said, "Great, glad you're here."

I asked, "Are we late?"

"No, but I wanted to catch you before you talk to Bruce."

"Uh-oh," said Jazz. "What's up?"

"Nothing," Liam assured us, "but early on, when I was convincing him to put Lady Jasmine in the show, he happened to ask your real name—your man name—and I didn't want to appear stuck, so I told him you were Jack. We didn't get into *last* names, thank God. So: if he calls you Jack, just play along."

"Got it. Jack, Jasmine, Jazz—same difference."

Crossing my arms and giving Liam the once-over, I said, "Cute getup—but *odd*. Are you in the show?"

"In fact, I am. Bit part in one of the acts. I'm one of the Bongo Boys, the only men appearing onstage as men tonight. You'll see it later—just before Jazz goes on."

She corrected him: "Before *Lady Jasmine* goes on."

"Jack!" said Bruce Tucker, bounding over to us, taking a break from his duties at the dressing table. "I've been *dying* to meet you."

Jazz, Liam, and I all tensed—this would be the moment of truth. If our subterfuge were to fail that night, it would probably be now. While Jazz and Bruce had never actually met—in the sense of being introduced—they had once spent several minutes in the same room together. Two days before the murder, Jazz and I were with Lanford Endicott at the guesthouse when Bruce arrived, thinking he had been summoned to give Maude Movay a hairdo. Learning that he was needed only to freshen up Maude's wigs, Bruce grew indignant, displaying rapid mood swings before leaving with the wigs. Jazz and I were standing nearby as this transpired, but Jazz never spoke, and given Bruce's flustered state of mind that day, I was banking that he wouldn't remember her.

He now said to her, "Liam tells me you'll steal the show tonight."

Jazz reached to give Bruce a limp handshake. "Whatever the outcome, it's all for a good cause. When I heard you were abandoned by that *slut* Darla Midnight, I thought it might be time to break out the stilettos again and brush up my act."

Bruce chuckled. "I must say, those knockers are first-class."

I was breathing easier now.

Lady Jasmine laughed merrily. "I was lucky to have a little help with *those*. A little help, plus good genes." Under her breath, she confided, "Genes are definitely involved."

Bruce tossed his hands, laughing with her. "*Come*," he said with a flourish, "let's get you settled, and I'll introduce you to the rest of the 'girls.'"

Liam and I tagged along as Bruce took her to the dressing

table. Wigs turned as Lady Jasmine seated herself regally in front of the mirror. I set some of her things on the table, including the Maude Movay paperback, which I propped up against the mirror. I unzipped the hatbox containing the magnificent wedge-shaped wig and passed it to Bruce, telling him, "Work your magic, maestro." Then I grabbed my satchel and asked our diva, "Will you be needing me for a while?"

"Dante, *dah*-ling. I'm a big girl." With a flick of her wrist, she added, "Run along, now."

Liam said, "Let me show you the setup."

We walked from the shadowy mayhem behind the scenes and out to the immaculate calm of the stage itself, empty except for the glittering silver backdrop curtain and a mirrored disco ball hanging overhead. From the front of the stage, a narrow runway extended about halfway into the audience, surrounded by the VIP tables in front and the rows of seating to the back. "Table twelve," said Liam, pointing, "that's yours." It was just one table removed from the runway.

I gave his arm a squeeze. "Looks good. Thanks."

"Dante?" he asked.

"Yes, Bongo Boy?"

"Um, I know we've danced around this before, and it seems the two of us were never quite on the same page. But let me give it another try: What if we got together for dinner some night?"

I shrugged. I liked the guy and definitely found him attractive, but I was afraid it could get messy. Since he had posed the question theoretically, I felt comfortable giving an evasive reply: "Sometime...maybe."

But then he got specific. "How about tomorrow? I know you'll be at Blade's brunch—Jazz invited me, too—sounds like fun. But later, that night, we'll be ready to eat again, and my evening's wide open."

I hesitated. Liam's suggestion of dinner *sounded* innocent enough, but we both knew the meal was merely a pretext for what might follow. Just that morning, I'd been pining to find some direction with Isandro, but he'd shut me out. I'd get no merit points for celibacy in his absence, so what the hell? "Liam," I said, "we're on. Think about where you'd like to go."

He winked at me. "Nice."

There in the club, easy jazz played softly while volunteers set up long tables for the event's silent auction. At the bar, servers helped the bartenders polish glassware. Near the stage, the tech crew spoke to each other through headsets, running cues.

I asked Liam, "Could I talk to the sound guy?"

"Sure." Liam went over and spoke to one of the crew, who then waved someone down from the booth.

A minute later: "Hi there, I'm Frank. You're with Lady Jasmine?"

I introduced myself, pulling a CD from my satchel. "I just want to make sure you've got the same recording of the song that Jasmine worked with." I handed him the Grace Jones album.

He looked it over, nodding, checking the running time of the track. "That's it—the extended mix—already on our hard drive, so we're good."

"Sorry we had to miss last night's rehearsal."

"Nah, no worries. Won't be the first time we've run an act cold."

I grinned. "I appreciate your confidence. Lady Jasmine is a bit of a perfectionist."

Frank gave me a look. "They're *all* divas, right?" After sharing a laugh, he said, "Wanna talk to Tommie? She's running lights—has a few ideas for this."

"Absolutely."

He waved her over.

A jolly lesbian in a vintage Texaco jumpsuit, Tommie told me, "I run the follow spot, and I fuckin' *love* that song. It's got this long instrumental sorta cha-cha intro that builds from nothing, and then, at the end, it's the opposite. So I thought, pencil spot! I'll start it real small, no bigger than her face, then slowly bring it up—full body—for the song itself, and then, at the end, shrink it down again, real slow, to nothing. And here's the thing: I'd love to gel it, so the light is *pink*."

I said, "*La vie en rose*—life in the pink. Sounds perfect, Tommie."

She gave me a thumbs-up, then turned and strutted off, walking tall in her chukka boots.

Backstage, the tension was building as eight o'clock neared—out front, the doors would soon open. At the long dressing table, the wild chatter was more subdued as Bruce worked his way down the line, giving the troupe a final spruce and spray.

Also working the line was a drag queen who didn't look like the others—paunchy and not convincingly feminine. Liam leaned to tell me, "That's Carlotta, the show's emcee. By day, Carl Asten is the organization's executive director and chief fundraiser. He does this *every* year—thinks it's *his* night to shine. We've had sponsors come forward and offer to pay a professional to run the show, but Carl won't hear of it."

As Carl stopped to gab with each member of the troupe, I saw that he was not only offering words of encouragement, but also passing a flask. Each time someone took a swig, he did the same. This concerned me, as Jazz had sworn off booze, a problem that had helped wreck her marriage. Her resolve had impressed me, but if anything could cause a relapse, the pressures of that night were probably tempting.

I stepped closer as Carl turned his attention to Jazz.

I couldn't hear what he said to her, but when he offered the flask, Jazz—now the fully transformed Lady Jasmine—rose from her chair and turned, towering above him in wig and heels. Wagging a finger, she cautioned him, "Watch that stuff, little man. Not good for your figure—or your 'performance.'"

Everyone howled—at Carl's expense—and while he was unaccustomed to finding himself the butt of a joke, he was drunk enough to join in the laughter.

The stage manager stepped back from the wings, clapping his hands like a schoolmarm. "Quiet, people! The house is now open."

Jazz took me aside. "It worked—the Maude Movay novel on the dressing table. As soon as Bruce Tucker started working on me, he noticed it. Went all gaga."

I asked, "Did he let on that he knew about the murder—or that Lanford was 'Maude'?"

"At first, he hesitated. But he must've figured that if *you* brought me here, I must be in the loop. So he said something like: 'I guess we're not supposed to talk about this, but isn't it awful? I was such a big fan of hers, but now I'm feeling sorta... *lied* to.'"

"In other words," I suggested, "losing the Maude fantasy is more upsetting to him than the real-world strangulation of Lanford Endicott."

Jazz nodded meaningfully. Her tall, angular Afro sliced the air.

I said, "Now the *big* question: Did he say how he learned about the murder?"

"He *said* that Mrs. Payne, who's a client of his, phoned and told him about it. That makes sense—it's credible—but then again, that's exactly what he'd say if he was hiding something."

"Okay," I said, "he's telling the right story, but we don't know if it's true. He'd be *highly* motivated to lie about it if he had even an inkling that you're actually a private detective working on the case. Or does he seem convinced that you're a guy named Jack who does drag?"

She smirked. "I'm *good*, baby. He asked me out for a drink sometime—maybe next week. And Bruce isn't the type to go trolling for *women*."

Within twenty minutes, it was evident to all of us backstage that the party out front was in full swing—the background music was now inaudible over the laughter and chatter of guests arriving, drinking, and mingling. With the silent auction in progress, the show wouldn't begin for at least another twenty minutes, giving people time to browse and bid before being seated.

I told Jazz, "I'll be happy to keep you company till you go on."

"Nah, I'll be fine. So get out there and entertain our guests."

I lifted her fingers and kissed the back of her hand. "As you wish, dear Lady Jasmine." I stepped away, but turned back momentarily, adding, "Break a leg."

When I arrived out front, I saw that the annual extravaganza was every bit as popular as it had been hyped to be. The cavernous space of the show hall was packed with noisy, happy revelers, many dressed in the spirit of things, as if this were *the* social event of the season—and for all I knew, perhaps it was.

Table twelve, I noticed, had already been found by our guests. Arcie the cop and Allison the lawyer were seated apart from each other, both busy on their phones. Blade Wade was playing host, standing nearby with Cooper Brant and Christopher Friendly. The men were drinking, laughing, and backslapping; the women were not.

When I approached the table, I was hailed by the others—who, in addition to Liam and me, were the only people there that night who knew Lady Jasmine's true identity. With a huge grin, Blade was first to ask me, "How's our girl doin'?"

I told all of them, "If self-confidence is any predictor of success, you're in for a treat tonight. And the look, the transformation—it's amazing."

They chorused their eagerness and enthusiasm. Only Allison seemed skeptical: "Now, *this* I've got to see." I couldn't help feeling she harbored a naughty wish to see Jazz fail in Christopher's eyes. Meow.

When a server delivered a round of drinks to the table, Christopher joined Allison, sitting next to her. Cooper then sat next to his wife, Arcie Madera. I remained standing with Blade.

Surveying the crowd, I noticed that Guy Kirby was there with Ramil Bagoyo. I explained to Blade, "They're the ones still staying at the guesthouse in Indian Wells. The older one is Guy, who hired Jazz to help clear him."

"Ah," said Blade. "Jazz invited them to tomorrow's brunch, but they have no idea—yet—that Jazz is in the show tonight."

"Who else will be there?"

He started ticking off on his fingers: "Arcie and Cooper, of course—"

I interrupted: "Hold on. Let's get Arcie in on this." I gave the detective a subtle finger-wag. She leaned to Cooper, excusing herself, then stood and joined us.

"Gentlemen?" she asked.

Blade said, "I was just going over the guest list for tomorrow's brunch." Arcie and I listened as he rattled off the names.

I then said to Arcie, "From the standpoint of the *investigation*, is there anyone else you'd like to have there?"

After a moment's thought, she asked Blade, "Are you planning to have any help tomorrow for serving?"

He shrugged. "It was all sorta last-minute, so: no. But it's not a bad idea."

Arcie asked me, "That younger maid at the Payne estate, Nina Rodriguez—she doesn't live there, right?"

I nodded. "She's day help, a college student. Need to talk to her?"

"I already have, out there at the main house, but Agnetha Berg was hovering, and Nina seemed uncomfortable. I think she'd open up to me—somewhere else. Maybe the brunch?"

Blade asked, "Got her number? I'll see if she's available."

Arcie was already scrolling her phone.

While Blade placed the call, reached Nina, and hired her to work the next morning, I kept my eye on the ebb and flow of the crowd—and made two significant sightings.

By then, I had not seen Isandro in six days, since spotting him with Krill Collie, the real-estate broker. But tonight in the crowd, there was Isandro, seemingly enjoying himself with someone else, an older man I didn't know. He was not only older than Isandro, at thirty-three, but considerably older than me, at fifty-two.

I also spotted—among the serving staff wending its way through the room with trays held aloft—none other than Zane Smith, who had a thing for Liam and once doused me with ice water. Tonight, like me, he was keeping a watchful eye on the crowd.

By the time they closed the silent auction, served another round of drinks, got everyone seated, and dimmed the lights, it was well after nine.

"Ladies and gentlemen," said an announcer's voice, "please welcome...*Carlotta!*"

Everyone broke into applause as Carl Asten stepped out to the fully lit stage to start the show, but we quickly realized it was going to be a long slog—listening to this bearded fright doing skag drag in a bad ball gown and a wig resembling blue cotton candy. Half sauced, Carlotta slurred her words, heavily laced with rambling vulgarities, which she then dialed back each time: "But remember, folks, it's all for charity." The tagline, though repetitive, invariably drew whoops and laughter from the crowd.

Taking a break from her shtick, Carlotta started trotting out the individual acts—a Streisand, a Garland, a Madonna—all the usual war-horses in their rhinestones and boas. The costumes and production values were top-notch—the lip-sync, hit-or-miss—but overall the well-rehearsed performances were heartfelt and credible, providing many shining moments from this troupe of dedicated amateurs. Some of the impersonations were genuinely beautiful, others wickedly funny, but all of them fetched enthusiastic applause from the audience—allowing lots of lavish bows.

The *problem*, however, was the auction. The silent auction had ended long ago, but the *live* auction was conducted onstage in the intervals between the acts. Works of art, meals with celebrities, private jet service, cruises—it went on and on—which raised some big bucks for a worthy cause, but it slowed things down and sapped the dynamics of the show.

So it was nearly eleven o'clock when Carlotta told the audience, "We just sold our last cruise package, so now it's time to go down to ... *Brazil!*"

Carlotta barely had time to skitter away before the perky ensemble of four Bongo Boys swooped onstage. Thumping the upbeat rhythms of "The Coffee Song," they ushered in a sassy drag queen with an extravagant headdress inspired by Chiquita Banana, who took the lead and lip-synced the silly lyrics of Rosemary Clooney's recording—extolling Brazilians and their billions of coffee beans. Liam looked great, now wearing a straw hat, like the other boys in the backup. The simple but effective choreography blended with the infectious appeal of the song itself, a quick little ditty that ended all too soon.

It was damn good, and the crowd loved it—a tough act to follow, as they say.

And only one other act remained.

When the excitement waned, Carlotta returned, telling the audience, "As some of you have probably heard, we've had a replacement in tonight's program ..."

Sitting next to me at the table, Blade Wade leaned to ask, "Is it just me—or are we getting nervous?"

With a grin, I quietly assured him, "She can handle it."

Carlotta concluded, "So I present to you ... Lady Jasmine."

The crowd was hushed as Carlotta walked offstage and the entire room faded to black in the dead silence.

And then, in darkness, we heard the quiet opening measures of "La Vie en Rose." Tommie, working the spotlight, had described this introduction as having a cha-cha rhythm, but she was off a bit. This radical, sultry interpretation of the sentimental torch song employed a syncopated bossa nova beat, and as it grew, the pencil-thin beam from Tommie's pink spotlight picked out Lady Jasmine's face on the blackened stage. The audience seemed to collectively hold its breath.

As the music built, Jasmine began to hum a few measures, as Grace Jones did, strutting slowly downstage toward the runway. And then, as the music fully blossomed, along with its sung words, Jasmine's spotlight opened and brightened, revealing her full figure—to our collective gasp. The black vinyl bustier and skintight pants. The six-inch stilettos and sixteen-inch Afro, carved into a sharp asymmetrical wedge. The fierce gashes of makeup defining her cheeks and brows. And the riding crop? That, apparently, wasn't good enough for Lady Jasmine—somewhere backstage, she'd found a long black bullwhip. It was coiled around her shoulder, and when she moved forward, she let it drop, dragging it like a snake on a leash.

Did I mention we gasped? Some might've wet their pants.

Couple this with the song itself—its sung and spoken words, its ecstatic vocal runs, all of it with Grace and Jasmine in perfect sync—and our reaction in the audience was awestruck, slack-jawed amazement as the music began to fade and the circle of pink light began to tighten around Jasmine's face.

It was almost hypnotic, nearly eight minutes of this, and when it ended in the dark, we were all breathless for a moment—but only a moment—before we rose as one, roaring our thanks, clapping our hands raw as Jasmine took bow after bow after bow.

And afterward, when some people began to leave, while others remained for a last drink, we waited at the table for Jazz to join us. When she emerged from a door near the side of the stage, all traces of Lady Jasmine and Grace Jones were gone, replaced by Jazz Friendly in a little black dress she'd brought along. No one who saw the act would recognize her—except, of course, those at our table.

We stood as she approached, all smiles.

Christopher reached for a hug. "Jazz, you were *fab*-ulous."

And I thought: Oh, *honey*. There you go again.

By the time I returned home from Saturday's extravaganza, midnight had come and gone. Once in bed, I was still keyed up, with preshow jitters replaced by the adrenalized afterglow of Lady Jasmine's triumphant debut. Sleep came slowly, but when it did, it was deep and dreamless.

I slept till nearly nine—not at all my habit. When I rolled over to read the clock, my first thought was that I had wasted the morning. But then I figured: It's Sunday, and you're not due at Blade's till noon, so relax and enjoy it.

When I got up, I splashed water on my face and finger-combed my hair. After pulling on a pair of gym shorts, I padded out to the living room and opened the door a foot or so for fresh air. I started a pot of coffee.

Waiting for it to brew, I fussed for a few minutes till it beeped. Out on the patio, I heard the squeak of the front gate but didn't think about it as I reached for the pot and filled my mug.

And then there came a gentle rapping at the door.

I turned.

Isandro stood there, looking sort of bashful and uncertain. He was dressed for the day—sneakers and jeans, as if out running errands—but that didn't seem likely on Sunday morning. He said, uneasily, "I noticed your door was open. Got a minute?"

"Of *course*. Um ... pour yourself some coffee." And I ducked out of the room to throw on a shirt and give my teeth a ten-second brushing.

When I returned, Isandro was seated on the little sofa, sipping from his cup, which he then set on the low table, where he had also placed mine. I joined him.

With a quiet laugh, he said, "That was quite a show last night—saw you there. Was I imagining things, or was it *Jazz* doing that Grace Jones number?"

"That was supposed to be a secret, but it doesn't matter now." I told him about the undercover ploy, relating to the investigation of Lanford Endicott's death, concluding, "... and we did, in fact, get a few new insights. But holy Christ—did she *nail* that song or what?"

Isandro agreed, "She was *fab*-ulous!"

Recalling Jazz's supposedly straight ex, I noted wryly, "That seems to be the consensus."

Isandro reached for his coffee and took another sip, getting quiet again. "Don't know if you noticed, but I was with friends last night."

I nodded. "Was there a group? I did see you with someone... older."

"That was Richard Gibbs. He'd popped for a whole table and asked me to join them."

I gave Isandro a quizzical look. "But who *is* he?"

Isandro grinned. "Ready for this?"

"I'm not sure."

"Richard owns that estate in Old Las Palmas—with the coach house for sale. I bought it from him. So he wanted to introduce me to some of his—"

"Hold on," I said with a skeptical laugh. "You *bought* it?"

He nodded.

"But how? You said you couldn't swing it by yourself."

"I admit, it was sorta dicey. My older brother in Chicago,

Márcio, he moved from Brazil before I did. He's *way* more es-tablished—big job—and he agreed to cosign for the loan. Don't get me wrong: I still need to figure out how to *pay* for it, which won't be easy, but this seemed like such a great opportunity, I didn't want to lose it. So, yeah, I took a chance."

"Wow. I'm impressed, kiddo. And I admire your resourceful-ness, not to mention your brother—what a great guy."

"Anyway, just wanted to let you know why I haven't been around lately. Friday was my first night over there. I haven't ac-tually moved in yet, but I wanted to sorta 'claim the space' and get the feel of waking up there."

I patted his knee. "I don't blame you. And how was it?"

"Terrific. But I still need to find someone to help with ex-penses—I'll post an ad online."

I swallowed. "We should talk about this. It seems we *are* talking again, correct?"

He touched my hand, smiled. "Seems so."

I told him, "I'm busy this afternoon, a brunch for Jazz. I'd ask you along, but it involves the investigation. Then, I have dinner plans later, but I can change that—if you'd like to go out."

"As nice as that sounds, and it truly does, I'm spoken for this evening. Richard does this Sunday cookout around the pool—a regular thing, I guess—and he'd like me to get to know his crowd, his neighbors, *my* new neighbors. I think I should be there."

"Of course you should. But help me understand this—even though it's none of my business. I'm curious about Richard. You seemed to be having a good time with him last night. Are the two of you...*involved*?"

Isandro eyed me sternly for a moment, then sputtered with

laughter. "He's old enough to be my *grandfather*."

I didn't need to remind Isandro that I wasn't much younger than his own father, so I knew firsthand that he had an interest in older men. Apparently, though, there was a line he wouldn't cross—with Richard Gibbs on the wrong side of it.

I suggested, "Monday, then? Dinner tomorrow?"

"Sure, Dante." He stood. "And maybe you'll want to take another look at the place."

Grinning, I stood. "Maybe."

He raised both hands, touching my face. "Don't hate me, but I've gotta go—stuff in the car—busy day ahead. Sorry."

I kissed his forehead. "You have *nothing* to apologize for."

"*Coração*," he said, "*eu era uma fera*—I've been a beast."

Laughing, I pulled him close, and we shared the sort of kiss that usually marked the start of something, a point of no return.

But then, alas, he did indeed need to leave.

Shame on me.

Driving over to Blade Wade's loft, I should have been figuring out the best way to let Liam Heimlich know that I needed to cancel that evening's dinner date. Instead, I was weighing *if* I needed to cancel with him. After all, he had merely suggested "dinner," and I was free that night, so nothing had really changed—not much, that is, except that all my recent pining over the loss of Isandro had suddenly been replaced by the prospect of a fresh start.

Why would I even *consider* jeopardizing that? I could no longer deny or defend it: my mental dithering was ludicrous.

A few minutes past noon, I parked in the lot at the strip mall and walked over to the row of shops and galleries. The mall was always busy on Sunday afternoons, a good time for browsing, so the lot was crowded, but I easily spotted Jazz's black SUV with its pugnacious crash bumper.

When I rang the intercom in Blade's street-level vestibule, someone buzzed me in without asking my name. The rush of chilled air in the stairwell carried the smell of bacon and the convivial sounds of conversation and music as I made my way up and emerged into the loft. Brunch was still being prepared, but the party was already in full swing. Most of the guests I knew, but several I did not, including three young men who turned out to be the other Bongo Boys (without their costumes and penciled beards), brought by Liam.

While complimenting one of the lads (the blue-eyed blond who couldn't stop looking at me) on his bongo skills (they had actually carried conga drums), I felt a gentle tug at the back of my shirt. When I turned, there was Emma, wearing her painter's smock over a flouncy Sunday dress the color of creamy lime sherbet.

"Hello, Dante!" Her dark eyes sparkled. "Want to see my new work?"

"That would be delightful, Emma." I had to laugh—it was no longer her painting or her project, but her work.

I took my leave of the blond Bongo Boy (I would later learn his name was Oswin) and followed Emma away from the main room, around the stairwell, and into the calm of the studio area, where one of the easels stood out. All the others displayed Blade's heroically scaled red paintings, in various stages of completion, while Emma's easel displayed a smaller canvas—smaller than Blade's paintings, but taller than Emma herself—and at first, I wasn't quite sure what to make of it.

Hunkering down, I peered into the brushwork, smiling. "What *is* this, sweetie?"

"It's an abstraction! A little like Monet—he changed the way we see."

I nodded. "Yes, he did. He saw things—like water lilies—in a new way, and he painted his *impression* of them, a kind of abstraction. Now, this painting of yours, is this an abstraction *of* something?"

"Oh, *no.*" Emma shook her head gravely. "My earlier work was. But this is nonrepresentational. Do you like it?" She quickly added, "You don't *have* to—that's okay. I'm still exploring the process."

I pulled her over for a hug. "I like it *very* much. And I wish you great success on your journey."

She giggled. "That's just what Mr. Wade calls it—a journey."

"Well," I said, standing, "don't let *me* interrupt you. Like the rest of the world, I'm waiting to see where you'll take this."

"Oh, *Dante.* That's silly. Nobody knows I'm painting—I'm only *four.*"

"But almost five, right? From what I hear, that can be a *huge* year." I leaned to give her a kiss, then handed her a brush. "So get busy, squirt."

Back in the main room, I told Jazz, "Talk about precocious. That kid is *amazing.* By the time she's ten—CalArts? Yale? Who knows?"

"I'm sure you're exaggerating, but thanks. She gets that from her father—*he's* the arty one."

Mm-hmm. Now, *why* didn't that surprise me? But I told Jazz, "Don't sell yourself short, Lady Jasmine. You've got tons of style—remember last night? You could hang up your pistol and take your act on the road."

"Last night was for *fun*," she said. "But now we've got a murder to solve."

While that afternoon's gathering was intended to celebrate a stunning faux-drag debut, both Jazz and I hoped to use it as an opportunity to uncover new evidence that might help us name who had strangled Lanford Endicott.

What's more, we hoped to prove that the killer was *not* Guy Kirby, who was not only the husband of the deceased, but also Jazz's client. He was still at the top of the antsy DA's suspect list, so time was running short—and he was right there in the loft that afternoon.

Guy had brought along Ramil Bagoyo, and both seemed more chipper than I'd ever seen them—before or since Lanford's murder—as if grief for the loss of their three-way relationship had transitioned to a more agreeable phase resulting from their sudden, exclusive couplehood. I knew, of course, that the new twosome's recent exclusivity was not absolute—at least it hadn't been eight days earlier, on the Saturday when Ramil took me out to lunch and then paid for a pricey hotel room, a splurge prompted by the windfall he'd just received from Lanford's estate.

In the open kitchen of Blade's loft, Nina Rodriguez—moonlighting from her domestic duties in Indian Wells that day—arranged a tray of bite-size quiches, with bacon or spinach, which she began passing to the guests, numbering a dozen or so. Most already had drinks in hand.

When Guy and Ramil each picked a quiche from the tray, they fed each other through linked arms, the way some newlyweds horse around with a wedding cake. They laughed as they did this, and Ramil nearly choked on the quiche, prompting Guy to offer a slurp from his cocktail, which looked like a gin and tonic.

Jazz and I stepped over to them. As we did this, I noticed Arcie Madera talking with Nina over the tray of appetizers. Arcie's husband, Cooper, was huddled near the stairwell with Blade Wade, talking art. Liam was hanging out with the other Bongo Boys, whose giddy conversation suggested that the cocktails in hand were not their first. Allison Harper and Christopher Friendly had gone up the spiral stairs to the sleeping area and stood facing the window, checking out the view of the valley and the mountains beyond.

Guy set his drink on the kitchen island, licked a few buttery crumbs of quiche from his fingers, then used his napkin to tidy his hands. Jazz said to him, "You seem in high spirits this afternoon," and she raised her stemmed glass of water as a toast.

"Well, that's *your* doing," said Guy, returning the toast. "What a show last night—the whole world seems a bit brighter today."

Ramil added, "We had a *great* time." He turned to me and winked. "And *you*, Dante—I understand you were the mastermind behind Lady Jasmine."

I deflected the compliment with a modest shake of my head. Today's celebration belonged to Jazz alone.

But she told Ramil, "I had my doubts—a white boy coachin' *me* as Grace Jones? I mean, c'mon. But you saw what you saw. Dante knows his stuff."

Ramil glanced at me while saying to Jazz, "Obviously, he's a man of many talents."

"Okay, *enough*," I said with a laugh. "Last night's little diversion had a higher purpose, you know. We're *trying* to pin Lanford's murder on someone other than Guy."

Jazz told them, "And I wish I could tell you we've figured this out, but we're not there yet."

Guy dismissed this glum assessment with a flick of his hand. "You'll get there, I'm sure."

I shrugged. "We appreciate your confidence."

"Look," he said, sounding serious but unable to hide his cheery smile, "I *know* I didn't kill Lanford, so the facts are *bound* to bear that out—eventually—and meanwhile, things have taken a *wonderful* turn."

Dubiously, Jazz asked, "How so?"

Guy explained, "For more than twenty years, Lanford was the love of my life, and to lose him as we did was shocking and painful at so *many* levels. Those circumstances will never change. But life itself does change, and this is one of those junctures. Lanford's death has *forced* me to move on. And, as luck would have it, Ramil was there for me all along—and still is. We've come to understand that Lanford's death points us toward a new beginning."

Ramil said, "We're planning to get married."

They turned to each other with sappy infatuation.

After offering our congratulations, Jazz and I stepped away, leaving them to dote near the kitchen, where Blade had joined Nina, setting up the brunch buffet.

As Jazz and I moved into the open space of the living room, I leaned near, asking her, "Guy isn't making this any easier, is he?"

"No, he isn't," she said with dry understatement. "And even if we take him at his word that he's not the killer, he's now given us a stronger motive pointing to Ramil—his future husband, who would have a *lot* to gain from their marriage."

I winced. "What if that's the whole point? What if Guy *wants* to cast suspicion on Ramil?"

Arcie Madera approached us with a smile, asking Jazz, "Still basking in the glow of last night? Honest, Jazz—you blew us away. You could make a *career* out of that."

"Thanks, but I'd rather do more with the career I've *got*. And my client just made it more complicated. Guy and Ramil are planning a wedding. So either one of them—or both of them—might've wanted Lanford out of the way."

Arcie nodded. "That seemed like a plausible theory all along, and a rush to marry just amps it up. But that's not the only development."

I noted, "You were talking to Nina Rodriguez."

"Right. I pulled her away for a few minutes. We're both Latina—I figured she might open up to me, and she did. According to her, Agnetha Berg was *highly* interested when Nina told her what she suspected: that Maude didn't exist and Lanford wrote the books. Turns out, Agnetha went to the guesthouse late in the morning on the day Lanford was killed."

This was consistent with what Nina had confided to me while I was lunching at the Payne estate with Zola Lorinsky. I told Arcie, "I got a similar story from Bruce Tucker, the hairdresser, who claimed he saw Agnetha when he returned the wigs."

Arcie nodded. "I've had that same conversation with him."

Jazz asked, "So that's not new information, right? But you mentioned a 'development.'"

I said, "Let me guess. By any chance, Arcie, did Nina *also* mention taking Mrs. Payne to a doctor's appointment?"

This was news to Jazz, who arched her brows.

"In fact," said Arcie, "Nina was glad to find me here and was eager to talk about it. They did some blood work on Mrs. Payne, who got word yesterday from her doctor: they found minute but suspicious levels of arsenic and have ordered further tests.

Mrs. Payne wants to keep things quiet till they know more, but Nina thought she should tell me."

Stunned, Jazz said, "George needs to hear about this. That cold case in Palm Springs involved arsenic—and Agnetha Berg."

Arcie assured us, "I just got off the phone with him."

"Well, now," said Jazz, "that *is* a development."

"But there's more," Arcie told us. "And this relates directly to Lanford Endicott's death. Just before I arrived here, I got a call from an assistant who's doing routine background searches on everyone related to the case. Remember Lanford's niece?"

Jazz snorted. "And how. Nicole Endicott Chang. Went for a visit two days ago in Redlands."

"She's had some issues," said Arcie.

My turn to snort. "*That's* putting it mildly."

Arcie continued, "But it's not just Nicole. Her husband, Saxon Chang, has had some drug trouble of his own. It was quite a few years ago, back when they were *both* doing a stint in rehab, which is how they really met—not at the university. Since then, he's sorted things out and gotten himself straight, but he does have a record."

I noted, "He also has a hot mistress and a nice inheritance from his wife's uncle, who all but gave Saxon his blessing—in *writing*, from the *grave*—to dump Nicole."

"And," said Jazz, "that's exactly what Saxon is planning to do. He gave Nicole an ultimatum—a setup that seems *designed* to make her fail."

Blade clanged a glass. Someone turned off the music.

"Everyone?" he said. "I'm not much at making speeches, but I'm sure you'll all want to join me in letting this lovely lady know what a fantastic job she did last night. Bravo, Jazz!"

We all gathered near her, clanging and raising glasses, offering a chorus of cheers and congratulations, then a hearty round of applause.

Even Emma made an appearance, wandering out from the studio, curious about the commotion. When she saw that her mother was the focus of these festivities, she wiped her hands on her smudgy smock and joined in the clapping.

"Okay, folks," said Blade, "brunch is served—help yourselves. And let's have some more music."

Someone asked, "Got any Grace Jones?"

"No!" yelled Jazz with a thrust of both palms. Everyone laughed as something tame and mellow began to play.

But then came a lull as people shuffled in place, no one wanting to be thought a pig for rushing to be first in line. So Blade insisted, "Jazz, you're the guest of honor—let's get this started while everything's hot."

So Jazz led Emma to the buffet and helped her make up a plate. The rest of us lingered while Jazz served herself, then we fell into line behind them.

When everyone was settled with their plates, Nina circulated, offering coffee or fresh cocktails. There weren't many takers for the coffee.

Emma ate quickly, whispered something to her mother, and skittered off to the studio, disappearing among the easels to get back to her painting—her *work*.

I hung with Jazz for a while, and when my plate was empty, I said, "Think I'll try the pasta salad. Can I bring you anything?"

She shook her head. "I'm fine, thanks."

When I stepped over to the buffet, Christopher Friendly and

Allison Harper set aside their plates, moved to where Jazz was sitting, and started gabbing with her—updates on the murder case and the book deal, no doubt.

As I scooped the pasta salad, I noticed Liam standing next to me—as if he had materialized out of nowhere. He asked, "What's good?"

"Everything, so far."

He plucked a shrimp from a huge bowl of ice. "Nice to indulge—but we'll be hungry again—by *tonight*." He ate the shrimp, then looked about for somewhere to dispose of the tail.

With a grin, I took it from his fingers and placed it on my plate. "Tonight," I said. "Weren't we planning on dinner?"

"Why, yes," he said, sharing the grin, "I believe we were."

"So, uh"—my grin faded—"we're still on?" At that moment, I was hoping he'd tell me that something had come up, that we'd have to postpone our rendezvous, our *first date*. Please, I thought, let it be *his* decision. Let him spare me the need to tussle with this, the need to juggle him with Isandro in my conflicting notions of loyalty versus desire. I wanted an easy way out. But no.

"Of *course* we're still on," he said with a wary laugh.

So. It was up to me. I could sit him down and begin a *very* difficult conversation—or—I could stand there and affect a breezy tone while asking him, "Where would you like to go?"

Having chosen the easier of my options, I now heard him reply, "Restaurants are crazy this time of year, especially on weekends, so I thought I'd cook—you know, at *my* place."

When I did not immediately respond, he added, "I'm pretty good at it—cooking. Thought I'd keep it simple. Are steaks on the grill okay? Eight o'clock?"

"Uh, sure."

"Great." He pulled a business card from his wallet, already prepared for me with handwriting on the back. "That's my apartment and the gate code—not far from the gallery in Palm Desert."

By three o'clock, after everyone had eaten their fill and imbibed their limit, after all the congratulating and hobnobbing had run its course, the party was breaking up.

Among the first to leave was Liam, who had shopping to do (and bedding to change, no doubt). The other three Bongo Boys were next to go—probably expected at a seedy tea dance somewhere. Oswin, the blond, made a point of giving me a goodbye peck.

The rest of us were most likely contemplating Sunday naps— I certainly was. One by one, or two by two, in dribs and drabs, the remaining guests thanked Blade, offered Jazz a last bravo, and headed down the stairs to the parking lot. Cooper Brant had driven his own car, needing to meet with a potential design client that afternoon, leaving his wife, Arcie, to chat with Jazz, Blade, and me while Nina Rodriguez cleaned the kitchen.

After two or three minutes, though, Jazz told us, "Know what? I'm beat. Hate to break this up, but—"

"Go," we said. "Get some rest." Blade added, "Emma's busy with her painting. If you want some quiet time, I could drive her home later."

"That's sweet of you," said Jazz, standing, "but you'd need to get a safety seat first." And she sauntered off toward the studio area. "Emma, honey, time to go."

While Blade, Arcie, and I carried some last dishes to the kitchen, we heard Jazz say, "Emma? No games, now. You hiding?"

We exchanged a quizzical glance, then moved over toward the

stairwell just as Jazz emerged from the jumble of easels in the studio. "She's not *there*," Jazz said with a look of panic.

Mumbling our confusion and concern, we agreed that we hadn't seen her since she'd returned to her painting after eating.

With frantic calls, we were joined by Nina in a hasty search of the entire loft, including bathrooms, closets, and under the bed.

Arcie Madera wasted no more time, phoning it in.

Jazz raced down the stairs. I followed as she ran through the vestibule and out to the parking lot.

The Sunday crowd of shoppers, mostly tourists, laughed and jabbered in the brilliant desert sunshine, toting newfound treasures to their cars. Birds twittered in the trees. "Emma?" shouted Jazz, darting from row to row of vehicles. "Please, honey, where *are* you?"

As her search grew more frenzied, her pleas grew all the louder. When she reached the outer row of the parking lot, she turned back to face the strip mall, shrieking to the universe:

"*Emm-mma!*"

Everyone froze, witnessing a mother's anguish. The surrounding mountains echoed her primal scream.

Hushed, the birds flew from their trees.

PART THREE
TOUGH LOVE

CHAPTER
THIRTEEN

Because the disappearance—and possible abduction—had occurred in Palm Springs, Arcie Madera reported it to the local police, rather than the county sheriff's department, where she worked. Still, she would be involved in the case as a witness and informant, having been on the premises not only when Emma was last seen there, but also when the child's disappearance was discovered.

Arcie joined me in the parking lot as we tried in vain to console Jazz, whose hysteria had melted into something of a breakdown. Sitting on the curb, contemplating the worst, she wept in bereavement, her sobs overtaken by the approaching sound of sirens.

The dismayed crowd parted as several squad cars and an evidence team's van pulled in and parked in front of the shops. The sirens stopped, then the flashers, as we got Jazz to her feet and walked over to meet them. I noticed Blade Wade waiting in the doorway of his loft's entrance; Nina Rodriquez stood nearby in her maid's uniform, wringing her hands.

First to emerge from one of the police vehicles—an unmarked sedan—was the plainclothes detective I knew only as George, the fit and handsome Latino cop who had befriended Jazz when she previously worked with him on the Palm Springs force. When Jazz saw him, she rushed the few remaining steps to collapse in his embrace.

"Tell me what happened," he said softly, but Jazz was incoherent.

Arcie took over, giving George a quick, detailed account of the afternoon's events. I held on to Jazz while he took notes. Arcie concluded, "There was no apparent intrusion, violence, or assault—she just went missing."

George dismissed most of the forces who'd arrived, needing only one uniformed officer and an evidence tech. The crowd, looking a tad disappointed, began to disperse, returning to their quest for souvenirs, T-shirts, or snacks. George said to us, "Let's go inside."

Blade and Nina led the way up to the loft, followed by George, Jazz, and the rest of us. While we ascended the stairs, with George in charge, I sensed a slight improvement in Jazz's condition, as if there was now at least a glimmer of hope because help had arrived and something was being done. She held on to the railing while climbing the last few steps, but she otherwise needed no assistance.

Once in the loft, the uniformed officer took Blade and Nina aside to get statements from each of them. We showed the others where Emma had been working at her easel, and the evidence tech began taking photos of the painting, as well as the taboret next to the easel, where Emma's paints, brushes, and palette were neatly arranged. The brushes were clean, and the tubes of paint had been capped. Her smock was draped over the back leg of the easel.

George told the tech, "When you're through with pictures, check the area for fingerprints."

Knowing that would be messy, I suggested, "Maybe you could move the painting—it's still wet." Emma had graduated from her earlier crayon-and-turpentine works to traditional slow-drying oil paints.

George gave the tech a nod. Then, walking us out to the main room, he said, "Now, tell me who was here—everyone."

Jazz, Arcie, and I recalled and agreed upon the guest list. When we mentioned Christopher Friendly, George said, "Emma's father? Did you check to see if *he* took her?"

With an embarrassed shrug, Jazz said, "No. Emma was supposed to stay with *me* tonight."

Arcie said, "Worth checking, though. I'll call him. It would be odd if he took Emma without mentioning it, but even if he didn't—he needs to know about this."

"Thanks, Arcie," said Jazz, sounding forlorn.

While Arcie stepped away to make the call, George asked us, "And the gathering here today—it was just a social occasion, a brunch, right?"

Jazz sighed. "Right."

"But," I explained, "it had a purpose. We were celebrating Jazz's performance last night. She was in a charity drag show—and brought down the house."

George looked up from his notes. "At Apockalippso? Grace Jones? Was that *you*, Jazz? My wife and I were there, at a table with friends—it's always such a great event."

She rolled her eyes, reddened by her tears, telling him dryly, "I'm glad you enjoyed it, but frankly, that's the last thing on my mind right now. And besides, I didn't do it for kicks. It tied in with the murder investigation—Lanford Endicott—in Indian Wells."

George made a note of this, nodding. He'd already helped Jazz on *that* investigation, digging up old dirt on Agnetha Berg. Surely, though, as far as Jazz was concerned, the murder case was now "just business," having suddenly taken a back seat to *this* investigation—Emma's foreboding disappearance.

George said, "This will sound like a ridiculous question, but I have to ask it, so don't be offended: Did Emma have any enemies? Do you know of anyone who might want to harm her?"

"Jesus fucking Christ," said Jazz, "she's *four*."

I added, "No enemies, George. Emma is cute, smart, and kind. You can't think of her without thinking 'delightful.' No one would want to harm her—at least no one who knows her."

George reminded us, "It's *possible* this was done by someone unknown to her."

Jazz asked him, "Any *other* cheery thoughts?"

"Well," he said, "here's an alternate theory: What if she just wandered off? Kids do that sometimes. Who *knows* what they're thinking?"

I recalled something. "Jazz, when Emma finished eating this afternoon, she whispered something to you before she went back to her painting. What did she say?"

Jazz instantly teared up. "Sweet Jesus—those were the last words I heard from her. She said something like: 'I'm going to change the way we see—so I need to get busy—it's a journey.'"

I smiled. "I had a talk with her shortly after I arrived, and it sounded a little like that. The 'journey' referred to artistic growth."

"But she's *four*," said Jazz. "Maybe she thought the journey was—you know—a *journey*, wandering the streets out there, following a trail of breadcrumbs or whatever."

"I really doubt that." But I didn't want to press the point, as the breadcrumb theory sounded marginally less ominous than the abduction theory.

Arcie, pocketing her phone, returned to us. "Christopher didn't take Emma. And when I told him why I was asking, he really freaked out. I mean, don't get me wrong—I *get* it. But honest to God, in almost thirty years on the force, I've never had a guy fall apart like that."

Deadpan, Jazz acknowledged, "He can be a bit... emotional." Mm-hmm.

George told Jazz, "If you want, I can visit him later and do a welfare check."

She nodded. "Sure. But he should be all right—he has the adoring Miss Allison Harper, Esquire, on call to hold his hand."

"Meanwhile," said George, "we need to issue an Amber Alert. Have any pictures with you?"

And they both took out their phones to set it up.

CHAPTER
FOURTEEN

Like many of my acquaintances, I had turned off the emergency alerts on my phone the first time I was needlessly roused and alarmed in the middle of the night, so I wasn't sure how effective they were. But I found it encouraging that Jazz embraced this procedure, as it gave her an active role in increasing the odds that Emma would be found and returned to her.

And there was more she could do—on her own—while George and Arcie availed themselves of the tools reserved for law enforcement.

Clinging to the notion that Emma's disappearance was not as sinister as it first seemed and that her daughter had merely wandered away on a path of childish curiosity, Jazz spent the remainder of the afternoon driving around the eastern edge of town, where Blade's loft was located, hoping to spot the little scamp and put an end to this nightmare.

I did the same in my own car—for a while—but quickly determined that Blade's neighborhood was not the sort of place a child would find attractive for exploration. These weren't tree-lined streets with storybook houses and parks and fountains. It was a commercial district with strip malls and car dealers and a few gravel roads, where a wandering toddler would not go unnoticed. Further, the entire area was cut off from the rest of the town by Highway 111, a busy high-speed thoroughfare not propitious for pedestrian crossings. If a four-year-old had tried it, we'd have heard about it—for better or, probably, worse.

So I gave up, although those were not words Jazz would want to hear.

From my car, I phoned her in her SUV. "I'm really burned out," I said. "I'm just going through the motions now—and not as observant as I should be."

"Then go home and get some rest," she said, unbothered. "I'd do the same, but I'm just too worked up. Christ, I need a *drink*."

"Ummm...," I said warily.

"Just a figure of speech, Dante. I lost Emma *once* because of booze—won't risk it again. I need to be strong for her."

"You *are* strong," I told her, no fatuous compliment. "If you need some company later—for dinner, or just talk—be sure to let me know."

"Thanks, but I won't be hungry—and wouldn't be good company. Christopher wants to come over, but he's a bigger mess than *I* am. We'll see."

So we rang off, and I drove back to my apartment.

The developments of that afternoon offered more than ample excuse to cancel my dinner plans with Liam—and if Jazz had wanted to see me, that would have been the end of it—but instead of phoning him then and there to call it off, I waffled, intending to decide later, wondering if a short nap might change my perspective. After all, Liam had presumably *shopped* for me already, making an actual investment in our plans that now outweighed my shifting druthers.

Arriving home just after five, I didn't see Isandro's car (he had a cookout of his own that evening), and I didn't see Zola sipping cocktails on the patio (she would have wanted to gossip and catch up), so I entered my apartment, closed the door and the drapes, left the lights off, slipped my shoes off, and stretched out on the bed.

Sleep came quickly.

When my phone woke me, I was disoriented in the blackness of the room. The glaring numerals on the phone informed me that it was nearly eight o'clock. And the readout told me Liam was calling.

"Hello?" I answered, barely able to speak.

Liam said, "I just got the *terrible* news."

"What?" Stupidly, I added, "Am I late?"

Liam paused, confused. "Dante, are you all right? Are you in the *car*?"

I switched on a light. "No—I'm so sorry—I fell dead asleep."

"I know you had a rough afternoon—the scare with Jazz's daughter. I just got a call from the police in Palm Springs. They're following up with everyone who was at the brunch. I hadn't heard about it." He seemed to hesitate. "What a shocker."

Imagining the worst, I could barely ask: "You mean ... they *found* her?"

"No. She's still missing."

Not good, I thought, but better than what I'd feared. "Uh ... look, Liam, I'm sort of—"

He cut me off: "I *understand*, Dante. I know tonight's not right for ... well, *you* know. But if you're hungry, I've got a couple of beautiful New York strips here, and I haven't started the grill yet, so it doesn't matter that you're running late. If you want to talk about things—or forget about things—come on over."

I inhaled deeply, considered his words, then breathed more easily. "Tell you what: I need a little time to put myself together, and the drive is another twenty minutes or so, which would get me to your place before nine. Is that ridiculously late?"

He laughed, reminding me, "I'm twenty-two. *Nothing* happens before eleven."

The Heimlich Gallery, where Liam worked for his uncle, was located in a swanky shopping district along El Paseo in Palm Desert, and the apartment complex where Liam lived was just a few blocks up the hill from the gallery, in a neighborhood best described as nice but nothing special. That said, Liam's apartment was larger, newer, and better appointed than my own, and considering the disparity of our years, I could objectively think of him as "privileged."

Not that there's anything wrong with that. He had never, in my experience, lorded his upbringing or his circumstances over those he dealt with or called friends. Why think less of him because he had lucked into good fortune and faced a promising future? All of this was simply part of who he was—like a custom-tailored suit—and he wore it well.

When he greeted me at his door, he wore not a suit but dressy jeans and loafers with a V-neck sweater, perfect for a desert night that had turned chilly. "You found it," he said with a smile.

"I know my way around." I handed him the bottle of wine I'd brought. There in his doorway, we leaned together for a hug, a pat on the back, a kiss on the cheek.

He closed the door behind me as I stepped inside, telling me, "Make yourself comfortable while I fuss in the kitchen."

The kitchen opened into the main room, so we could gab while I nosed around.

Either he had an exceptional eye for decorating or, at twenty-two, he had an exceptional budget and a decorator. The place had a warm, comfortable feel—in marked contrast to the modernist interiors I saw so often, which were tasteful, bright, and disciplined, but cold.

Liam's living room felt more masculine and clubby, with dark, muddy walls and a floor of ruddy terra-cotta tile. Some of the overstuffed furniture was upholstered in buttery tan leather, the rest of it in a nubby brown tweed. A selection of top-notch paintings lined the walls, including one of Blade's big red squares—on loan, I assumed, from the gallery. A corner fireplace with a curved adobe surround was topped with a rustic wooden mantel. The fire within glowed and crackled, spreading warmth over a big sheepskin rug and its assortment of plump cushions, ideal for lounging.

"If I didn't know better," I told Liam, "I'd think you were planning to seduce me."

"I *was*," he assured me while whisking vinaigrette, "but after what happened with Emma—and the awful uncertainty—hot sex would seem sorta tacky." He set the bowl aside, adding, "Even so, later on, a cuddle by the fire might be in order."

Yes...it might.

He asked, "Can I get you a drink?"

I hesitated. "Not yet, thanks. Maybe just wine with dinner."

"It won't take long, now that you're here. We can eat indoors or out on the patio. Your decision—take a look."

I'd already noticed the round dining table in an alcove near the kitchen. Dinnerware was stacked there, but not yet placed. Walking around the table, I opened one of the French doors along the back wall and stepped out to a small but charming patio.

Festive swags of soft, amber lights were strung overhead from the slats of a brise-soleil, lending an air of fantasy to the setting. A tidy little table for two sat within a few feet of the grill, which had been heating, adding warmth to the night air. An uplit ficus hedge served as backdrop to a large stone sculpture, an abstracted figure resembling the work of Henry Moore—also, I assumed, on loan from the gallery. Beyond, the mountains formed a jagged silhouette against the black velvet sky, pierced by stars and maybe a comet as the planet gently tilted toward spring.

"Pretty, isn't it?" said Liam, standing in the doorway.

"Gorgeous. Let's eat out here."

"Not too cold?"

"No problem." Having driven in my open convertible that night, I'd worn a sweater.

Liam told me, "I'll put the meat on. You set the table."

Within twenty minutes—it was now nine thirty—the table was set, the flowers were primped, the wine had breathed, and the steaks were grilled and rested. When we sat, Liam poured wine for both of us, then raised his glass. "Welcome, Mr. O'Donnell. This is long overdue—but better late than never."

I winked at him. "I'll drink to *that*." And we both sipped.

Everything was served together on our oversize plates—the salad along with the steak and tiny sautéed potatoes, as well as Liam's thick vinaigrette, used as an all-purpose sauce. And it was, without exaggeration, *fab*-ulous.

After exchanging compliments on both the food and the wine, we were able to relax with our meal and settle in for some serious conversation—with plenty to talk about. Topmost in both of our minds, of course, was Emma.

"I talked to Blade," said Liam, "right after I called you, around eight."

"No news, I assume?"

Liam shook his head. "Blade said the cops were at his place

for a couple of hours, taking pictures and such, but he didn't think much came of it. When they left, they asked him to call if he had any ideas, and they didn't seem to have any theories of their own—or if they did, they didn't let on. He's worried sick—for both Jazz *and* Emma."

"So am I. When Jazz discovered that Emma was missing, she had a total, instant breakdown—I've never seen her like that before. When we last spoke, she sounded more herself, focused on the mission, but that's an act, that's her job. I know she's torn up inside, and it'll get much worse if Emma isn't found soon— safe and sound."

Setting aside his fork, Liam asked, "What's *your* best theory, Dante? How did she disappear? And why?"

"Well, sorry to say, I don't think she just wandered off, so the only other possibility is that she was taken. *Abducted*—God, that sounds awful. And I highly doubt that some intruder sneaked in from the street and hauled her away, meaning, whoever did it was probably there at brunch. But that's crazy, right? Everyone there was well known to us—except the Bongo Boys, of course. Well, *you* know them. And while we're on the topic, what can you tell me about Oswin—he of the turquoise eyes and flaxen hair?"

"Stop that," said Liam, managing a laugh.

"Sorry," I said, smiling in return. "Oswin sorta commanded my attention, but I'm asking about the *group*—all of them. What do you know about them?"

Liam shrugged. "They're *kids*."

"If you say so, gramps. But they're old enough to drink—I saw them."

"I *mean*, they're peer volunteers at the Safe Palms Community Center, working with at-risk gay youth. I don't know them very well, except for rehearsing the Brazil act together. To the best of my knowledge, they have no connection to anyone who was at the brunch, including Emma."

"Which leaves us"—I tossed my hands—"nowhere."

Liam topped up his wine, but I declined with fingers covering my glass.

"On a slightly happier note," I said, "may I ask how things are going with you and Zane Smith? It seems you keep bumping into each other—and I'm delighted to report no further incidents involving ice water—so I can't help but wonder if you boys are achieving some sort of *rapprochement*."

"Too early to tell. I think he's ready, but I'm not."

"Why not?"

"Well, he's great in *bed*—"

(This didn't surprise me.)

"—but it's just that I've still got this unresolved itch. For you, Dante."

"Ahhh...*that*," I said, enlightened.

"Yes, that. And unless I'm mistaken, there's something unresolved with someone in *your* life, too."

"Oh, Liam," I said with a sigh. Extending my arm across the table, I offered my hand. When he took it, I explained, "There's this neighbor in the apartment complex where I live. His name is Isandro. We've been 'seeing' each other for about two years, off and on. More recently, for about six months, we've been 'dating,' and that's gotten more frequent, but not what you'd call 'exclusive'—at least *I* wouldn't call it that."

Liam nodded, grinning. "So it's complicated."

"Yes, it is. But he and I *might* be on the verge of something, and if that was meant to be, I don't want to screw it up." I paused, truly confused, adding, "At least I don't *think* so. Am I making any sense?"

"*No.*" Liam laughed, dropping my hand and leaning forward, elbows on the table. "But you obviously need to sort this out—and the timing is right, because *I* need to sort things out with Zane—which means, you and I are *not* destined to become great lovers, at least not in the foreseeable future. But we can still be friends. We can still have dessert. And if you're interested, later on, we can still get cozy by the fire."

So we talked and talked. We had dessert—a crème brûlée that he torched before serving—and we talked some more. We cleared the table.

And then, around eleven thirty, Liam closed the patio doors and dimmed a few lights, suggesting, "Cuddle time?"

"But no sex, young man," I reminded him with mock gravity.

He took my hand and led me over to the fireplace—a convincing setup with gas-fired logs, which he dialed down to a flutter of dancing flames. We slid our shoes off, then settled next to each other in a nest of cushions on the sheepskin rug.

With an arm around his shoulders, I took a deep breath and closed my eyes, sated by the meal and exhausted by the day.

He asked softly, "All talked out?"

I chuckled. With my eyes still closed, I said, "We didn't exactly solve the problems of the world, did we?"

"We gave it a good shot."

I opened my eyes and turned my head to look at him. Our noses touched. "Thank you," I said. "I didn't know it, but this is just what I needed tonight."

"Happy to oblige." He winked, which looked comical—with our faces so close, we were staring cross-eyed at each other.

Backing off a few inches and blinking to pull the room into focus, I thought of something. "Bruce Tucker," I said.

Liam seemed unfazed by my non sequitur, saying, "A talented guy—a wiz at hair and makeup. What about him?"

"The Bongo Boys—Bruce must know all of them, right?"

"Sure. Bruce is on the youth center's board, and we both worked on the committee for the fundraiser. In fact, it was *his* idea to recruit the four of us as backup to the Brazil act."

I thought aloud, "But he has no connection to Emma or Jazz."

"None that I know of," said Liam. "Except, he worked on Jazz backstage before the show—but he thought she was a guy named Jack."

"Yeah." I mulled this, then recalled, "The day I brought Zola Lorinsky into the salon, you were with Bruce, getting a haircut."

"A Friday morning," said Liam, "week before last."

"It was two days after the murder at the Payne estate, and the reason I brought Zola in—other than a *much*-needed styling— was to sound Bruce out. He had delivered Maude's wigs to the guesthouse not long before Lanford was killed on Wednesday. I wasn't even sure if he knew what had happened."

"He did," said Liam. "He talked about it while he was cutting my hair—said Mrs. Payne gave him the news. I imagine he'd told a *lot* of customers about it by then. He's highly valued as a stylist—*and* a gossip."

I pushed myself up on one elbow, looking down at Liam. "And that's what I found so strange about my conversation with him that day. At first, he didn't let on that he knew about the murder. But later, as I was leaving the salon, he got his story mixed up, referring to Lanford as a 'poor guy' and hoping I'd 'figure it out.' So he *knew*. But if he already knew about it, why would he pretend, at first, that he didn't?"

Liam pushed himself up and sat facing me cross-legged. "That's easy," he said. "Bruce was probably sounding *you* out, hoping for fresh details for his hot gossip."

I sat up, mirroring Liam's crisscross pose. "Well, duh—stupid me. That makes perfect sense. And here I was, thinking Bruce tried to hide something from me—to *thwart* the investigation—which made him seem all the *more* suspicious."

With a quiet laugh, Liam shook his head. "You were reading him wrong, Dante. Bruce wasn't trying to hide anything from you. In fact, he later told me that he was afraid he hadn't told you *enough*."

That caught my attention. I asked, "Like what?"

"According to Bruce, when you were at the salon and discussing his delivery of the wigs to Lanford Endicott, you asked Bruce if he'd talked to anyone else while he was there."

"Right. And Bruce told me he'd said hi to a maid. The woman he described was Agnetha Berg. She's been a suspect from the start."

"But," said Liam, "even though you asked Bruce if he'd *talked* to anyone else, you didn't ask if he'd *seen* anyone else. And he did. He wondered if it might be relevant, but when he told me about it—turns out it was nothing."

"Fill me in."

Liam explained, "After delivering the wigs and picking up his signed book, Bruce left the guesthouse, and while he was getting into his car, another car pulled in. A well-dressed woman got out. She carried a briefcase and wore 'big red glasses.' I told Bruce that she was surely Allison Harper, the lawyer responsible for Maude's book deal—nothing suspicious about that. She'd set up the rental to make sure that Maude, meaning *Lanford*, was able to get the book written. And ever since Lanford was killed, she's been pressuring you and Jazz to solve the murder. If she was at the guesthouse that day, she was simply checking on progress."

While this bit of news was unexpected, Liam's reasoning was spot-on. If Bruce's reported sighting of Allison was correct, it revealed no inconsistency with the facts already known. Most crucially, Allison had a huge interest—both financial and professional—in seeing the terms of the book-and-film deal fulfilled, with no conceivable motive to strangle her own client, Lanford Endicott, a.k.a. Maude Movay, a.k.a. the cash cow.

I leaned forward, giving Liam a chaste peck on the lips. "You're every bit as clever as you are cute. Now, where were we?" And I flopped back into the nest of cushions. When I patted the space on the rug next to me, Liam joined me, lying down at my side.

He snuggled closer, and once again, I reached an arm around his shoulders as he rested his head on my chest. We didn't speak, lazily enjoying each other's presence, the cozy setting, the flickering yellow of the fire. I stifled a yawn.

He said, "I know you're wiped out—if you want to doze off, be my guest. I'm not going anywhere."

I pulled the phone out of my pocket and checked. It was just before midnight, and no one had called or texted. "If anyone needs to reach me, they know the number," I said while tucking the phone away again.

As my eyelids drifted shut, dimming the fire's glow, the long day ticked to an end, and the woozy contentment of sleep quickly swept over me.

Just as quickly, it seemed, I was roused by the buzz of my phone.

"Sorry," I mumbled, digging it out to take a look.

"No problem," Liam told me, sitting up, smiling. "I was awake."

I also sat up, shaking my head, trying to clear the brain fog. Squinting at the phone in the middle of the night, I saw that it was just past two o'clock. I had received a text from Jazz: "Any chance you're up?"

I typed: "I am now. Any news?"

"Nope. If your offer's still good, company would be nice."

"I need a half hour."

Jazz: "I'll be here."

Setting down the phone, I told Liam, "Gotta run. But I really enjoyed this."

"So did I, Dante. Good luck with everything—including your guy."

I kissed the tip of my finger and touched it to his lips.

In the dead of the night, there's nothing like a brisk ride in an open convertible to wake you up and jerk you back to the grim reality of a murder and a child's abduction. There was plenty to vex me as I zipped along Highway 111—but at least there was no traffic. None.

When I parked the Karmann Ghia outside the apartment building where Jazz Friendly had so painstakingly rebuilt her life—committing herself to sobriety and a new career, struggling to gain joint custody of her daughter, and finally establishing a fragile truce with her ex-husband, working together to raise their child with both a mother's and a father's love—after everything Jazz had been through, I couldn't begin to imagine the heartache she was feeling that night. And I hoped she hadn't hit the sauce.

I climbed the outdoor stairs to the second floor of the building, and as I approached her door, it opened. Jazz stepped over the threshold. "I heard you pull up. Quiet night—too quiet."

When we hugged, she told me, "Thanks for coming."

I could smell coffee on her breath—no booze. Stepping inside with her, I asked, "You holding up okay?"

She closed the door. "Let's just say I've had better nights. I *hate* this—when nothing's being done."

"Well," I said wryly, "if *anyone's* capable of rushing the sunrise, it's Jazz Friendly."

"Hah," she said, not quite allowing a laugh. "I know it's stupid. 'The law never rests,' they say, but everyone needs sleep—even when there's a lost kid—except, I'm afraid I'll dream." Leading me over to the kitchen area, she said, "Coffee's on. Want some?"

I shook my head. "Thanks, but I'm so out of sync already, coffee's not the answer."

She shrugged. "Sorry, no liquor in the house. So whataya want—*milk*? I've got some." Needlessly, softly, she added, "It's Emma's."

"You know," I said, hardly believing my own words, "that sounds pretty good."

"Comin' right up." She fussed in the kitchen, pouring coffee for her, milk for me, and setting out a plate of cookies for both of us.

From where I stood, I could see into the little bedroom that was Emma's—when she wasn't staying with her father. Tonight, of course, she wasn't at her father's, and she wasn't here, either, but the night-light was turned on, keeping a silent vigil next to her bed. The frilly pillows were plumped and ready. Her ragdoll cat, named Oliver, was curled at the foot of the bed, waiting to jump up and greet Emma when she rushed in for a hug and a heart-to-heart, swapping stories about their adventures of the day.

Holding the plate of cookies, Jazz asked me, "Couch? Or kitchen?"

"Don't want to get too comfortable—might drift off. Kitchen's fine."

She set everything on a brightly lit section of bar-height countertop, where we could sit facing each other on stools. She asked, "Did you get *any* sleep?"

"Couple hours this afternoon, then again tonight, so I'm fine, just out of whack. Now, tell me: What have you heard?"

"Not much of substance, but Arcie and George have both been good about giving me updates. Emma's information has been entered in the FBI's missing-person database, and the Amber Alert went out. Did you get it?"

"Somehow, I missed it." How could I tell her I'd blocked those?

"It already brought in several reported sightings—mostly from around here, but one from Nevada, which *really* freaked me."

I asked hopefully, "And?"

"Every report was checked, and all were dismissed as mistaken identity. It's been quiet for a few hours, but George says everything should be back in gear after daylight."

"What about Arcie?"

"She's busy with it, too. Offered to set me up with a county caseworker. I have law-enforcement background, though, so the plan for now is, we'll just keep the lines of communication open. But if this drags on..." She didn't finish the thought. Instead, she broke off half of a chocolate-chip cookie, bit off the tip, and dropped the remnant back onto the plate.

I took a whole one and ate most of it, drinking milk between bites. Even at that weird hour, even under such horrible circumstances, the combination had a comforting, unaffected appeal. After swallowing the last of my cookie, I told Jazz, "These are good."

She gave me a look. "They're from a bag."

I said, "I assume you've talked to Christopher."

Nodding, she said, "Arcie was right—he's a total mess. Meaning, I need to 'remain strong,' not only for Emma, but for my ex. I almost wish there was a way I could *blame* him for this, but there isn't."

"And besides," I said, "that would be petty and irrational."

"Yeah, yeah, yeah…" She dabbed at a few cookie crumbs, then licked them from her fingertip. "He was here, by the way. Left about an hour ago."

"Then *we're* not the only ones losing sleep."

"Christopher has a truly good heart. I know: I bad-mouth him a lot. But I married him cuz I loved him, and he's still the father of my child, and he loves her same as me. He's a sweet man."

Mm-hmm. I'd noticed that.

Jazz looked at her watch and groaned.

I asked, "What's wrong?"

"It's nearly three. It's now been *twelve* hours since we discovered Emma was missing. Each hour we lose, it's less likely that—"

I interrupted: "Don't go there, Jazz."

We remained in the kitchen, nibbling cookies, bucking each other up, wasting yet another hour—knowing that each minute mattered—but our only current option was to worry.

A few minutes past four, I glanced at a text that arrived on my phone. Jazz had been saying something, but her words trailed off in a slur. Then her head jerked as her eyes sprang open and she gripped the edge of the counter—nearly falling from her stool.

"*Whoa*," I said, standing. "Time for someone to lie down and get some rest."

She nodded, stood. I walked her over to the sofa, gathered a few throw pillows, and got her comfortable, telling her, "Your phone's right here on the coffee table, in case you fall asleep."

"Not gonna happen, Dante." But her eyes were already closed. And I left.

Closing the door to her apartment, I stepped out to the open stairway. Somewhere, maybe, newspapers were being printed or bread was being baked or cows were being milked, but there on that quiet street in Palm Springs, no one stirred, nothing moved. Stars still shone brightly in the sky's utter blackness.

Even in my sweater, I found the night air cold—how spoiled we were in the desert, where fifty degrees could feel like thirty. I trotted down the stairs and walked over to my car. Getting in, I took a minute—another lost minute—to close the roof. Then I pulled out my phone to read that last text again: "I need to talk to you. Call me when you can." It was from Christopher.

The text had been sent only five minutes earlier, so he was obviously awake, and I placed the call. When he answered, his voice sounded soft and distant: "Dante! Did I wake you?"

Sitting in the dark confines of my little car, I said into the phone, as if whispering in a confessional, "No, you didn't wake me. Who can sleep?"

"Have you talked to Jazz lately?"

"Just left her. She's resting now."

"Does she, uh...does she know I texted you?"

"No, I didn't mention it." I wondered, of course, why he would ask that, but he offered no explanation—at least not directly.

"I've been wanting to talk to you—I mean, in person. My place or yours, doesn't matter."

"I'm in the car right now, so I'll come over."

"Fine. *Fine*, Dante. You know where it is, right?"

"I do."

And off I went, cruising through the city's empty streets, heading toward a north-side neighborhood near the historic Movie Colony, but not in it, which offered a measure of panache at a less princely price. This was the stomping ground not of the megarich, but of the highly affluent—a good fit for Christopher Friendly, founder of a prominent local law firm, who, at forty, was still on his way up.

Within fifteen minutes, I parked near the low wall surrounding the Friendly residence, got out of the car, and walked toward the gate.

"Dante," said a voice from the shadows, speaking in a stage whisper so as not to disturb the neighbors. A hand swung the metal gate open—a squeak in the stillness. "Come in. Please."

I followed his silhouette to the light at the front door, which was open. When I stepped inside, he closed it, telling me, "I can't believe you're here. I mean, at *this* hour. Thanks for coming over." It was now four thirty.

I said, "You've certainly piqued my curiosity. What's up?"

Leading me into the living room, he said, "Well, it's sort of… personal." Turning to me, he added, "It's not the kind of thing I can discuss with just *anyone*—but I think you'll understand."

He looked at me with the barest hint of a smile, an uncertain expression that verged on pleading. He'd clearly not gone to bed that night, as he was wearing the same outfit he'd worn to yesterday's brunch—nicely tailored gabardine khakis with a crisp oxford shirt, striped pink and gray. His clothes were now a bit rumpled, and he needed a shave, which gave his handsome face an attractively rugged edge I hadn't seen before.

I asked, "How can I be of help, Christopher?"

He hesitated. "Want some coffee?"

"Uh...sure." Why fight it? In an hour or so, the dark of night would begin to wane as Monday morning, still beyond the horizon, crept our way.

Christopher said, "Got cereal, too, if you want some. It's Emma's, so it's sweet."

"No, thanks."

He led me through the dining room and into a big, bright kitchen, where I settled at the table while he poured coffee. From where I sat, I could see into Emma's bedroom, as I had done at Jazz's apartment, but here, their daughter's room was bigger, more lavish, loaded with oversize stuffed toys and all the lacy whatnot befitting a little princess. Strikingly similar, though, was the night-light—left on, still burning softly, keeping a hopeful vigil.

Christopher brought two mugs of coffee to the table—a square with four chairs—and sat not across from me, but at my side, telling me, "I'll come right out and say it: Allison Harper has the hots for me, and I *ought* to find that exciting, but I need to be honest with myself."

I nudged: "Yes...?"

"Truth is," he said, "I'm still consumed with regret about leaving Jazz, and now, with Emma missing, I don't think I can *cope*."

(So much for any fantasies I'd harbored.)

Christopher continued, "And that's why I didn't want Jazz to know I reached out to you. Do you think I stand *any* chance of getting her back?"

I doubted it, but I told him, "Only Jazz can answer that. She's involved with Blade Wade, of course. But the bigger issue, I think, is her ... let's call it her 'independent nature.' The divorce was an awful blow to her, but it transformed her, and she's really come into her own. She discovered what she's capable of. My hunch is, she won't be inclined to be tied down to *anyone* right now. Sorry."

Christopher heaved an exhausted sigh. Then he touched my arm. "I guess I needed to hear that—even if I didn't want to."

"Sometimes," I said, "truth hurts. They call it tough love."

He grinned—then winked at me.

"Besides," I said, "you've got Allison to lean on."

"True. But I've already explained to her—or *tried* to explain—that I still have unresolved feelings for Jazz. Plus, there's Emma. Jazz and I will *always* share that connection."

"Still," I said, "you and Allison aren't just professional colleagues, but *friends*. And right now, you're a friend with a crisis. Since Emma went missing, I'm sure Allison has been a much-needed source of support—*and* affection."

"Oh, sure, absolutely. Allison's been great. We've *talked*, of course—on the phone. But I haven't seen her since yesterday."

"Why *not*?"

"She's dealing with a crisis of her own up in Idyllwild—something involving her mother."

Recalling an earlier conversation about Allison's upbringing, I asked, "Inez Norris?"

"Right," said Christopher, "Inez. According to Allison, her mother has a history of mental issues, and something set her off again, so Allison had to rush up there—said she *plans* to be back in the office today, but I thought it sounded iffy. So I went over there tonight, after visiting Jazz. Then, when I left the office, I texted you."

Confused, I asked, "You went to your office? Why would you do that in the middle of the night?"

"Because Jazz reminded me that she still hadn't gotten a copy of the Maude Movay contract, which Allison agreed to give her. So I went to the office, checked Allison's files, and dug out a copy." Christopher got up, stepped over to the counter, and brought back a heavy legal-size document with a black pressboard cover, bound at the top with a two-prong fastener. It landed with a thud as he dropped it in front of me, saying, "Enjoy."

My eyes bugged—it was more than an inch thick.

Sitting, Christopher added, "Or just pass it along to Jazz."

I opened the cover and started browsing through it, trying to get an idea of how it was organized, as it covered a number of interdependent agreements. I asked Christopher, "You've never seen this, correct?"

"Correct. Allison completed that deal in LA, before joining my firm."

Our conversation continued in spurts while I turned the pages—a blur of mumbo jumbo. At times we didn't speak at all. Christopher got up to refill our mugs—twice, maybe—and I occasionally asked him for the meaning of Latin terms that seemed intended more for obfuscation than for clarity.

Christopher's explanations were concise and helpful, but I could tell he was preoccupied with the looming gravity of his daughter's disappearance—which grew only more serious with each passing, wasted minute.

I closed the contract's oblong cover, resolving to stay focused on the plight of Emma, Jazz, and Christopher. I asked him, "When you left the brunch with Allison yesterday, did you say goodbye to Emma?"

He shook his head woefully. "God forgive me—I didn't. There wasn't time. There was a three o'clock lecture at the museum I planned to attend, but I'd started gabbing with one of the Bongo Boys at the brunch—"

"Oswin?" I asked.

"Yes, in fact. He was *quite* engaging, and I lost track of time. Running late, I ducked into the studio to tell Emma I was leaving, but she wasn't at her easel. I just *assumed* she went to potty —so I left." He looked at me, forlorn, as a tear leaked from one eye, then the other.

"So," I said, "neither you nor Allison saw Emma."

He waggled his hands. "Sorry, I wasn't clear. Allison and I didn't leave together because we didn't drive there together. She had zero interest in the lecture, so she took her own car. Then, at the brunch, when things started winding down, maybe two thirty, I noticed she was on her phone a lot. I went over to ask if something was wrong, and she told me about the situation with her mother—she was *really* upset. So she apologized for bugging out early, told me to enjoy the lecture, and off she went."

"Think carefully," I said. "Did you see her actually head down the stairwell—alone?"

"Well, *no*," he said, as if I were dense. "I needed to get back to *Oswin*."

Mm-hmm.

When I laid everything out for Christopher, reminding him that he had rebuffed Allison's desire to play house with him—and when I further reminded him how he'd told Allison that little Emma was the glue that forever bonded him to Jazz—only then did his glowing memories of the gabfest with flaxen-haired Oswin seem trivial.

I then emphasized that he must not talk to Allison about anything we had discussed, concluding, "You need to play along with me on this, Christopher—for *Emma's* sake."

With a sober, earnest nod, he agreed.

I had the Maude Movay contract tucked under my arm as I left the house and walked through the gate, out to the dark street. Stars still filled most of the sky, but I noticed the first hint of light to the east. I checked the time: five twenty-five. Estimating that Jazz had gotten an hour's sleep—not much—I was nonetheless certain she would want me to wake her. I placed the call.

After a few rings, she answered groggily, "What?"

I asked, "Are you gassed up?"

"I *beg* your pardon?"

"I just had a talk with your ex, and I think we need to zip up to Idyllwild." After explaining why, I said, "Those roads can be scary, and there's still some snow up there, so we'll need your SUV. Up for some mountain driving?"

"*Hell* yeah. Give me twenty minutes—I'll pick you up at your place."

"Dress warm," I told her, and we rang off.

I barely had time to drive home, rush into my apartment, and brush my teeth—long overdue. There wouldn't be time to shave, so I grabbed a jacket to wear over the sweater I'd had on since last night, then darted out the door. But I stopped, went back inside, and took the bound contract I'd brought in from my car.

Standing at the curb in front of my building, I noticed that the sky had brightened to the twilight of early dawn. At a quarter till six, the quiet was shattered by the roar of a menacing black SUV turning the corner and heading my way.

It screeched to a halt just long enough for me to open the door and hop in. We were moving before I had the door shut.

"Morning, Jazz," I said while buckling up. "Wide awake?"

"No—but the adrenaline makes up for it. Do you know where we're going, exactly?"

"A week ago, Allison told us that her mother's name is Inez Norris, and she lives at a family retreat they built, called Zenithgate. The town is so small, we should be able to stop anywhere and get directions."

While heading out of Palm Springs toward the freeway, Jazz asked me, "So *if* you're right, and *if* Allison took Emma up there, what was it supposed to accomplish? What do you think we'll find?"

I shook my head. "Honestly? I have no idea. I assume you've let Arcie know what's going on—or George?"

"No way. They'd just send in a fuckin' SWAT team. If my kid's up there, she's been traumatized enough. And if anyone's gonna be firing weapons, it's gonna be me." She pulled back her jacket to expose her shoulder holster—and the Glock 19 in it.

Good God, I thought—we were in this alone.

Idyllwild was only ten or twelve miles from Palm Springs—by *air*—but the drive was closer to fifty miles and would take over an hour, requiring us to travel west on the freeway to the Banning Pass, where we would turn south and then backtrack up the far side of the mountain on a steep route of hairpin curves rising to six thousand feet.

Leaving Palm Springs, merging onto the 10, we found that the traffic heading west was already brisk at that early hour, much of it bound for LA. But it was moving steadily, and the thrum of the tires created a monotonous drone within the vehicle. Music might have improved this annoying ambience, but the radio was off—this was no joy ride, and there was plenty to think about.

I had placed the Maude Movay binder in my seat pocket and now pulled it out, setting it on my lap. I told Jazz, "Christopher found the contract you wanted and asked me to give it to you. It's pretty dense, but I've been skimming."

"Skim away," she said, gunning it as she found an opening in the fast lane.

It was difficult to concentrate, but the task helped pass the time, and before long, we were exiting the interstate at Banning and heading up the mountain road.

When we started the climb, the sky was fully lit, though the sun itself had yet to breach the eastern horizon. We'd left the palm trees behind us on the valley floor, and a few miles later, pines appeared along the craggy roadway. A few miles after that, patches of snow lingered in the curves, with embankments of rock on one side, boulders below.

I kept my eyes on the contract, flipping pages, reading, trying to ignore the road—one lane up, one lane down, most of it with no passing, plus an unpredictable mix of drivers, some seasoned and others skittish, heading in both directions. I tuned out Jazz's running commentary—"slow down, asshole"—"step on it, fuckface"—while elevation signs whisked by, marking every thousand feet. And the dashboard thermometer kept dropping.

"*Oh, my God!*" I said.

Jazz turned to me with a quizzical look. "What? We're cool. Slowing down—almost there."

"No," I said, "the contract. I found something. Something that might be...*relevant.*"

"What?"

I read her the clause.

"My, my, my," she mused while braking to pull in at an old-timey shingled gas station with a little convenience store. We had arrived in the tiny community of Pine Cove, adjacent to Idyllwild. The temperature hovered just at freezing as the first pricks of sunshine streamed up from the east, glinting through the frosty red branches of manzanitas. It was a few minutes before seven o'clock—sixteen hours after Emma had disappeared.

"You go in," Jazz told me. "A Black woman asking for directions might make someone think a phone call to Inez Norris is in order. Just tell them you're a friend of Inez's daughter, who invited you up to see Zenithgate. She said you should stop here for a map."

Worked like a charm.

And a couple of minutes later, we were winding our way

through wooded back roads—"forked," as they say—but we knew all the turns, and when we drove slowly over the crest of one last ridge, where asphalt changed to gravel, there it was. Two stone pylons flanked a needle-strewn driveway, spanned by a primitive sign of woven twigs: ZENITHGATE.

Inside the pylons was a makeshift parking court and, near the main house, one vehicle—a husky old Chevy Suburban, classic two-tone, maroon and cream. Frost covered its windshield. Above, a woodpecker rattled the trunk of a fat oak, sending debris to the ground, where chubby gray squirrels and crow-size mountain jays foraged for their breakfast.

Jazz parked on the road, just beyond the sign, and killed the engine. She checked her gun (oh, Christ), then quietly opened her door and got out. I did the same and put on my jacket. A cello sang quietly in the distance, surely a recording—unless Yo-Yo Ma had dropped by for *his* breakfast, which seemed doubtful. We carefully nudged the doors closed. Trying not to crunch the gravel, we walked softly, but not softly enough, back to the gateway and entered between the pylons.

The woodpecker stopped. The cello stopped. The front door of the house opened (oh, Christ), and a woman appeared, tall and imposing with frizzy silver hair, wearing a full-length embroidered tunic of sorts—or it could have been her nightclothes.

"Good morning," she said without menace. "Is there something I can help you with?"

I watched Jazz tug the lapels of her jacket, as if straightening it, but her hands came to rest within an inch of her gun. She said, "Mrs. Norris?"

"It's *Ms.* Norris, but yes, I'm Inez."

"Good morning, Inez. My name is Jazz. Jazz Friendly."

And out from behind Inez scampered Emma. "Mommy!" she called, running toward us with open arms and a big smile. "Hi, Dante!" She seemed delighted to see us, but nothing in her manner suggested she felt imperiled or even stressed.

Jazz, on the other hand, was a blubbering mess, crouching to smother her daughter with kisses, smoothing and primping her little dress, the color of lime sherbet—though it looked just fine.

Inez came out to meet us. "Please," she said, "come in from the cold."

All four of us walked back to the house. When Inez closed the door behind us, she said, "We weren't expecting you till this afternoon."

Jazz and I glanced at each other.

Inez continued, "Hope the place wasn't *too* hard to find. Care for some coffee?"

"Uh, sure," said Jazz warily as Inez walked us through the main room toward an open kitchen. The house was rustic in style, but lovely in its concept and furnishings, with a soaring timbered ceiling—very Ralph Lauren. A big fieldstone fireplace warmed the space, which was filled with the welcoming smells of coffee, toast, and cinnamon. If little Emma was being held captive—or whatever—her accommodations weren't too shabby.

Plus, she had landed in a veritable playpen of arts and crafts. Inez was apparently involved with pottery, weaving, sculpting, and other creative pursuits. A sunny workroom opened from the far side of the kitchen, where Emma now busied herself. We watched as she practiced knotting the fibers of a composition that looked something like macramé.

Inez asked us, "Kitchen table okay?"

A handsome old pendant light with a globe of milk glass hung over the round oak pedestal table. Jazz and I took chairs that gave us a direct view of Emma in the next room. Inez set out the mugs of coffee and a colorful ceramic plate of cinnamon rolls, their shiny frosting still gooey. The very sight of them made me realize I was hungry.

When Inez sat with us, Jazz asked her, "Why did you say you were expecting us?"

Inez looked confused. "Because ... that was the plan. Wasn't it?"

I said softly, "Inez, this is the first we've heard of *any* plan. What did Allison tell you?"

Inez hesitated. With a look of concern, she closed her eyes in thought, then exhaled heavily. When her eyes opened, she leaned forward, speaking in a confidential tone, "I thought something didn't sound right. Why is Emma here?"

Jazz assured her, "We don't know, not exactly. But didn't you get the Amber Alert?"

"I block those." Inez shrugged. "Doesn't everybody?"

"Here," said Jazz, taking out her phone and tapping the screen. "Here's how it posted to Instagram, with a picture." She passed the phone to Inez, who looked at it, dismayed.

Jazz continued, "Emma's last name is Friendly. I'm Jazz Friendly, her mother, and I'm a private detective." Jazz pulled out her wallet and displayed her state-issued investigator's photo ID. "Since yesterday afternoon," Jazz continued, "I've been frantic over Emma's disappearance. We were at a brunch party, where Emma was abducted by Allison, who happens to work for Emma's father—my ex-husband, Christopher Friendly. If you don't believe me, I can—"

Inez interrupted, "I believe you, Jazz." Then she lolled back her head and spoke quietly to the ceiling, "Ughh, Allison, what the hell have you done?"

I repeated my earlier question: "What did Allison tell you?"

Inez swallowed hard. Planting her elbows on the table, she explained, "Allison called me yesterday, around two, and said she was managing a 'crisis situation' for a client involved in a custody battle. Her 'team' had just 'rescued' a little girl from a dangerous situation with her father, and Allison wanted me to hold her 'in sanctuary' overnight. So she drove Emma up here later in the afternoon. She instructed me not to discuss any details with Emma, who was supposedly 'unhinged' by the situation, and I was simply to play nice with her until her mother arrived to pick her up—today, this afternoon."

Jazz rolled her eyes. "So: Allison is sending someone up here to pose as Emma's mother and take her away, but we have no idea where or why. As far as you know, Inez, is that plan still in effect?"

"I haven't heard otherwise. In fact, I haven't heard *anything* from Allison since she left last night—said she had to get back to Palm Springs, busy day at the law office."

"I'll just bet," Jazz muttered.

"Inez," I said, "do you understand that Allison lied to you—about *everything*?"

Woefully, she shook her mop of radiant silver hair. "Nothing surprises me anymore, not where *she's* concerned. Of *course* she lied to me. She has no sense of right, or truth, or even reality. I used to joke with Gordon, her late father, about how *different* she was from both of us. '*That* one fell pretty far from the tree,' he used to say. I'd laugh with him, and then he'd say, 'Hope she finds her way.' But I didn't think she would."

Jazz reached to touch her hand. "Inez—for *my* daughter's sake—can we count on you to help us set this right?"

She smiled. "Of course you can. Emma's *such* a sweetheart. What do you want me to do?"

"For starters, obviously, don't tell Allison that we've been here or that you've figured out what's going on. Simply go along with her plan. Meanwhile, Dante and I will take Emma back to Palm Springs, and I'll fill in the sheriff's department. They'll put a surveillance team in place to apprehend whoever comes to pick up Emma. When is 'mommy' supposed to arrive?"

Inez said, "According to Allison, 'early afternoon'—maybe one or two? She said she'd call me to confirm everything, so I expect I'll be hearing from her."

"Great. I'll stay in touch, and I think you'll also be hearing from Detective Arcie Madera. She's with the Riverside sheriff's department, which covers Idyllwild as well as the Palm Springs area."

Emma called from the workroom, "Inez? I have a question."

With a grin, Inez said, "Excuse me," and she left to help Emma with her knots.

Jazz reached for her phone, itching to put the plan in motion. But I said, "Wait. Here's another idea: Let's call a meeting at your office today—say, two o'clock. The pretext is that Arcie has made important headway on Lanford Endicott's murder. You or Arcie could invite Allison to be there, since she's been so concerned about clearing Guy Kirby. Guy should be there; Ramil, too. Plus, of course, Mr. and Mrs. Saxon Chang. He has a Monday lab this morning, but ought to be free this afternoon. Both he *and* Nicole should be itching to attend—since they each want to pin the murder on the other." I twitched a brow, asking Jazz, "Whataya think?"

With a nod, she got busy on the phone with Arcie.

I called Christopher, letting him know that his daughter was safe. I also filled him in regarding what we knew about Allison and the plan to apprehend her co-conspirators in Emma's abduction. He readily swore that Allison would hear none of this from him.

Finally, Jazz took the phone, telling Christopher, "I'm up to my eyeballs today, so I think Emma's going to need to be with her father when we get back. Can I bring her over to the house around ten or so?" She waited briefly while he replied, then made a kissy sound, saying, "Thanks, baby."

Jazz rang off and handed the phone back to me just as Inez returned to the kitchen from the workroom.

"She really is the most *remarkable* child," said Inez, refilling our mugs, then sitting. "I'm sixty-seven years old, and I've never encountered such an inquisitive young mind—or such a pureness of spirit. I envy you, Jazz. Whatever you've done, I wish *I'd* known about it—with Allison."

"Any mother," said Jazz, "she can only follow her heart and do her best. Early on, I *wasn't* the best possible mom for Emma, and I damn near lost her—in fact I *did*, for a while, but then I got a second chance with Emma, and today, I got a third. Thank you, Inez."

Tracing a finger around the rim of her coffee, Inez said, "I feel I didn't even get that *first* chance with Allison. It's as if we've never truly known each other."

I recalled, "V. Allison Harper. When I asked about her first name, she wouldn't tell me—just said she never liked it."

Inez grinned. "Her first name is Venus."

"Cool," said Jazz. "What's wrong with that?"

"Don't ask *me*. Her father and I thought it was beautiful—she was the product of our love. Plus, it was sort of cute."

I asked, "Cute?"

"Her father was Gordon Harper—the astrophysicist?"

It took me a moment. "*Really?* Nobel Prize, right? UCLA?"

Inez nodded. "He was wonderful—the only man I've ever loved. I'm a lesbian, in case Allison hasn't mentioned it."

Jazz and I glanced at each other, shook our heads.

"No surprise," said Inez. "Allison *hated* her unconventional upbringing. Gordon and I never married, never took each other's names. His head was in the stars—quite literally—while I saw myself as a social crusader. Many described me as a feminist lesbian. A few even called me a radical, *militant*, feminist lesbian. Gordon and I laughed at them. We shared a creative, *expansive* mindset, and Zenithgate became something of a commune at times—artists, dancers, poets, *thinkers*. But Allison? She'd have none of it. *Her* childhood dream was single-minded: She wanted to be a lawyer. And carry a briefcase. And help the rich get richer."

Inez heaved a sigh of lament. "Wouldn't you just know it? She turned out *Republican*."

CHAPTER
SIXTEEN

Jazz told Emma, "Put your headphones on, honey."

We had left Zenithgate around eight thirty, parting with a round of hugs and comforting words for Inez. She gave Emma the macramé piece she'd been working on, along with some extra supplies, and they kissed goodbye.

Now, driving out of Idyllwild in the SUV with Emma ensconced behind us in her safety seat, Jazz and I needed to talk.

She told me, "When I called Arcie, her first instinct was to go over to the law office in Palm Springs, wait for Allison to show up for work, then nab her and be done with it."

I said, "But it seems Allison is still coordinating with the other 'mommy,' so her arrest would muck that up—and we'd *never* learn details of the ultimate plan."

"Exactly," said Jazz. "Arrest her right now, she gets charged with simple kidnapping. On the other hand: keep her in the dark, then arrest her later when the whole scheme is exposed, and she probably gets charged with much worse." Jazz wagged her head, looking through the windshield to the open sky. She mused, "What's the *deal* with Allison? I mean, her mother thinks she's screwed-up—I get it. But lots of us have 'issues,' and we don't steal other people's kids. What *drove* her to that?"

I hesitated. When I had phoned Jazz before dawn while leaving Christopher's house, I had recounted key details of my conversation with him regarding Sunday's brunch—specifically the timing of Christopher's and Allison's separate departures from Blade's studio, which had led me to reason that Allison was responsible for Emma's disappearance. In the telling, however, I had avoided the delicate issue of Allison's motive.

I now explained to Jazz, "Christopher told me that Allison has the hots for him—his words."

Jazz rolled her eyes. "She's made no secret of *that.*"

"No, she hasn't. But she never got her way with him—not even close. Christopher confided to me that he now regrets divorcing you, and I confided to *him* that I didn't think you were interested in getting back together—hope I wasn't out of line."

Jazz shook her head, grinned. "It's the truth. I'm doin' fine on my own. Best he knows it."

I said, "And here's the point: Christopher had also told Allison that he was off-limits because Emma would always be the glue that keeps him emotionally attached to you."

Jazz blew a low, thoughtful whistle.

"Allison," I noted, "seems highly intelligent, with a great head for business and strategy and deals, but in her warped thinking, she must've concluded that the only way to win Christopher over was to remove Emma from the equation."

"Jesus," Jazz mumbled. Glancing over at me, she added, "And to think—I was always wondering if he might be gay."

I told her honestly, "I think he's bisexual. I also get the impression you've been the only woman in his life."

She shrugged. "That's something, I guess. But he deserves to be happy, and I think he needs a man... someday."

I thought so, too, but I shifted the conversation back to our immediate purpose. "Anyway," I asked, "Arcie liked the idea of meeting at your office?"

"You bet. Showdown at two o'clock. She's already working on our list of 'invitees.'"

"I wonder if Agnetha Berg will be on that list."

Jazz singsonged, "I don't think so." With eyes on the road, she explained, "Arcie said that George talked to Mrs. Payne's doctor yesterday afternoon, and the doc called her into the emergency room for a urine test as a follow-up to her blood work. Definite signs of slow, deliberate arsenic poisoning, which could easily account for Mrs. Payne's anxiety and wacky behavior."

Goes without saying, our mood driving down the mountain was considerably improved over our glum mindset during the drive up, but our work was far from finished. And even though we could now bask in the joy of knowing Emma was safe with us, I still hated to contemplate what might have been her intended fate.

We cruised into Palm Springs shortly before ten that morning, and Jazz decided to drop me off before taking Emma over to Christopher's house. When we pulled up to the curb outside my apartment, I exchanged blown kisses with Emma, who was still busy humming along with something on her pink headphones. Getting out of the SUV, I asked Jazz through the open window, "Quarter to two?"

She gave me a thumbs-up—"Seeya then"—and drove away.

Which meant, I had a few hours to myself. I'd already phoned Sunny Junket to let them know I wouldn't be in that day. I'd been away from home since the previous evening, and I'd gotten only two hours of sleep overnight, so I knew what needed to be done as I walked through the gate and headed around the pool to my apartment.

I unlocked the door, stepped in, and closed it behind me.

Switching off the lights I'd left on, I went into the bedroom and undressed. I needed a shave—the stubble was driving me nuts—so I padded into the bathroom and took care of it. Back in the bedroom, I set my phone to wake me at one o'clock. Then, as I stretched out on the bed, I worried that the events of the past nineteen hours, since Emma's disappearance, would not let me sleep. But within a minute or two ... those thoughts ... evaporated ...

When the troubled, noisy dream woke me, I was disoriented. The bedroom's curtains were closed, but the sunlight beyond the doorway to the living room left my brain in a confused muddle. As my head began to clear and I recalled why I was in bed in the middle of the day, I reached for my phone and saw that it was just a few minutes before one o'clock. I canceled the wake-up alarm, satisfied that I'd gotten nearly three hours' sleep.

I wasn't hungry (Inez Norris had sent us on our way with a bag of her fresh cinnamon rolls, three of which I ate during the drive), so I got into the shower and cleansed myself for the start of a new day—some six hours later than usual. Then, while I primped at the bathroom mirror, my phone rang. It was Jazz.

"Just wanted to make sure you were awake," she said. It was ten minutes after one, and I planned to leave in about twenty minutes.

"Wide awake," I assured her. "I had this weird dream. Noisy. Pulled me out of a deep sleep—but now, ready to go."

She asked, "Isn't there a noisy dog next door to you?"

I laughed at myself, feeling stupid. "Of course—it was Mitzi."

"Whenever you're ready, come on over." And we rang off.

Within five or ten minutes, I was dressed, looking good, and decided to be on my way. The bedroom curtains were still closed, and I'd be returning home in the daylight, so I flung them open. The drapery panel nearest my nightstand caught a framed photo that was displayed there, toppled it, and knocked it to the floor with a loud clatter. Luckily, the glass didn't break.

But the eruption of barking from next door was instant.

Ughh.

I gathered my things, left the apartment, then walked through the front gate and out to the curb, where I had parked the Karmann Ghia.

A boxy van, a rental, had just pulled up behind my car, with its motor still running. As I approached, the driver killed the engine.

Both doors opened, and the driver hopped down to the street. He was burly and unkempt, wearing a T-shirt. From the passenger side, an attractive male leg—silky gym shorts at one end and a sexy-looking sneaker at the other—reached out to the curb. The guy the leg was attached to, now standing on the sidewalk, was neither burly nor unkempt. It was Isandro.

"Dante!" he said. "It's moving day. Huck's helping me."

Huck laughed—a low, burly chortle.

"*Darn*," I said, "I'd offer to help, but I'm due at a showdown."

With a hoot, Isandro told me, "Like ducks. Have fun, *coração*. Are we still on for tonight?"

"Why, yes"—I grinned—"I believe we are."

Huck flashed me a sly look as I got into my car.

Parking on Palm Canyon Drive near the Huggamug building, I noticed that both Jazz's SUV and Arcie Madera's unmarked cruiser had already arrived.

When I climbed the stairs from the rear lobby and walked through the door to Jazz's outer office, she rushed out from the conference room with a wild look in her eyes. "You won't *believe* what happened." The words, taken at face value, might have seemed ominous, but her tone carried a lilt of delight. "Come look." And she retreated into the conference room.

I followed, then froze in the doorway, bug-eyed. Arcie Madera was there, arranging a stack of file folders, seated at the table— but it was no longer the battered old folding banquet table. It had been replaced with a classically modern Parsons table with a flawless black-lacquer finish, and it looked a *lot* like the one I'd seen in the garage space at the coach house that now belonged to Isandro.

Jazz said, "*Isandro* brought it over during the noon hour. He hired a guy with a truck for his move out of the apartment— and he said you thought I might like this. I *love* this!"

Then I noticed the painting, a big one, mostly red, surely one of Blade Wade's. Jazz said, "He sent it over on Saturday afternoon—sort of a good-luck gift before the drag show that night. Lookin' pretty good, huh?"

The dreary, windowless conference room, seemingly hopeless, was now fully transformed. The brown walls, red painting, new carpeting, Thonet chairs, and the clean lines of the Parsons table—it all pulled together perfectly. What else could I say? "Fabulous."

"Very nice," agreed Arcie, reminding me of her presence— and our purpose.

Jazz told me, "You can sit *there*," indicating the chair to the left of hers. She would sit at the head of the table, nearest the door. She and Arcie agreed to save the seat at the far end of the table for Allison Harper. Arcie would remain in her current chair, adjacent to Allison's. Guy Kirby would sit on my side of the table, across from Arcie. The chair between Guy and me would be for Ramil Bagoyo. This would leave two open seats across from me for Nicole and Saxon Chang, filling out Arcie's side of the table.

While waiting for the others to arrive, Jazz asked Arcie, "Anything from George yet?"

I, too, had been wondering if the handsome Palm Springs police detective had made any headway in reopening the investigation into the suspicious demise of Agnetha Berg's long-ago, short-lived husband—and the implications it might have regarding Agnetha's odd relationship with her addled employer, Marjorie Payne.

"Uh...*yes*," said Arcie with a tone of understatement. "Up-to-date DNA testing of physical evidence from the original case, coupled with the current forensic evidence that Mrs. Payne is a likely victim of arsenic poisoning—these new facts linking the two cases have been sent straight to the district attorney. Peter Nadig is a glutton for sensational headlines, so I think it's safe to assume that Agnetha will find herself in custody by tomorrow—if not tonight."

I was pleased, of course, to know that Mrs. Payne was out of danger, but I was sure that Agnetha's absence from the estate, after so many years, would be a difficult adjustment for the lady of the manor.

As if reading my concerns, Arcie told us, "I've given Nina Rodriguez a heads-up. She intends to make sure that Mrs. Payne gets the help—and the care—that she needs."

While reflecting on this, we heard Guy and Ramil enter the outer office. Jazz went out to get them, then ushered them into the conference room.

They knew that Emma had been kidnapped (but not found) because they'd attended yesterday's brunch and had since been reached for routine interviews, along with all the other guests. Now, of course, they commiserated with Jazz about the awful turn of events, and she put on a convincing act—stiff upper lip—expressing confidence that her daughter would be found.

I suggested that Ramil might want to sit next to me, which he readily agreed to. This, as planned, put Guy in position next to Ramil, across from Arcie.

Next to arrive was V. Allison Harper, attorney-at-law, who lugged in a fat briefcase and offered consoling words to Jazz regarding Emma's disappearance. "Frankly," she said, "I'm amazed you're even *working* today. I can't imagine what you must be going through."

Stoically, Jazz replied, "I've placed my faith in law enforcement—they know what they're doing. Meanwhile, we've got a murder to solve."

Arcie then suggested, "Why don't you sit down here, Miss Harper, at this end of the table?" She paused before adding, "Next to your *client*."

Guy's expression signaled he was concerned by the sound of that.

Allison took her seat and busied herself pulling stacks of paperwork from her briefcase, arranging them in piles on the table. She took out her phone, checked it quickly, and set it in front of her.

At the opposite end of the table, Jazz lifted a slim canvas tote from the floor and set it in front of her, near me.

Allison checked her phone again. So did Arcie.

And soon—it was just a minute past two o'clock—Lanford Endicott's surviving niece, Nicole, arrived with her husband, Saxon Chang. They apologized for running late (traffic) and expressed their concern for Jazz's missing daughter. I wasn't sure how they knew about this; maybe they hadn't blocked their Amber Alerts.

They took the two remaining seats, across from me and next to Detective Madera, who had a few things stashed under the table. She reached down and brought up a folded beach towel—old and faded, with red, blue, and yellow stripes—which she placed in the center of the table, directly in front of Saxon. Both he and Nicole eyed it with evident terror, as if it were some venomous creature that might pounce and bite.

"Now, then," said Jazz, "it seems we're all here." She began reviewing the circumstances and some of the known facts of the murder of Lanford Endicott, who was "ruthlessly strangled while attempting to write a book." As Jazz continued speaking, Guy and Ramil, like Nicole and Saxon, hung on her every word, waiting for the hammer to fall—on anyone else.

Arcie Madera, however, and Allison Harper didn't seem to be listening at all. Instead, they were both busy with their phones—swiping, reading, typing—and the detective's manner was decidedly more calm than the lawyer's.

Jazz said, "… and although we identified more than a half dozen viable suspects, Lanford's killer was shrewd and evasive."

Detective Madera looked up from her phone, cleared her throat, and gave Jazz the slightest nod.

Jazz, in turn, gave *me* the slightest nod, telling the others, "I'd like Dante to summarize some recent developments he figured out."

I paused, drawing curious stares from around the table.

"Twenty-three hours ago," I said, "we discovered the disappearance of Jazz's four-year-old daughter, Emma, setting in motion a desperate search involving the sheriff's department, the Palm Springs police, and even the FBI. *Everyone* rallied, *everyone* cared—everyone, that is, except Venus Allison Harper." I looked her in the eye.

Startled, she averted my gaze, took off her big red glasses, and set them on the table.

I said, "That's right, Venus. We visited your mother this morning. She told us your name, and she mentioned that you hated it."

She spat the words: "Inez and Gordon—they thought it was *cute*."

Jazz said, "Your mother told us that she and Gordon named you Venus because you were the product of their love."

"Oh, *yeah*? A couple months before I was born, they got this big slobbering black Lab, and they named *him* Jupiter. Did she tell you *that*?"

"Uh, no," I admitted, "that never came up."

Guy Kirby said, "Excuse me, but I must be confused. How does this relate to Emma?"

Jazz told him and all of us, "Venus... Allison... whatever the hell her name is, she *took* Emma, kidnapped her, and hid her up in Idyllwild with her mother while she schemed to make her next move."

Guy, Ramil, Nicole, and Saxon looked stunned.

I explained, "Something was afoot—we didn't know what. But Emma is back home in Palm Springs this afternoon, in her father's care."

Venus gripped the edge of the table and caught her breath.

Arcie Madera set her phone aside. "And *now* we know the plan." Watching Venus, she told the rest of us, "Agents have just reported apprehending a woman and a man of Serbian extraction who arrived in Idyllwild to pick up Emma, as arranged by Miss Harper here. The woman was to pose as Emma's mother, who would take her away to 'protect' her. What was really going to happen, however"—Arcie turned to address the remainder to Jazz—"they were going to fly Emma to Eastern Europe, where a paid adoption was being arranged. Emma was to permanently 'disappear.'"

Trembling, Jazz rose, leaning forward on the table, glaring at Venus, sitting eight feet away at the other end. "You fucking piece of *shit!*"

I was glad she didn't have her gun on her.

Guy Kirby looked stricken. *"Allison,"* he said, "I've known you and worked with you for *how* many years? I couldn't be more disgusted..."

"Oh, come *on*," said Venus, dismissively. "It's not as if they'd *kill* her. She'd have a *very* nice life over there. The agency screens only the *best* people for—"

Guy interrupted: "You were going to *sell* the girl? For *money?*"

"It wasn't *about* the money. It was—"

Jazz screamed and began to move, stepping around the table.

I grabbed her, and Arcie rushed over to help get Jazz seated again. Arcie hunkered down to eye level with Jazz, assuring her, "We'll take care of this—trust me."

Panting, Jazz calmed herself, closing her eyes.

Arcie reminded her, "And we're not quite finished, are we?"

Jazz opened her eyes, smiled.

Arcie resumed her seat next to Venus, then turned to Nicole and Saxon, sitting to her left. Fingering the beach towel she'd set in front of them, Arcie said, "We know *one* of you drove back to Indian Wells from Redlands on the morning when Lanford Endicott was killed."

Saxon insisted, "I had *classes* that morning—an early lab, followed by a lecture at eleven."

I told him, "Yes, you did. And I confirmed it with several of your students who attended that lecture."

"Noted," said Arcie. "So, Nicole, tell us about your return visit to your uncle that morning."

Nicole Endicott Chang hung her head. "I drank myself sick the night before, so Saxon and I spent the night and left early in the morning. Before we left, though, I found Uncle Lanny's wallet in the bedroom where we slept—and a stash of cash in one of the drawers—so I helped myself. When Saxon and I got back to Redlands, he got out of the car at the university, and I drove myself home. The money I took—it was a lot, and I needed it. But I knew I was in for *big* trouble if I didn't fess up and return it. So I called Lanny and told him I needed to see him, soon. He said he was working, but invited me to drive back. He gave me directions to the private gate and said I should call when I got there."

Arcie said, "He received a call from your number at ten thirty that morning. Is that when you arrived?"

Nicole nodded. "Sounds about right. The gate opened for me, I drove in, and he met me at the door of the guesthouse. I brought a few things in the car—hoped he might let me use the pool while I was there—it's so beautiful, and I thought it might cheer me up. As soon as we went inside, I told him what I did and showed him the money and tried to give it back—but he wouldn't *take* it. He said something like 'If you stole it, you must've needed it, so keep it, Nicole—an advance on next Christmas.'"

Saxon looked dumbfounded, telling his wife, "You never said a *word* about this."

Paying no attention to him, she continued, "So Uncle Lanny went back to work on his book, and I took a swim. When I finished, I left the towel hanging on that *awful* statue—just a joke. Uncle Lanny came out to kiss me goodbye. He said he would open the gate, and I left."

Arcie said, "Explicitly: the last time you saw Lanford Endicott, he was alive and well, correct?"

"Yes, he was, Detective. I swear I didn't kill him."

Arcie paused to survey everyone else in the room. She told Nicole, "I know you didn't." Then she slid the towel closer to Nicole, saying, "We no longer need this as possible evidence. If you'd like to take it, you can leave."

Nicole and Saxon glanced at each other, grabbed the towel, and hurried out of the room. We waited to hear the closing of the outer-office door.

Arcie explained to us, "I'm certain Nicole didn't kill Lanford Endicott—because now we know who did."

Guy and Ramil shared a look of deep apprehension while their lawyer sat stone-faced.

Jazz nudged her canvas tote in my direction.

I withdrew from it the bound copy of the Maude Movay contract, asking Venus, "Recognize this?"

She eyed it askance, as if she'd been betrayed.

I told her, "Jazz asked you twice if she could see this, and twice you agreed to take care of it, but you didn't. So last night, Christopher Friendly—your employer and the object of your affections—dug it out for us. I got to read some of it last night, and then more of it this morning, while riding up the mountain to visit your mother. It wasn't quite what I'd call *pleasure* reading, but then, one particular passage really grabbed me. I'm no lawyer, so I'm not sure if you'd call this a paragraph or a section or maybe a clause—an 'escape clause'? Here's what it says: 'Blah, blah, blah … While time is of the essence in fulfilling the terms of this agreement, if the author should become incapacitated by reason of severe illness or death, the schedule of deadlines shall be paused for sufficient time to acquire new talent to complete the project described herein ... blah, blah, blah."

After a moment's silence, Guy blurted, "I was the principal *agent*. I never signed that. I never *saw* that."

"You did sign it," I told him, displaying the signature page, "but I have a hunch you never saw that clause. I think your lawyer slipped it in."

"Ughh." Guy covered his face with his hands. "There were *dozens* of rounds of changes. I didn't read the whole damn thing each time—I relied on Allison to guide me through it."

She shrugged, "So we missed something, Guy. Big deal. And it's a damn good thing we had that language in place."

"It sure was," I said. "When Lanford died—because someone *strangled* him—that clause kicked in and you could simply invoke it while finding a ghostwriter. But that's not how you *told* it. After the tragedy, you bragged to everyone about how you had this brainstorm and how you did all this last-minute heavy negotiating and how you saved the day by getting everyone on board with the new idea of a ghostwriter. But it was there all along. Guy and Lanford weren't aware of it, but you were—you *wrote* it."

She put her glasses on again. "So what?"

"*So*," I explained, "when it became apparent to you that Lanford was *not* going to complete Maude's manuscript on time, it gave you a multimillion-dollar motive to invoke the escape clause and save the deal—by killing him."

Guy and Ramil gasped, but Venus laughed. "Watch it, Mr. O'Donnell," she said, "you're skating perilously close to slander and defamation. It's wild speculation—you can't prove it."

I raised a finger. "I think maybe we can. You placed several calls to Lanford on the morning he died. Nothing suspicious about that—you were bugging him to write the manuscript. We assumed those calls were from your office in Palm Springs, but one of them was perfectly timed to place you at the Payne estate's private, unmonitored back gate shortly before the murder. Coincidentally, a hairdresser was leaving the guesthouse just then, and he saw a woman arriving, whose description fits you—and your red glasses. Once you were inside, it's safe to assume you found Lanford at work in Maude's bedroom, working at her laptop, even wearing one of her scarves. But one look at the computer screen was enough to convince you that he hadn't even *begun* Maude's contracted novel—and would never be able to finish it on time. Instead, he was horsing around with a new obsession, a planned exposé of that creepy Agnetha Berg. And then, you suddenly had a strong motive *not* to see him alive and working, but dead and buried."

Jazz laughed merrily. "Motive, means, and opportunity, Venus. The only thing standing between you and a murder charge is proof that you were in Indian Wells that morning."

Arcie slid a computer printout from a folder and placed it on the table. Tapping it, she informed Venus Allison Harper, "We got the drilled-down report of your call activity on the morning of the murder. Around eleven thirty, a call from your phone was placed through a cell tower near the Payne estate in Indian Wells."

Guy Kirby, literary agent and former husband of the late Lanford Endicott, took a sharp breath, balling his fists on the table.

Venus raised her bowed head, turned to him, and reached to place her hand on his. Without emotion, she told Guy,

"Lanford was going to blow the whole deal. There was no other way to save it. So remember—everything you now have, you owe to me."

With a look of revulsion, Guy withdrew from her touch.

Arcie pulled out a pair of handcuffs. "Phew—kidnapping, child concealment, conspiracy, not to mention first-degree murder—I'm not sure where to begin."

Helpfully, Jazz suggested, "How about: 'You have the right to remain silent...'"

Alone and defenseless, Venus wept.

F lowers? Wine? Why not both?

Isandro had texted me later that afternoon: "Can't wait to see you tonight, but all fagged out from chores with Huck. Not up for clubbing, so let's keep it simple. I'll cook (if I can find my way around the new kitchen). Six thirty? xoxox"

I replied: "xoxox"

So that night would be—I hoped—a reunion, a reconciliation after nine days apart. But it would also be something of a housewarming for Isandro, the first time he would entertain in his new home. I couldn't show up empty-handed. Flowers *and* wine would cover the bases.

I parked the Karmann Ghia inside the back gate of the Old Las Palmas estate and walked around to the front of the coach house, facing the pool terrace. I climbed the flight of stairs—roses in one hand, a festive bottle of Veuve Clicquot rosé in the other—and managed to stretch a finger to press the doorbell.

"Awww," said Isandro, opening the door, "you shouldn't have."

"Of *course* I should," I told him, stepping inside. Something smelled wonderful—a hearty stew, perhaps.

When I handed him the flowers, he kissed me. "Thank you, Dante."

I handed him the champagne. "For us to share tonight."

He flashed me a stern look of disappointment.

"What?" I asked.

"I thought you might bring a little overnight bag. You know—pajamas?" Then he laughed.

"Goofus," I told him, mussing his hair. I'd be overnighting, all right.

He led me back to the kitchen, where he put the bottle in an ice bucket and began fussing with the flowers.

I said, "You may be in for a bit of 'special treatment' tonight. Jazz couldn't *believe* you sent over the Parsons table. She's highly grateful—and so am I."

He countered, "You may be in for some 'special treatment' yourself—rescuing a four-year-old and nailing a killer in one fell swoop. You deserve everything you've got coming—later."

I liked the sound of that. His engine, it seemed, was already running.

While he took the flowers to the table, I wandered into the main space of the loft and nosed around. He'd moved in that very afternoon, and nothing was arranged yet; much of it hadn't even been unpacked.

He joined me. Looking about, he said, "Gonna be great, once it gets organized. But I should leave that to someone who has a better eye for it."

No question, I could make some magic in this space. I asked, "Did you get around to posting that ad for a roommate?"

His head wobbled. Coyly, he told me, "Thought I'd hold off and see how things go tonight."

My cramped apartment was on a month-to-month lease, so that would be no problem. And I certainly wouldn't miss sharing a bedroom wall with a deranged rat terrier. The only thing holding me back was the fear of defining my relationship with Isandro—*if* I moved in.

"Tell you what," he said. "The *picadinho de carne* won't be ready for a while. So why don't we take the champagne out to the pool? It's beautiful down there."

"Yeah, I *noticed.*"

When we headed down the stairs—he with two champagne flutes, I with the wine bucket—the sun had slipped behind the nearby mountains, but the sky was still aglow, rosy to the west, sapphire above, a gorgeous spring evening in the desert. We settled on chaises near the far end of the pool, with the champagne on a low table between us.

Isandro filled the two glasses, passed one to me, and raised his. "To starting over," he said.

I hesitated, but said it: "To us."

We clinked, then drank.

"Yoo-hoo." A door from the kitchen of the main house had opened, and the older man stepping out had a martini in hand. I recognized him as Richard Gibbs, who owned the estate. He asked from across the pool, "Mind if I join you, Isandro? I'd love to meet your friend."

We both waved him over—it was *his* pool, after all—and we stood for introductions. Then I moved a chair so he could sit with us.

He said, "You're *everything* I've heard, Dante. Hope we'll be seeing more of you." With a sweeping gesture toward the coach house, he added, "What do you think of Isandro's new digs?"

"I'm sure he'll be very happy here."

"I'm *sure,*" he echoed. With a frisky wink, he plucked the olive from his glass.

As he ate it, I said, "Your place is spectacular, Richard—truly a showplace."

He'd doubtless heard this many times. Setting aside the toothpick, he turned to study the length of the pool and the terrace surrounding it. "It's lovely, yes, but I've always been vexed by the *symmetry* of everything—the matching fountains, the columns. Perfectly proper and classically correct—but it's so damn *predictable*. I'd love to give it a *jolt*, an unexpected 'hero element,' so to speak."

"Something like...a distinctive oversize sculpture?"

"Exactly." He laughed. "But *what*?"

The three of us chatted for a while, comfortably sharing hot gossip and off-color jokes and nuggets of profound philosophy, sounding a bit like old friends. But as the sky darkened, the evening turned chilly, and Richard got up from his chair, saying, "Thank you, gentlemen, for letting me intrude on your time together—it's been delightful."

We said our good-nights, and he returned to the house.

Isandro sipped the last from his glass and set it down. "The stew should be ready. Hungry?"

"You bet."

The bottle of champagne was still half full, about right for dinner, so we gathered our things, walked back to the coach house, and started up the stairs.

Glancing over the banister toward the pool, I saw a spot on the terrace where I could easily envision the giant stone figure of an Inca warrior upsetting the symmetry, lording over the otherwise serene setting, churning the water with his fierce reflection. Richard Gibbs wanted to give a jolt to his backyard paradise, and Mr. Big could do the trick. What's more, I had a hunch he might be available.

Over in Indian Wells, Marjorie Payne was still in the throes of her obsessive death-cleaning project, and unless I was mistaken, she would probably be willing to part with the statue, which served as a monumental reminder of her late husband's not-so-secret past. It had also stood as a silent, stoic witness to the many years she had lived as a virtual prisoner in her own home, cowed into submission by the surly Agnetha Berg.

My thoughts returned to the present when Isandro and I reached the top of the stairs and paused outside his door.

He wrapped an arm around my waist and hooked a finger through one of my belt loops. Pulling me close, he shook his curly dark hair aside, looked up with a playful grin, and once again posed the question: "Your place or mine?"

"Ours," I heard myself say.

Palms rustled in the night sky as I stepped inside with him. He nudged the door closed behind us, and in the quiet of the dim, lofty room, I heard his breathing. I felt his warmth.

Michael Craft is the author of nineteen novels, four of which were honored as finalists for Lambda Literary Awards. His 2019 mystery, *ChoirMaster*, was a Gold Winner of the IBPA Benjamin Franklin Award, and the first installment of his Dante & Jazz series, *Desert Getaway*, was a 2023 MWA Edgar nominee for the Lilian Jackson Braun Award. In addition, his prizewinning short fiction has appeared in British as well as American literary journals.

Craft grew up in Illinois and spent his middle years in Wisconsin, the setting for many of his books. He now lives in Rancho Mirage, California, near Palm Springs, which provided the setting for his current Dante & Jazz mystery series.

In 2017, Michael Craft's professional papers were acquired by the Special Collections Department of the Rivera Library at the University of California, Riverside. This comprehensive archive, along with every edition of his completed works, is now cataloged and made available for both scholarly research and public enjoyment.

Visit his website at www.michaelcraft.com.

ACKNOWLEDGMENTS

First and foremost, I want to thank you, my readers, for embracing the Dante & Jazz mystery series, which employs a stylistic departure from much of my previous work. Your enthusiasm for last year's *Desert Getaway* was not only deeply gratifying, but it served as validation for the series as a whole and has led directly to this second installment, *Desert Deadline*. Thank you for wanting more.

I am forever grateful to Lee Goldberg for his many efforts to establish the series and promote the first book. This sequel has now moved to another publisher, and I am indebted to Jim Thomsen, whose incisive editing and thoughtful guidance have been invaluable in fleshing out and polishing the manuscript.

While writing *Desert Deadline*, I once again relied on David Sirek and attorney David Grey for their assistance with various plot details. Barbara McReal and Larry Warnock served as early readers of the manuscript, lending countless suggestions for improvement.

Hugs to fellow gay mystery novelists Michael Nava, Anthony Bidulka, and Rob Osler, who graciously contributed early endorsements of this book.

As always, Mitchell Waters, my literary agent for more than twenty-five years, has been tireless in helping me navigate the mercurial currents of the publishing world.

And finally, my husband, Leon Pascucci, has been a steady font of patience, support, and good cheer.

My heartfelt thanks to all.

— *Michael Craft, 2023*

ABOUT THE TYPE

The text of this book was set in Garamond Premier Pro, a 2005 interpretation and expansion of Adobe Garamond, which was designed in 1989 by Robert Slimbach as a digital revival of Claude Garamond's original array of metal typefaces dating from the mid-1500s in France. Garamond is a serif typeface classified as "old style," meaning that its strokes and serifs have a slightly more organic, handwritten feeling than transitional or modern serifs.

Known as the most conspicuous example of French Renaissance typography and one of the key font families worldwide, Garamond can be easily recognized for its elegant forms and excellent readability. Its smooth curves and simple serifs convey a classic and easygoing beauty, well suited for long blocks of text. Among print designers, Garamond is often favored as a timeless choice for text that is authoritative, highly legible, and slightly dressy.

Printed in the USA
CPSIA information can be obtained
at www.ICGtesting.com
LVHW101914230823
756086LV00013B/34/J

9 798218 137953